DOUBLE NEGATIVE

A VICKY BAUER MYSTERY

OTHER BOOKS BY LEONA GOM:

NOVELS

Housebroken
Zero Avenue
The Y Chromosome
After-Image

POETRY

Kindling
The Singletree
Land of the Peace
NorthBound
Private Properties
The Collected Poems

DOUBLE
Negative

A VICKY BAUER MYSTERY

by

LEONA GOM

SECOND
STORY
Press

Canadian Cataloguing in Publication Data

Leona Gom, 1946–
Double negative

(A Vicky Bauer mystery)
ISBN 0-896764-07-X

I. Title. II. Series.

PS8563.083D68 1998   C813'.54   C98-932046-4
PR9199.3.G66D68 1998

Edited by Charis Wahl
Copyedited by Beth McAuley

*Second Story Press gratefully acknowledges the assistance of the
Ontario Arts Council and the Canada Council for the Arts
for our publishing program. We acknowledge the financial
support of the Government of Canada through the
Book Publishing Industry Development program.*

Printed and bound in Canada

Published by
Second Story Press
*720 Bathurst Street Suite 301
Toronto, Ontario
M5S 2R4*

ACKNOWLEDGEMENTS

I would like to thank Dale Evoy for his advice and support, Charis Wahl and Beth McAuley for their editorial assistance, George Clulow for helping me research the B.C. Social Studies curriculum, Franco Marino and Charles Ennis for their expertise in Criminology, and Neil Besner, the Canada Council, and the University of Winnipeg for providing me with a place and time to begin this novel.

A selection from this novel has been published in *Books in Canada*. The excerpt from Wordsworth's "Ode: Intimations of Immortality" is from *The Norton Anthology of English Literature*, Vol. 2.

This is entirely a work of fiction.

For Dale

AFTER

$\mathcal{T}$HE POLICEMAN PUSHED open the door, dragging along a dazed-looking man wearing a green windbreaker, jeans and handcuffs. With every step, the man's knees bent too far, and it seemed that only the grip on his elbow kept him from sinking to the floor.

There was blood on his jacket. Vicky shuddered, and Amanda squeezed a little closer to her on the bench, as though the man might be coming to sit between them.

"What you got there?" said the officer behind the desk.

"B 'n' E," said the constable, taking off his hat with his free hand and scratching his neck with his thumb.

"Okay." The other policeman pushed a button that released the door, and the constable, putting his hat back on and rocking it back and forth to anchor it, propelled his captive through the doorway.

"Shit," Vicky heard one of them say as the door clicked shut behind them.

Amanda patted her hand. Hers was even colder than Vicky's. "Hang in there," she said.

"Why are they making us wait so long?"

"Don't worry. They'll come for you soon."

"I'm sick of waiting," Vicky said. "Maybe I'll just go home."

"Come on." Amanda sounded alarmed. "You have to do it their way."

"I can't stand this waiting, this sitting here waiting."

"You've got nothing to worry about. You didn't kill him."

"Are you sure?"

"Please," Amanda said. "Don't say things like that." Her voice was low, and frightened.

Vicky sighed, nodded. She leaned her head back against the pockmarked wall and let her eyelids slide almost closed, her lashes pulling a gray gauze over the harshly lit room. She had taken a Valium in the police car on the way here, and she could feel it starting to cut in, making her feel drowsy, a little stupid. Why had she taken one, anyway? She had to be sharp, to pay attention, to be careful what she told them when they came for her, when they took her down the hall to whatever room they used for their interrogations.

She concentrated on the buzz of a fluorescent light overhead and let her eyelids close all the way. What would she tell them? Where would she begin?

Part I

THAT
WEEK

MONDAY
MORNING

S HE HAD TOLD herself this call could come someday. Still, as she struggled awake, her right hand reaching instinctively for the pencil and notepad as her left fumbled the receiver to her mouth, it was the last thing she expected.

"Hello?" She cleared her throat and repeated the word, trying to sound eager and awake.

"Good morning! Karen at the Dispatch Centre. Is this Vicky Bauer?"

"Speaking."

"I've an assignment for you today. Can you take it?"

"Yes." She sat up.

"It's a one-day assignment, so far, anyway. Two Socials 11, a Socials 9. For a Mr. Polanski. At Fraser Secondary. You need the address?"

Her pencil stopped dead on the upstroke of the "k" in "Polanski." Fraser Secondary. Somebody had made a mistake. Polanski must be new at the school. He must have told the Dispatch Centre just to send anybody. She ran her pencil up and down the spine of the "k" so hard the paper began to pucker.

"Hello? Are you there? Is there some problem?"

What could she say?

"No. No problem. I know the address."

"Great. Check in with the principal. Mr. Taylor. Classes start at eight-fifty. Have a nice day!"

Not likely.

She hung up, sat staring at the notepad. *Mr. Polans*— Today she would have to go back into Fraser Secondary as though nothing had happened. She tried to swallow the pebble of fear in her throat.

She shuffled, shivering, into the living room and turned up the thermostat. She knew she should try to program the timer to come on at six-thirty since she was getting job calls almost every day now, but she had lost the instructions, and she didn't want to experiment. Setting the timer had always been up to Conrad.

She went into the kitchen and turned the tap on, hard. Today was going to be difficult enough without thinking about Conrad, about if only, I wish, it's not fair, why me. She plugged in the kettle, went down the back steps into the little added-on porch, and opened the door for the cat. He complained loudly and wiped his wet fur around her bare legs.

"You horrible, ugly thing," Vicky said, surprised, as she always was, by the sudden intensity of her affection for a creature who seemed equally fond of her legs and those of the coffee table.

He sat purring in the bathroom sink as she dressed, in the brown suit jacket and skirt she always wore the first day of a new assignment. She checked herself in the little vanity mirror: the thick, black hair Amanda cut for her; the dark eyes of her Blood Indian mother; the nose not quite symmetrical; the mouth drooping more at the corners than it used to. And was that fattiness under the jaw something new? She tilted her head back slightly. There, all gone. She stretched a smile across her face so wide she could see the filling in one of her molars. "Hello," she said. "I'm Mrs. Bauer and I'm your sub today." She could see the rows of students, the sudden whispering, *Isn't she the one ...*

She knew she should eat something, but her stomach was already reconsidering whatever was in it, so she only poured herself a cup of black coffee and drank it standing at the small east window looking out at the darkness of Semiahmoo Bay, at the lights across it of Blaine in Washington State, at the cold rain that could turn to snow any time.

The phone rang just as she was reaching for her coat. Maybe she shouldn't answer. But what if it was the school, or the Dispatch Centre, telling her there'd been a mistake, that she wouldn't have to go after all? She grabbed the receiver.

"Vicky?" She had told him a hundred times not to phone her so early. But that's when I know you're home, he'd say. "I want you to get me some socks."

"Socks?"

"Yeah. Not like those last pair, though. The elastic was too loose. I want the ones with the wide blue stripes."

"Dad, I'm late for school. I have to go."

"Get them on your way home."

"I probably won't have time."

"I'll see you after school, then. Remember, the ones with the wide blue stripes."

"Good*bye*." How long had it been since she'd had a conversation with her father when he hadn't annoyed her?

She put on her coat, and the cat, fearful of being locked outside, scuttled across the room in a belly-to-the-ground run he evidently thought was furtive and crawled under the sofa.

"I can still see your tail," Vicky told him.

Her old Toyota started reluctantly, sounding like someone being asphyxiated. It needed a tune-up, but where was the money to come from? She leaned back against the cold headrest and looked at the sun visor folded against the roof.

It had been a month since she'd had to lower it. Before moving to the West Coast, she had lived for over thirty years in Alberta, and she thought with a sudden longing of its sunny winter days.

As she backed out of her driveway and into the alley behind her house, she noticed the moving van next door. The McClintocks, an unobtrusive older couple, had, to her dismay, moved out yesterday. On the other side of her property a boxwood hedge separated her from Mrs. Birdsell's, but on the west her yard merged into the adjoining one, so it was impossible to avoid whoever lived there.

The movers were setting something large and gangly on the back lawn. She groaned. A swing set. Young children. There would be noise—screaming, laughing, shouting noise—the special torment of children as she sat in her house, alone.

A man wearing jeans and a grey sweatshirt and holding an empty laundry basket came out onto the back porch and said something to the movers. She peered at him from the alley, through the web of branches from his pear tree: about her age, blond, a little on the short side maybe, muscular torso—

He looked up suddenly, right at her, and how could she possibly have thought she was inconspicuous in her wheezing red car only thirty feet from him with its lights shining practically straight down his driveway? He lifted his hand and waved. So she had to wave back, discovered.

"Shit, double shit," said Vicky. A bad beginning to a gruesome day.

She had to stop for gas. Her car was so old it was still supposed to take leaded; she should find out more about using additives before she burned her engine out completely. What a nuisance. A few years ago, she thought, she would never have considered an environmental improvement a nuisance. During the two years she had spent with Conrad in Germany they had even joined the Green Party. When she came back to start her PhD in Film Studies and discovered her teaching assistantship had vanished, she had taken a year of teacher training instead, and she had majored in Social Studies primarily because of her environmental concerns. And now look at her—she probably wouldn't even return her pop cans if it weren't for the deposit.

She jerked the nozzle out, hung the hose up. A man at the next pump was finishing just as she was, and she couldn't stop herself from glancing at him, from remembering Amanda saying the other day, "Ever notice how men give the gas nozzle a shake before they hang it up?" This man didn't. Vicky looked quickly away. Amanda could embarrass her even in absentia.

She got to the school early, so she sat in her car in the visitors' lot and watched the students arriving in their fancy cars. A SAAB was pulling in now. It reminded her of a personalized plate she'd once seen on one: SNAAB.

She began looking for students she recognized. For one in particular. The one who'd gotten her fired. Well, not fired, exactly. Getting fired was a privilege reserved for those with real jobs.

She had had a real teaching job once, at the school in Edmonton where she'd done an impressive practicum. And then Conrad, who had with no regrets ended his own long teaching career, came back from Germany and said he'd found a cousin in Vancouver who had offered him work translating documents for German tourists and did she want to move there? The West Coast, she'd thought. Ocean. Mild winters. Living with Conrad again. Why not? "With your qualifications you'll get a job like that," he'd said, snapping his fingers.

Like that turned out to be two years of subbing and

humiliating interviews, of two principals in one week telling her, "You people from Alberta can't expect to come here and get hired over our own teachers." So it was back to the sub list (*sub* for *subhuman*, Amanda said), hoping to get noticed, hoping to get asked back, hoping to be kept in mind when a permanent job came up, hoping not to make enemies. She had tried hard, had been diligent and deferential. Until what happened with Jeremy Mill.

And that was him, she was sure of it, getting out of the red sports car. Or was it? It had been a whole year since she'd seen him.

Maybe she wouldn't run into him; the Dispatch Centre hadn't given her any Grade 12 courses. Maybe he wouldn't even remember her; maybe once he and his parents decided not to file charges he just forgot about her.

She couldn't put the day off any longer. She tightened her hand on her purse strap as though she were heading into an alley of muggers and got out of the car. The rain beat at her face. As she walked she could almost feel her hair getting heavier, a million straws sucking up water.

Inside, photos of old graduating classes looked down at her as she headed for the general office. It was like walking back into a house she'd lived in years ago, everything familiar yet not, inhabited now by new owners. She had worked here for only two months, replacing someone on maternity leave; but, after the stress of a new school every day, this had started to feel permanent, the principal hinting that if the teacher decided not to return the job would be Vicky's. She had only herself to blame for screwing it up. She should be grateful they let her teach again in the district at all.

Only one of the three secretaries looked familiar, and she glanced at Vicky without any sign of recognition. Finally, one of the others, an anorexic young blond, came up to the counter and asked her what she wanted.

"I'm Mr. Polanski's sub."

"Oh. Yeah. Right." The secretary bounced her pencil on the counter and looked vaguely over her shoulder. "Mr. Taylor's with somebody right now. But the vice-principal probably has the stuff for you."

The vice-principal. She tried to remember the man's name, but all she could think of was: Jesus Christ. It was what everyone, even Mr. Taylor, called him behind his back. She wasn't sure whether it had been his humourless fundamentalism or his intrusive nitpicking that had made people, when they saw him coming, groan, "Jesus Christ, what does he want now?" But that was how the joke had started.

Then she realized: the secretary wouldn't expect her to know him. "The vice-principal. And what's his name?"

"Bob Cross. His office is right there." Vicky let her gaze follow the woman's pointing finger, as though she needed to. Bob Cross. Of course. That name suited him, too. *Nomen omen.*

She made herself walk over to the office. Yes, there he was, chunky, grim, wearing the look of a man trying not to fart. He glanced up at her impatiently. Three yellow pencils of identical length, their tips ground to the vanishing point, were lined up on his desk and pointing at her.

"Mr. Cross? I'm Vicky Bauer. I'm Mr. Polanski's sub." Months of practice proffered the phrases with the expected mixture of apology and confidence.

"Vicky Bauer." He peered at her, frowning. She could tell he was trying to remember. "Oh." He remembered. "I didn't think you'd be back here."

"The Dispatch Centre sent me. You can call them to check."

"It's rather late for that now. Well, never mind. Mr. Polanski, let's see." He fumbled together a pile of books and papers. Vicky watched his fingers: short, thick, barely prehensile. He poked at the top page with a paper clip. "Here's his timetable. I'm sure you'll find everything set out in the daybook. Mr. Polanski is one of our more organized teachers." He looked up at her, forcing a smile. His thin lips disappeared completely when he smiled, as though he'd sucked them into his mouth.

"Well. Thank you." She picked up the texts and papers, the daybook binder, glad to have something to hold as she backed out of the room.

"Mrs. Bauer."

He was frowning now at the paper clip in his fingers. A *trombone*, Vicky thought absurdly, staring at it, too. Amanda always called paper clips by their French name, and Vicky could see a small, delicate trombone in the shape now, squeezed between Jesus Christ's thick thumb and forefinger.

"You're all right now, are you?" He didn't look at her.

"Yes. Thank you. I'm fine."

"I'm glad to hear that. Have a good day, then."

She walked away, feeling his eyes on her back. What did he care, she thought bitterly, if I'm all right? What he was really asking was, am I fit to be trusted in his school? If it had been up to him she'd have been blacklisted forever.

She went directly to the classroom, not wanting to face the other teachers in the staff room. They'd been her colleagues, her friends even, but when she had needed them they had been embarrassed and evasive, quick to turn her back into a substitute, peripheral to their lives. Maybe they even made jokes about her as they did about Jesus Christ.

She sat down at the desk and looked at Polanski's timetable. Two Socials 11 in the morning, a prep period, then in the afternoon a Socials 9 and, surprisingly, another prep period. She scanned the lesson plans for her morning classes. The chapter on Quebec. Students were to read it and make written answers to the questions on page 173. What a relief. She had taught the same chapter last week to a chaotic class used to a debating style. She couldn't remember whether the "Separatism, oui" or the "Separatism, non" side won, but she would vote for separatism herself if it meant she wouldn't have to teach it that way again.

A warning bell sounded. She could imagine the tide of students heading in her direction, eddying people out into various rooms as it came. She took a deep breath. These few moments were the worst, were the ones she had never gotten used to.

It was a large class, about thirty, but she didn't see any faces that looked familiar. She made herself smile and tell them who she was, not writing her name on the board as she usually did, took the roll, and gave out Polanski's instructions. They muttered and groaned but settled down to work, and Vicky allowed herself to think this might not be worse than any other day.

But of course she was wrong. She knew it the minute the next class started to straggle in. She began to recognize some of the students—yes, that one had been in Socials 10 last year, and that one, and the two coming in now. She pretended to be absorbed with marking the assignments from the previous class. She could smell her sudden, acrid sweat.

As she began taking the roll, she could see the whispering begin, the story leaking down the rows like a breaking dam. She forced herself to continue, to keep her voice steady. When she finished, the room was dead silent, twenty-five faces looking at her eagerly, excited.

"You are to read the chapter in your text on Quebec, and answer—" she saw the hand raised in the second row, knew what it must be wanting "—the questions on page

173." She couldn't pretend she didn't see it. "Yes?"

"Are you the Mrs. Bauer who was here last year?" The tall brunette, in a green silk blouse unbuttoned to show the top of her bra, leaned forward. Her raised arm lowered but only to the level of her shoulder.

"Yes," Vicky said. She turned and wrote on the blackboard, *p. 173*. She was holding the chalk so tightly it could easily snap. She turned back. "I taught here for two months. I think you were in my Socials 10, weren't you?" She gave the girl a disarming smile.

It didn't work. "Are you the ..." The girl paused, shifted in her seat. Maybe she wouldn't; maybe—

But then Vicky heard the hungry whisper, "*Ask* her!"

"Are you the teacher that broke Jeremy Mill's finger?"

There was a small collective noise from the class. They stared at Vicky as though she were something they would have to write a test on in five minutes.

"Yes. I am." She took a breath, let it out. "It was an accident. I'm not going to break anyone's fingers today. Unless you don't get at this work." She forced a smile, tapped the blackboard.

None of them laughed. She sat down, opened the daybook, underlined words in it, randomly. And finally, mercifully, she was aware of them opening their own books, their whispers not at a level that demanded attention. But she could feel their eyes glancing up at her as though they had to check that she was still Dr. Jekyll.

Her hands were shaking. She clasped them in each other, as though for mutual comfort, and pressed them between her knees, relieved that her desk was the kind with the board in front that went right to the floor.

After a few minutes she went back to her marking. But now that she had spoken of it, that terrible day, she couldn't stop thinking of it, seeing it on the pages in front of her.

Q: List two likely positive results and two negative ones of independence for Quebec.
A: Two positive results are ...

She is standing beside her desk and the bell has just gone to end the period and the students are picking up their map projects, and Jeremy Mill is standing there, too, holding his and saying, "I don't deserve a C for this, I worked really hard on it. Mrs. Chalmers would give me an A. I think you should take this back and mark it again. This isn't fair—" and she is passing out assignments and trying to read the instructions for the next class and trying desperately not to think about what had happened last night and how she began drinking when she heard although she knew she shouldn't, and she is saying to Jeremy, "I'm sorry, that's the grade it deserved. If you don't like it you'll have to work harder next time," Jeremy just standing there inches from her face and trying to make her take his assignment back and saying, "It's not fair. I don't get C's in this class. You have to mark it again." And suddenly she is screaming, "Get out! Get out!" and she has picked up the big Geography 12 book on the desk and is beating at his chest and shoulder and arm with it. When he steps back and stumbles on the wastebasket and grabs the desk for support, she realizes what she is doing, and she lets go of the big Geography 12 book and it drops, the hard, sharp corner of the cover landing on his index finger.

... that Quebec could control itself better and that they could protect their French, and two negative results are that the US would not want to deal in French and also some anglo phones who have a lot of money would be outa there.

Vicky joined the "o" in "anglo" to the "p" in "phone," underlined "outa," and put a check mark in the margin.

The class began handing in their assignments, starting their pile on the desk corner farthest from her. Well, at least if she wrote anything in their notebooks they might actually read it, looking for madness in her choice of words, the way she shaped her letters. They were a ghoulish lot at this age. It surprised her to find this amusing.

Her next period was a spare (or prep period, as she must remember to call it), so she continued her marking. When the noon bell sounded, she stretched, ate her cheese sandwich, jotted notes in the daybook for tomorrow, and had time to indulge in what she thought of as her Nasty Sub Habit.

Not that it was really nasty, not like the one she had given up because it was, well, a little disturbed: she had occasionally taken something from one teacher's desk—nothing *that* important (a pen, a packet of aspirins, some lengths of staples, a tampon, a pad of Post-it Notes)—and left it in another teacher's desk. Just a small compulsion, doctor, a small rebellion, a minor hostility. She had replaced this infraction with one less visible, benign by comparison: she wouldn't take anything, would just snoop through the desks looking for something interesting. Once she had found two bottles of rum; once a baggie of marijuana; once several pictures of a girl (whom Vicky had just had in her class) wearing a virtually invisible bikini, the bottom no more than a thread.

Polanski's desk yielded nothing of interest, however, except for a well-thumbed Bible in the top drawer. She took it out, let it drop open on the desk, in case it had some particular advice for her today. Her eyes had just snagged on "Holofernes" when the door burst open and someone shouted, "Aha!"

Vicky jumped to her feet and slammed shut the Bible, putting a significant wrinkle in Holofernes.

"Amanda! You nearly made me shit myself."

Amanda laughed, her big mouth pulled back in a toothful grin. She dropped her plentiful rump into a desk and stuck her legs out into the aisle. She was wearing a white blouse and tunic, a long flowered skirt, and her usual black nylons.

"I couldn't believe it when I heard you were here," she said. "Why didn't you tell me?"

"I just got called this morning. What are *you* doing here?"

"This is my second week. I told you." Amanda shoved her finger up along the bridge of her nose, ramming her glasses back into place so hard she seemed to be trying to embed them into her skin. A large fingerprint smudged the right lens from a previous miscalculation.

"No, you didn't. I'd have remembered."

"Oh. Maybe I didn't. Well," Amanda added defensively, "I didn't know if it would bother you."

"Why should it bother me? You think I expect you to boycott the biggest school in the district because of me?"

"Okay, okay." Amanda picked up a pencil from the floor and used it to scratch at the back of her head, where her brown, snarly hair always looked as though it had last been washed with chewing gum. She never set it anymore, not since she had missed taking out one of the rollers at the back and had taught all day like that, nobody, not even the other teachers, telling her. "So—does Jesus Christ know you're here?"

"I had to check in with him."

"I wish I could've seen his expression. My third day here he came sauntering into my French 12 class and just stood in the back, watching me. I was babbling away in

French, and without thinking I said to him, '*Est-ce que je peux vous aider?* Of course he didn't understand me, and one of the kids started to giggle, so he walked out in a huff. After school he said if I wanted to teach here again I had better improve my attitude. *My* attitude!"

"What did you say?"

"What fucking—" Amanda snapped a quick look at the door "—choice did I have? I mean, this is my first chance in a *year* to go more than five consecutive days. I'd have kissed any bodily orifice he wanted, and he's got more than most people."

Vicky laughed, but she understood such desperation too well. If a sub was hired for a sixth consecutive day on the same assignment her salary virtually doubled to real teacher rates. That it took six days before this could happen was of course unfair and arbitrary, but, as Amanda had sarcastically observed all too often, subs were only new grads teaching for the experience or housewives working for fun; they liked the flexibility; they didn't need the money. Subs were a clause in a contract written by and for other people. They were not, actually, supposed to be called substitutes anymore. They were "teachers on call," making them, Amanda said when she saw the memo, officially "call girls."

"I know," Amanda sighed, tossing the pencil she'd been poking into her hair back onto the floor. "We should be glad we have work at all, et cetera."

"*I* should be, anyway. I didn't expect the board to ever let me back into a classroom."

"Oh, come on. If I'd gone through what you just had I'd have been strapped down in a psych ward." Amanda shifted in her seat. "So what's with the Bible?" she said, changing the subject a little too quickly.

"It was in the top drawer of Polanski's desk."

"I hear he swears by it." Amanda snickered. "No, really.

Polanski's one of Jesus Christ's boys. A real brown-noser."

"How do you know?"

"We go to the same proctologist."

Vicky giggled, glancing at the door.

"Jesus Christ's done a lot of the new hiring here and he's brought in a nice little network," Amanda said. "Take a look at how many cars in the staff lot have fishy symbols on them. And fundamentalists breed in captivity, you know, not like the rest of us."

"Somehow I can't imagine Jesus Christ breeding."

"Oh, guys like him are very good at it. You know what the men consider foreplay?"

"I've heard that one before. They ask, 'Are you awake?'"

Amanda grunted. She hated having her jokes undercut. "Well, Jesus Christ would probably ask, 'Are you asleep?'"

Vicky laughed, glancing again at the door. A bell rang suddenly, making them both jump.

"Oh, hell," Amanda said, struggling out of the desk. "I didn't get my photocopying done. Well, play nice now."

MONDAY
AFTERNOON

ALREADY SHE COULD TELL the Grade 9 class would be a problem. Two boys staggered in, punching at each other so hard it might not have been in play, and then several girls ran in, shrieking, pursued by an over-muscled boy snapping what looked like a condom at them. Others came in, in groups of three and four, talking loudly, shoving at one another. The looks they gave her seemed hard, challenging. If the gossip about her had drifted down over the lunch hour it apparently hadn't intimidated them.

Vicky thought of the Unclear-on-the-Concept cartoon Amanda had drawn for her once: a sub walking into a Junior High classroom with a smile on her face. Vicky had never been particularly good at discipline, but, especially when she'd had her own classes, she'd had a toughness and a sharp tongue the troublemakers respected. After what had happened with Jeremy Mill, however, her confidence had been shaken, badly. Be careful, the voice in her head kept saying now: better they perceive you as weak than as crazy.

The boys in the back row began throwing things—balls of paper, a ruler, a sock. Another boy sat with his eyes closed, playing with great intensity an imaginary guitar. He was, Vicky thought, probably on drugs.

She stood up, feeling like an animal walking into a blaze of headlights. Only worse. She had watched a nature show once that said humankind had an evolutionary advantage in being able to anticipate the future, that it made civilization possible. Some advantage, Vicky thought, as a paper airplane, possibly made from a page from the text, sputtered down the centre aisle. A tall boy in front with a shaved head that looked to Vicky like a large thumb winked at her.

She began taking the roll, trying to make her voice deep and severe. She suspected some of the students were answering for absent friends. When she looked up the thumb-headed boy winked at her again, but this time she thought it might be a facial tic.

"Open your books to page 82," she said grimly. "We're going to read and discuss the section on Bismarck."

"We already did that," said one of the girls, indignantly, from the window row. She was as well-developed as an eighteen-year-old, and wearing a nose ring and so much eye make-up it must have hurt to blink.

"Yeah," said several others immediately. "Bismarck. We already did him."

Vicky hesitated. Perhaps Polanski *had* written the wrong page in the daybook. But more likely it was just the old sink-the-sub game. She shouldn't have let them see her hesitate.

"Well, we can do it again," she said. Another mistake: she had made it seem they were right. Hurriedly, she chose a name from the roll. "Carol, start reading, top of page 82."

There was some snorting and laughter, a farting noise, and then someone lifting his desk and letting it drop, but at last a wispy girl near the front began to read, laboriously. The room felt hot and close, as though the accumulated restlessness and boredom were sucking out the air. Twice she had to demand that two girls in the centre row stop talking. The one in front yawned, making a little deliberate noise on the exhalation, as she turned around.

"All right," Vicky said, relieved, when Carol finally reached the end of the paragraph. "So why did Bismarck introduce all these reforms? You." She pointed at the over-muscled boy bending over to pick up the pen someone had thrown at him.

"Me?" He straightened, looked at her insolently, pumping up his shoulders a little by tightening his hands and forearms. She thought of her cat puffing his hair out when he felt threatened or wanted to impress.

"Yes, you."

"What was the question again?"

The room burst into laughter. Vicky felt a hot surge of anger.

She had gotten angry at Jeremy Mill.

The memory of that day flooded back to her, and then the horror of the night before, the police at the door, the constable with the neutral voice saying, "Mrs. Bauer?"

She took a deep breath, squeezed her fingers, hard, into the covers of the text she was holding, forced the anger away.

"Why did Bismarck introduce reforms?" She enunciated each word carefully, as much for herself as for the boy.

"I dunno," he said, shrugging, making the muscles move under his tight shirt. The girl behind him punched him in the back, obviously something he took as approval. He began to giggle, sounding suddenly like an eight-year-old.

"Look at what we just read. Do you think he really cared about the people?" She thought someone said, "Who cares?" but she pretended she hadn't heard. "No, of course not," she continued. "He hated the Social Democrats, but he wasn't able to stop them by force so he tried to stop them by giving them some of the things they wanted. Was it a good plan? Do you think a government today could be successful doing that? Robert? Glenda?"

No reply. She could smell fresh nail polish. Someone was passing a magazine down the window row.

"Write down your answer," she said, giving up. "Then read to the end of the chapter and answer the first three questions. Mr. Polanski will expect them done." Another cop-out: the babysitter's wait-until-your-parents-get-home.

But, as she patrolled the rows, she saw that most of the students were attempting written answers. She tried not to notice the others, reading comic books or skin magazines inside their texts, passing notes, doing their math homework, daring her to say something. As long as they were quiet, she told herself. As the period itched to a close she began collecting the assignments. More marking: the price of a little peace during class time.

At last, the merciful bell. The students boiled out of the room. The boy with the imaginary guitar was the last to leave, his eyes half-closed, his fingers plucking tensely at the air.

The possibility of a fresh coffee lured her downstairs to the staff room for the last period. She felt drained, hungover, the adrenaline pulling back, making her pay. The one other person in the room was, Vicky was grateful to see, a man she didn't recognize, and she sank down on the couch, leaned her head back, closed her eyes. She had come back to the place of her nightmares and survived.

If subs had no prep to do during a spare they were required to report to administration to be given other work. She had better get busy marking before Jesus Christ spotted her.

As though she had invoked him, he appeared suddenly beside her. She looked up at him with what she hoped wasn't as much alarm as she felt.

"Mrs. Bauer?"

She nodded. Of course she was Mrs. Bauer.

"Could I speak to you in my office?"

"Yes, sure."

She followed him out. She could see the other teacher watching them from across the room.

What could he want? Had a student complained? Had he been listening outside her door? Maybe he'd been eavesdropping during the noon hour when she was talking to Amanda. By the time they reached his office she was too nervous to think. She sat down in the chair he pulled out for her, a phony chivalry that made her feel even more vulnerable. He sat down behind his desk, reaching up and carefully smoothing his tie along his chest and buttoning his suit jacket over it.

"Mr. Polanski called to tell us he'll be away again tomorrow."

"Oh. I see." She was limp with relief. "Well, that's no problem. I'll be able to come back."

"Ah. Yes. Well." He leaned back a little, pressed his fingertips together and steepled them under his chin. "I discussed the situation with Mr. Polanski and we decided it would be better to ask for another on-call teacher."

Vicky simply sat there, looking at him. *Damn* him.

"I've done this assignment competently," she said finally, trying to keep her voice from trembling. "I've the right to continue if it goes beyond today."

"I'm not disputing what you've done here to*day*." He made a grimace she supposed was intended as an ironic smile. "But in light of your history with this school, it's best you not return."

"But the board's assessment said—"

"The board removed your name from the teachers-on-call list. They suspended you."

"For two months. And they cited the doctor's report that said I was in shock that day, I wasn't fully responsible for my actions."

"That may be, Mrs. Bauer. But *someone* has to be responsible. And the safety of this school is my paramount concern. I'm afraid that takes precedence over your desire to continue with us."

"What does Fred think about this?" It was a risk, saying "Fred" instead of "Mr. Taylor," but it was what she had begun to call him, after all, when she was here.

The man across from her, whose real name had fled her mind again, leaned forward abruptly. His hands dropped on the desk with an audible slap. "Fred leaves these decisions to me," he snapped.

"I see." She shrank back in her chair.

"Now, I've asked one of the secretaries to bring your coat down from the classroom, so you can pick it up on your way out. And you can leave the marking with her when you've finished."

There was nothing she could do. She stumbled to her feet, the chair almost falling over, turned and fumbled for the doorknob.

"This is nothing personal," she heard Jesus Christ say behind her, his voice smooth and smarmy now.

·

It was only when she was half way home, stopped at the light at No. 10 Highway, that she began to cry. She turned the radio up, loud, to drown out the awful sound. When she got home she sat in the driveway, not turning the motor off, thinking about how the house would be cold and empty and how much she wanted Conrad to be there to say that who cares what old Jesus Christ said.

She watched the rain sputtering through the hole in the gutter above the kitchen window, running down the old stained stucco. She put her head down on the steering wheel and thought about crying again, but thinking seemed to discourage it. A drink. That's what she needed. Just one. She could feel it already in her throat, that sweet deception.... No. Don't. Don't.

Someone tapped on the window. She jerked erect, hitting her elbow on the door. But it was only Mrs. Birdsell, her neighbour. She was a short, stout woman in her late sixties, with a perpetually flushed face and a nose intended for someone twice her size.

Vicky rolled down her window.

"Hi," the woman shouted, slapping her arms at herself to keep warm. "I just wanted to be sure you were okay. Not carbon monoxided, or anything." She banged her fist twice on the car roof, for no apparent reason, and began to walk away, stepping carefully around the puddles because she was just wearing bathroom slippers.

Oh, Birdy, Vicky thought. A little of her, Conrad had once said, went a long way. Quickly Vicky opened the door and called after her, "Thank you."

Birdy turned and waved her right arm a little. "So long as you're okay."

"I was just feeling a bit down. Maybe," Vicky said, not knowing what she wanted to do until she heard herself say it, "I'll go and see Conrad."

Birdie had started to turn away and she stopped, looked at Vicky. She hesitated a moment, and then she said, in a voice that, whatever its intentions, sounded churlish, "You give up too much of your life for him. It's not fair."

"Of course." Vicky smiled. "Of course it's not fair."

.

When she got out of the car the rain was heavier, a north wind sweeping it in sheets at her. A gust pressed so strongly against the door of the Matheson Pavilion that it seemed a vacuum inside was sucking it closed.

"Rotten weather, isn't it?"

Vicky was relieved to see it was Nurse Nice on duty today, not Nurse Ratched. Not that Nurse Nice was really all that much nicer than Nurse Ratched, or that Vicky didn't know their real names; it was just some distancing game she had begun with herself when Conrad first came here.

"Yes," she said. "I hope it doesn't snow. My tires are so bald they'd skid on sandpaper." She hung her coat on the rack by the door. "How is he today?"

"Oh, you know. He had a little angry spell this morning and gave me a punch on the arm, but he seems okay now." Nurse Nice smiled. Her young, pretty face with all its features slanting upward seemed unsuited to the things she had to tell people.

"Oh, dear." Vicky gave the nurse a vaguely apologetic smile and moved off down the hallway. The walls had been freshly painted, the same off-white as before, and there was still a smell of paint in the air, mixing unpleasantly with the antiseptic.

Conrad's room was almost at the end of the corridor, which meant it was quieter but also that the nurse probably didn't check on him as often. Vicky tried not to look in at the other rooms as she passed; she kept her eyes on the red Exit sign at the end of the hallway. She had walked this corridor almost every day for eight months, but she had never gotten used to it, deliberately perhaps.

Room 121. She fixed the smile on her face and went in.

He was sitting in the chair by the window, dressed in his light blue shirt and grey cardigan. He was rubbing one of the sweater buttons between his fingers and had almost worked it loose of its threads. He turned, looked towards her. The face with its perfect features that had unnerved almost everyone who ever met him was no longer one people would describe as handsome. The large blue eyes, they would say now, were sunken, not deep-set; the mouth was no longer full and clearly defined but nicked with wrinkles; the skin was too pale even for a blond and had the invalid's dry and papery look.

"Hello, Conrad."

There was no recognition on his face. Every time she came she told herself she didn't expect any, but every time she felt, somewhere deep and uncontrollable, a sigh of disappointment. She sat down across from him. His gaze drifted across her face, settled on the painting of the ocean on the wall.

The few times his cousin Ernest had come with her to see him he had said Conrad looked "peaceful." It had chilled her: *peaceful,* as though he were dead.

Ernest and his wife, Helen, had been their best friends in British Columbia, but she rarely saw them now, and if they came to visit Conrad she wasn't aware of it. She had felt at first they were blaming her somehow, as though she were the drunk who had hit him that night. Even when she understood that it might just be too painful for them to keep in touch with her, it didn't lessen her bitterness. She knew they would help her in an emergency, but what she wanted from them was more than that; it was their friendship, which they had pulled away from her, like a loan they called in when she lost her collateral.

The button Conrad was twisting suddenly pulled free and fell to the floor with a small metallic ping. Conrad's eyes flickered down from the painting for a moment, looked at the frayed threads in his fingers.

"Well, that's good," she told him. "You know something happened." At first when she had said such things her voice had a phony, brittle sound to it, but she had become used to getting no answer.

She picked up the button, keeping a watch in case he wanted to flail at her. He had done that only a few times, and then rather halfheartedly. But sometimes his motions would be so specific she had to stop from thinking they were communications. Several times he had pointed suddenly and dramatically out the window, but when she had gone eagerly to look she saw just the same putter of traffic on the street. She had resigned herself to thinking of such gestures as some residual memory stored in the muscles of his hands, unconnected to conscious will.

It was how she had come to think of the words he spoke sometimes, as impulses stored in his throat. "Rooms," he said once, very clearly. And, another time, "feathers." And "mechanic." And "shoelace." Sometimes the words were in German, his mother tongue, but the only one she had ever understood was "*Bilder.*" Pictures. She had made a note of all the words and puzzled over them in case they might be a kind of code, a message she could read if only she knew the key. But now she would just smile and say, "Yes, I know. Trees."

She hooked her elbow over the back of the chair. "You wouldn't believe my day," she said. "I got called to Fraser Secondary this morning. So what could I say? I had to go. Anyway, when I got there ..."

She went on, telling him about the whole day, getting upset again when she came to the last part about Jesus Christ. "And then he had the nerve to say, 'This is nothing personal.' Can you believe it?" She kicked at the leg of the bed, hard enough to make the covers shiver. "Nothing personal."

Conrad reached up and scratched at his cheek, then let his hand fall, palm up, back into his lap. His eyes had dropped to the room's other bed, its beige blanket stretched tightly across it like a large bandage, which had been occupied by another head injury victim transferred to Vancouver General last week.

One of the junior nurses was at the door with the supper trays.

"Oh, good, you're here," she said, setting the tray on the raised platform beside Conrad's bed. "You'll be wanting to feed him, then." She was gone before Vicky could answer.

Feeding Conrad was not something she enjoyed. But she supposed it was better she do it than someone paid to.

Conrad had taken no notice of the meal's arrival. Occasionally he had reached out for the food, but, like his few gestures and words, it was something Vicky had learned not to see as significant. Dr. Kittridge simply shook his head when she reported these things to him. "The mind is a mysterious thing," he said.

She wondered if that was what he had said in his report to the insurance company, if that was why they kept refusing to settle, saying they had to assess the "final condition." She knew it was just a delaying tactic, but she didn't want to dispute it, didn't want to have to say, "This is it—this is his final condition." He had, after all, come out of his coma. Still, it was eight months since then, and she couldn't pretend she didn't know the facts, the prognosis. He wouldn't be in extended care if they expected him to improve.

She lifted the cover off the main dish and the faintly metallic odour of mashed potatoes and hamburger and cauliflower steamed up at her. She tucked the napkin in at Conrad's collar and lifted a forkful of potato to his mouth.

He sat unresisting, like a simple machine built to open, close, chew, swallow, open. A bit of cauliflower fell from the fork and landed on his upturned wrist. When Vicky picked it up she let her fingers rest there for a moment.

She felt the slow pulsing of his blood, his body alive under her touch. They had been in the shower together once, and he had been soaping her back, getting lower and lower, and then he was rubbing the washcloth into the crease between her buttocks, saying, "Why, what's this? Good grief, you're split down the middle—" and she had grabbed at his wrist, just here, just here.

Don't. Don't. Don't. It was a kind of mantra she had begun to use. Don't.

Conrad's mouth was open again, his empty eyes looking beyond her. She began to spoon up the pudding for him. He ate it all and then turned his head to stare at the painting of the ocean.

"Well, yes." She looked at the picture, too, for a while. Finally she said, "I guess I should go," and she got to her feet. "See you tomorrow." This was the worst part, this unshared and repetitive leaving.

In the hallway an old man was pushing a walker, with extreme slowness, towards her. Her steps faltered as she recognized him, but this time he did not, as he had the last time, gesture in a desperate clawing motion for her to come over, and, when she did, say to her in a wheezing voice, "Under your dress! Under your dress!" She had told Nurse Ratched about it, and she had laughed and said, "It's the last thing they think about, I swear. They're lying there, dying, and with their last bit of strength they try to feel you up."

Vicky stopped at the washroom, sat in a cubicle looking at the graffiti on the door. *The meek don't want it.* It took her a minute.

"You had a long visit today," Nurse Nice said, coming out of the storeroom carrying a box of syringes as Vicky was leaving the washroom.

"I guess I did. I had a lot to tell him."

Nurse Nice smiled, set the box down and pulled up the sleeves of the puffy pink cardigan she always wore over her uniform. "You're so conscientious. I mean, some of these people don't get visitors for months at a time, and they're dying to see someone."

"So to speak."

"No, really." The woman, Vicky realized, hadn't intended to make a joke. "I mean, it's, well, courageous of you to come, every day nearly, for so long."

"Courageous!" Vicky almost laughed. "No, no. That's not what it is."

"What would you call it, then?"

"Oh, I don't know. But not courage. No."

Outside in the car, waiting for the motor to warm and the windows to clear, she thought about what she might call it. It wasn't courage, and it wasn't the opposite, cowardice, nothing that simple. Habit? Duty? Guilt? Hope? No, not quite. She would have to think about it.

She and Conrad had never had a traditional kind of marriage. She had married him at sixteen, when he was thirty-three, teaching at her school in the far north of Alberta and determined to save her from the self-destructive life she was heading for after her father left and her mother, sunk into her own despair, could no longer care for her. She and Conrad had lived separately as much as together over the next twenty years, driven apart by the differences not just in age but in temperament (the deficiencies, she was more than willing to admit, being mostly hers). When they'd parted in Germany she'd thought, not really believing it, that perhaps if he found his missing childhood and she her missing adulthood they might be able to live together again, and to her surprise something like that did indeed seem to have happened. Since they had moved to the coast they had gotten along better than they had for many years.

Only to lose him here, to a goddamned accident.

She pulled out onto the highway. A car moved up fast behind her, swerved with excessive drama into the other lane and shot past her. The kind of driver who'd hit Conrad, she thought, feeling the rage push her own foot hard on the accelerator. It made no sense, of course, this speeding, this rushing to get home—she had hurried there after school today, too, and then she couldn't even get out of the car. Home: she thought of the board games she'd had as a child, where she would race her token around a host of pitfalls, eager to reach the safety of home; but what was it except an empty circle, a dead zone?

She pulled into her driveway. She could hear, as soon as she got out of the car, the water splattering out of the leaking eavestrough—and another sound, unfamiliar, a grating noise, next door, to the west. The new neighbours: the man she had stared at this morning. She'd forgotten all about that. She made herself keep walking, up her back steps; if she turned around she would be looking right into their back yard. She had the key in the lock before the sound she was hearing—a creaking, then a pause, then the creaking again—overcame her desire not to appear nosy, and, assuring herself she really was invisible this time because she hadn't left her outside light on, she turned to look.

The neighbouring yard was unlit, too, but she could see, dimly, a repetitive movement matching the sounds and coming from where the movers had left the swing set. A child was there, swinging, in the dark and the drizzle. She could see the legs thrusting out on the upswing, contracting under the seat on the downswing, the bending of the knees coinciding with the creak of the chains. For some reason Vicky couldn't take her eyes from the shadowy, pendulum movement.

A car horn sounded, made her start, and she turned quickly and went inside. By the time she had walked through the house to the front door and picked up her mail she was no longer wondering about the child next door. Still, when she would think back on this day (as she was doing now, sitting on the hard bench beside Amanda, waiting, in the police station) it would not be because of what happened at Fraser Secondary. It would be because it was the day her new neighbours moved in.

TUESDAY

*T*HE PHONE BROKE into her dream about a plane trip to South America. She groped for the pencil and notepad.

"Vicky. Where were you? You were going to bring me those socks."

"Oh, for god's sake." She dropped the pencil, let herself fall back into bed.

"I phoned and phoned and there was no answer. Not even your stupid machine. You could at least have called and said you weren't coming. Is that too much to ask?"

"I didn't say I would come, Dad. I had a hard day and I didn't have time."

"A hard day. What do you mean, a hard day?"

"They sent me out to Fraser Secondary."

"The school where—"

"Yeah. Then the damned vice-principal more or less ordered me out of the place."

Her father cleared his throat. "What did you do this time?"

She took a deep breath, pulled the quilt up around her ears. "Nothing. Forget it. Forget I mentioned it. Why do you need a new pair of socks all of a sudden, anyway?"

"'All of a sudden, all of a sudden.' It was yesterday I asked for them."

"If I have time I'll get them. Okay?" She added, "God," under her breath.

"When?"

"When I have time. If I have time."

"Later today, then." He went on, quickly, before she could reply: "So, where were you last night that you were so busy?"

"You know where I was," she said stiffly.

"How am I supposed to know where you were?"

"I was visiting Conrad." If he says, Vicky thought, *Why do you bother?* I am going to hang up in his ear.

"I don't know why you bother."

"Bye, Dad."

One of these days, she thought, she'd be able to do it properly, not say goodbye, just hang up. She pulled her arm in under the covers, glanced at her bedside clock. Eight.

She sat bolt upright. *Eight o'clock.* The Dispatch Centre hadn't called. Jesus Christ must have complained. She'd been getting work every day for a month, and there was a flu going around—it was too much of a coincidence that she not get a call the day after Jesus Christ told her to get out of his school—

She threw the quilt back, in a kind of horror, as though she had seen a rodent crawl into it, and jumped out of bed. But by the time she reached the living room she was reminding herself that she had forgotten to turn her answering machine on yesterday, that she had not even come into the house after school, and that most teachers were calling her directly now the night before. She rubbed her hands up and down her arms, soothing the goose bumps. She would wait a day before panicking.

Meanwhile, she had the day to herself. What she felt most like doing was getting back into bed and onto the plane that had been taking her to South America, but there were chores to be done: vacuuming, laundry, fixing the board under the back step, cutting off the branch of the elm tree that had cracked and fallen across her front walk so that the letter carrier had finally left her a rude note. She sighed. So little time and so little to do, some wit had said.

She was in the grocery checkout line resisting the lurid urgings of *The National Enquirer* to turn to page 43 when she thought of her father's socks. She began to slam down her groceries onto the counter with such ferocity that the woman in front of her looked back, alarmed, and moved the stick separating their purchases ahead a little, protectively.

Her father had vanished from her life when she was fourteen. An injury to his leg at the service station where he worked had given him the excuse. "I'm sorry. Better off without me," said the note he left behind. Despite his generally surly disposition, neither Vicky nor her mother considered themselves "better off without him," and Vicky's mother, losing the conditional respectability marriage to a white man had allowed her in their remote northern community, sank into an alcoholic and self-destructive state from which she was released only by what they decided to call a heart attack, a few years later. And if Conrad, out of compassion mostly, had not married Vicky and insisted she stay in school, she would likely have followed her mother.

Her father occasionally sent, from constantly changing addresses, money and short letters about work he had found, but these had both stopped abruptly after a few years, and Vicky hadn't heard from him again. Until two years ago: a phone call from a voice she no longer recognized, saying hello, this is your father, I guess you're living in B.C. now, too, what do you mean, how did I find you, I kept track, I always knew where you were.

Better off without me. Vicky had repeated those words to herself a thousand times, accumulating her anger, thinking of what she would say to him if they ever met again. But when it had actually happened she had listened to Conrad, who had lost both parents in the war and who said, "But he's your *father*," incredulous that she would not welcome a second chance, a lost parent. So she had said to her father, making herself mean it, that in spite of everything she was glad to see him, and she had let him get away with his stubborn refusals to talk about why he had left, why he had stopped writing, why he had never come back.

But what annoyed her most now, she realized, was that she was going to put the groceries into the car and then drive to the mall where she knew exactly where to buy his socks with the two wide blue stripes. And then, still angry, she would drive over to his apartment where he would yell, "Come in!" but the door would be locked, so she would reach up above the door frame for the key, and that would make her angrier than ever, because she had told him a hundred times not to leave it there, and why wouldn't he trust her with a key of her own, anyway?

This time he had the security chain on, too, so the door jolted to a stop and she banged her foot walking into it. "Dad! Come get this chain off."

She could hear the squeak of his wheelchair. Then he was peering at her through the door, with his huge blue eyes that seemed to have sunk further into his face every time she saw him. Or maybe it was that his nose was growing bigger—it jutted from his face like a ploughshare. He hadn't shaved in several days, and even from this distance Vicky could smell his breath, stale, necrotic. He pushed the door abruptly shut, and she heard the chain rattle free. She opened the door again, because she knew he wouldn't do it. When she stepped inside he was wheeling himself to the kitchen table.

The apartment was a small, standard one-bedroom unit. The bedroom and bathroom were off to the right, and the living room, by ending its worn brown carpet near the far end, turned into a linoleumed dining area big enough to hold a small chrome kitchen table and four chairs. The kitchen was surprisingly large and, given the mess it was usually in, mercifully screened from the living room by a wall open on both ends.

"Here are your socks." Vicky dropped them on the coffee table on top of the newspapers and biscuit crumbs.

"The ones with the two blue stripes."

"Oh, of course. Two blue stripes."

A noise from the kitchen startled her, although by the time the person there came out from behind the separating wall she had deduced who it was. Leo. A small-featured, fair-complexioned man with a perpetual nervous smile and a short, muscular body that must, at his age, which was somewhere in the mid-fifties, have been abetted by weightlifting, he lived next door to Vicky's father. But they had known each other from before, from jobs they had both held once, her father had said vaguely.

Usually Vicky was glad Leo was around; he seemed to be her father's only friend, and he was helpful when he wanted to be. He was generally shy around her, but there were times when he seemed nosy and downright leering and when his mangled platitudes and non sequiturs negated whatever charm he had. Even her father would sometimes shake his head and say things like, "He's not the brightest bulb in the pack."

"Hi, Vicky," Leo said. "I just made coffee. Want some?"

"No thanks. I can't stay."

He was disappointed, she could tell by the way he nodded with greater vehemence than necessary.

"I've a lot to do today," she said, picking at her purse strap.

"Sure, sure," Leo said. "But it's there. The coffee."

"Thanks. I know you make good coffee."

Leo grinned, glanced over at Vicky's father in apparent

triumph.

Her father only grunted. "How come you're not teaching?" he asked Vicky.

"I didn't get called today. I hope it's not because of that damned vice-principal, that it's just coincidence."

"There's no such thing as coincidence," Leo said somberly.

Vicky sighed. She knew he expected her to ask so she did. "Why not?"

"Power corrupts," he insisted, scratching at his neck hard enough to leave marks. "I had a job like that once. I didn't want to get too powerful. California was better."

"I suppose it was." Trying to follow Leo's logic, she had learned, was often futile. It was usually better just to agree up front.

A phone rang in an adjacent apartment. "Is that yours?" Vicky asked, hopeful.

"Could be. Them guys were gonna call. You have some coffee, Vicky, okay, if you want," he said, going to the door.

He'd only been gone a few seconds before the phone stopped ringing. Vicky doubted Leo would have had time to get inside his apartment, but he didn't come back.

"I better go, too," she said.

Her father wheeled his chair to face her. "Wait. I want to show you something." He was actually smiling, a little slyly.

Oh, god, she thought; it's going to be something awful. She let herself drop onto the sofa, which, like the coffee table, the two armchairs, the record cabinet, the bookcase, had either been left behind by the previous tenant or scrounged for him by Leo.

Her father pulled himself up from the chair and, holding onto the table as he moved, shuffled to the kitchen. He was wearing an old pair of Bermuda shorts (Vicky had told him a hundred times to dress more warmly), and she noticed how the skin of his knees was sagging, stretching down into two ovals the size of small tennis rackets. But he was walking better than he had been the last time she was here, and she thought cynically that he must have forgotten the precise level of decrepitude he had faked for her then. She heard him rummaging around in the kitchen, opening a drawer, closing another.

She leaned her head back on the sofa, let her eyes find the photograph on the record cabinet. Her father must have taken it shortly before he left them, perhaps having already made his decision, planning, as he framed them in the viewfinder, a souvenir of a life he had once had, people he had once known. Vicky was fourteen in the picture, and she was standing beside her mother, the two of them with their outfits cut from the same pattern and fabric, their black hair the same length and pinned on the left side with two bobby pins, their round faces and small noses that looked as though neither of them had outgrown childhood. They were standing in front of the wooden fence around their back vegetable garden in Worsley, Alberta, and her mother's right arm was draped along the top of the boards, her dangling hand making her look lighthearted and casual, but Vicky could still feel, even after all these years, the other arm which encircled her, tightly, protectively.

It wasn't that her father had been especially cruel to them, not in the way she understood, even at fourteen, fathers could be cruel. He had never hit them, or, as far as she could tell, had any desire to do so. His dissatisfactions seemed less with them than with the other failures in his life, first with the farm on what turned out to be two sections mostly of muskeg and then with the job at the garage in the village, where, eventually, the half-ton truck loaded with barley slipped its brakes at the pumps and smashed his right leg.

The accident had given him more excuse to drink, and it was when he drank that his bitterness would spill onto them: they were ungrateful; they were selfish; they were women. But his words were without much passion, were brewed in such obvious self-pity that Vicky learned not to be hurt by them, learned, as her mother had, to shrug and forgive him.

But what she could not forgive was his leaving. Maybe it was that anger at him that had really pulled her back into his life, an anger fueled daily by his crankiness and demands and her capitulation to them.

She looked at the picture of her mother. Vicky had so few photographs of her, especially of her and Vicky together. But the last one, a little off-centre and blurry, taken by a neighbour on Vicky's seventeenth birthday, was the one she had taken out and looked at for a long time the day her father phoned her, out of the blue, two years ago. She had thought of the day that picture was taken and the present her mother had given her. In an envelope, wrapped in tissue. She still had it, in the same envelope, the same tissue, tucked into her high school yearbook between pages 22 and 23. She had remembered the way her mother's fingers had been trembling when she handed it to her, saying, her voice crackly, "Maybe you won't want or appreciate this now, but you might later. Maybe you will later."

Someday, when Vicky was so angry with him that she was willing to give up the one edge she felt she had over him, she would show that envelope to her father.

He was coming back from the kitchen, shuffling over to his chair and not holding onto the table at all now, and he was carrying something covered in a dishtowel. He was holding it so carefully that Vicky thought: it's an animal— good grief, he's got himself a kitten and the building has a no-pets policy and how was she going to deal with this one.

But when he dropped himself into his chair and folded back the towel, slowly, keeping her waiting, what she saw made her cry out in revulsion.

"God! Where did you get that?"

It was a gun, black and oily looking, lying in the palm of his hand with the barrel pointing towards her. She shrank against the back of the sofa.

"Leo got it for me. In the States. There's no trouble at all getting them down there. You know Leo. He has to buy two of everything."

She nodded, staring at the gun, remembering when Leo had come over to her father's to show Vicky and Conrad his two new identical wrist watches, one on each arm. Conrad had shaken his head later about Leo. "Those watches," he said. Vicky laughed. "A fearful symmetry," she agreed.

"What on earth do you want a gun for?"

"Everybody's getting broke into. Leo got broke into twice."

"Leo was away down East for a month. You're home all the time—"

"So it's better they break in when I'm here? Well, maybe *now* it is." He set the gun in his lap, his right hand decisively over it.

"You don't have a license or anything. It's illegal!"

"So is breaking into people's places. I have the right to protect myself. You should have a gun, too, living alone like that. Leo could get you one."

"Oh, god, Dad." She stared at the ugly black thing in his lap. The more she argued with him, the more resistant he would become. She should have told him it was a wonderful idea.

"I know how to use it, you don't have to worry about

that." He patted the gun affectionately. "The war."

"The war," Vicky said. The man was crazy. He might shoot her. Or he'd shoot the Meals-on-Wheels person and then call her and tell her to take away the body. Her mind felt like Algernon after the smart drugs wore off and all he could remember was that once there had been a way out of the maze. How could she leave her father here with a gun? His key was out on the sill for anybody to find, and he would sit inside waiting, holding a gun on his lap. She could imagine the questions the police would ask her: "But you knew he had an unregistered gun, Mrs. Bauer. Surely you knew it was your responsibility to report it. And surely you knew that in the condition your father was in—" And they would gesture at him, slumped in his wheelchair in convincing, drooling senility.

"So," he said. He folded the dishtowel back over the gun and set it on the kitchen table.

"So," she said dully. She sat watching the towel. "Well, I might as well go." She stood up, abruptly, bumping the coffee table and jarring a section of the newspaper and some crumbs to the floor. When she bent to pick up the paper the hostile headlines of last week's news looked back at her.

"Getting messy in here," her father said. "Next time you come bring the vacuum cleaner."

When she didn't answer, he said, as she opened the door, "How was Conrad?"

She stopped, unprepared for the question. He didn't care about Conrad—it was just a way of delaying her.

"The same," she said, not turning around.

Her father grunted. Vicky waited. Maybe he would say something more, something that would make her finally go through the door and not come back.

"Okay. Thanks for the socks."

Oh, he was clever: now he would say thank you, when he hadn't said thank you to her a dozen times in his bloody life.

"You're welcome."

When she got home, she watched the McClintocks' old house as she walked towards her back door with her bags of groceries, but there was no sign of anyone at home. Beige curtains were up and pulled across the windows. There might have been a car in the carport, but if so it was pulled forward far enough to be out of her sight. Don't stare, she told herself, and turned without pausing to go up the stairs. When she put her foot on the top step she felt the whole staircase shift under her weight, nearly pull free of the house. She fought the feeling of helplessness in which she knew she could not indulge, and then she went inside, put the groceries away, found a hammer and some long nails in the basement, and went back outside. At least it had stopped raining.

She began to pound back the piece of wood that had been helping to support and balance the steps as the house had shifted and settled over the years. She had to hammer awkwardly, sideways along the ground, digging up chunks of muddy soil when she missed the piece of wood, but once she got it started it wasn't difficult. With the steps raised, she was able to hammer in nails where the top part had pulled loose from the house.

The cat prodded the door open from inside and looked at her skeptically, as though he remembered that Conrad had always been the one who fixed such things. Sometimes he had taken the pliers or screwdriver or wrench right out of her hand, had said, "Here, let me do that," and why should she resist? He did it better and faster than she. She would stand back and watch, relieved and resentful both.

Vicky bounced lightly on the middle step. Nothing

collapsed. "Not bad for a girl," she told the cat.

She took the hammer back down to the basement, and, cheered by her success with the stairs, found a saw, its handle wrapped with gummy black tape, and went out to tackle the branch of the elm tree fallen across her front walk.

It was a large limb, half a foot in diameter, with lots of smaller branches attached, and she saw that even if she could release it from the tree, to which it was still attached like some huge hangnail, it could fall even farther across her walk and she might not be able to drag it away. And what nasty note would the letter carrier leave her *then*? But she hadn't much choice.

The saw had barely broken the bark when her arm started to ache, so she switched to her left hand. She began to sweat. She paused, wiped her face with the back of her work glove.

Across and down the street she could hear the barking machine—that was what Birdy had called it and how Vicky thought of it now, not as some wretched dog left tied outside all day, but as a noise machine its owners turned on and left running until they came home. Birdy had gone over once to complain, but they had told her coldly that since they took the dog inside when people were home from work there was no problem. Listening to the sound now, beating at the quiet afternoon, Vicky wondered how Birdy had restrained herself from going over and strangling the creature.

She switched the saw back to her right hand. Now that the teeth had cut a track the blade didn't wobble and leap out of place as often, and she made more progress. Maybe this job wouldn't take two weeks, after all.

"You're pretty slow, aren't you?"

She nearly dropped the saw. The person who had spoken was a child, about nine or ten years old, standing right beside her.

"Oh! Well, yes, I suppose I am."

"That's a stupid saw to use, anyway."

"Well—"

"And the handle looks all broke and everything." He pointed at the black tape. "Why don't you use a real saw?"

Why don't you mind your own business, Vicky wanted to snap, but she made herself smile politely. He was a beautiful child, with short blond hair and large eyes with thick lashes, a mouth with a perfectly outlined Cupid's bow. But the critical and unsmiling way he was looking at her made his face look tight, hostile. Where had he come from, anyway?

Next door. The child in the swing. Of course.

"This is the only saw I have," Vicky said. She resumed her work, hoping he would take the hint.

"It's not even 'lectric."

She ignored him, kept sawing, squinting against the sawdust starting to blow into her face.

"Jason!"

Thank goodness. An unmistakably parental voice.

The boy didn't answer. Vicky, her arm aching, transferred the saw to her other hand.

"Is that your father calling?"

"Yeah."

Still he just stood there, but his gaze dropped to his shoes, a pair of untidily laced runners. He began kicking at the ground with his right foot.

"Don't you think you should go home?"

"Yeah." But he didn't leave. His foot had made a hole in the grass and he was kicking at the dirt.

The man who must have called was walking over to them. Vicky didn't know whether to be relieved or dismayed. He would collect the child, but she would have preferred better circumstances under which to meet, given the way she had gaped at him the other morning in the alley.

The child, seeing him approach, began to sidle away from her.

"Jason!" The man was only a few yards from her now. "Are you bothering the neighbours already?"

"No," the boy said. He began to move off across the lawn, still kicking a little at the ground, casting quick, dark looks at his father and then at Vicky.

The man paused, as though unsure of what to do next, but then he continued towards Vicky. He was only slightly taller than she was, slim, and blond like his son, his hair thinning slightly on the top. He had deep-set large grey eyes, strangely rectangular in shape, a perfectly straight nose, a full-lipped mouth in a somewhat asymmetrical smile now but with the same clearly outlined Cupid's bow that his son had. He was, Vicky realized, a very handsome man.

"Hello," he said, putting his hand on the broken branch and looking at her over it. He was wearing jeans with greenish stains on the knees and a brown V-neck sweater with a white shirt underneath. "I hope Jason wasn't bothering you."

"No, no, that's fine." She brushed at a bead of sweat hanging from the tip of her nose.

"We've just moved in," he said, gesturing next door, where the boy was now sitting on the front steps, playing with a small wheeled toy. "My name's Richard Menard." He pronounced it with a French accent. "And I guess you've met Jason."

"I'm Vicky Bauer. Pleased to meet you." She began to extend her hand, then realized she was wearing dirty gloves, so, with a nervous laugh that dismayed her, she pulled her hand back and clamped it on the saw handle.

"Vicky," he said. "Hello."

She gave him a clumsy grin, one she imagined would look appropriate on a stroke victim. "So, are you all unpacked?"

He lifted his hand from the tree, made a gesture Vicky thought must refer to something of the usual trauma of moving. "Oh, it will take months, I expect. Jason is completely refusing to co-operate."

"Are there just the two of you?" Immediately she realized how it must sound. She inserted the saw back into the cut in the branch, fixing her eyes on it.

"Yes," he said. "I'm divorced. And you?"

Well, she deserved that bluntness. "My husband's in the hospital."

"Oh. I'm sorry. I hope it's nothing serious."

"Well, yes, I guess it is. Fairly." She blinked at a mist of rain that had appeared again in the air and began to saw, unable to think of anything else to say, to do. The blade started to stick and grate, and she felt so annoyed that she wanted to throw the implement into Birdy's hedge.

"Here. Let me." He stepped around to her side of the branch and put his hand on the saw, right above hers.

Here. Let me. It could have been Conrad's voice.

She tightened her hand on the handle. Immediately he dropped his, took a step back. "I'm sorry," he said. "I don't know why I should assume I could do it any easier."

"Well, you probably could. I'm not very good at this." Great. Now she had made herself sound incompetent.

"Do you want me to give it a try?"

"All right." It would seem rude to refuse.

He took hold of the handle and began to saw, as clumsily as she had at first, then, as the saw bit deeper, with long, heavy strokes. She watched the blade grind through the fleshy wood, the white dust and chips spurting into the air.

Suddenly the branch snapped, broke free, and fell to the ground with a grunt, a clatter of snapping twigs. Richard Menard jumped back, the branch missing his feet by inches. He laughed.

"It's still blocking your walk," he said, dropping the saw behind him. "But we can drag it out of the way. What do you think? Over to the hedge, maybe, for now?"

"Well, yes ..." When what she really wanted to say was no, leave it alone, I can do it; but she couldn't have done it, could she? She had just been thinking that, that when the branch fell it would be too heavy for her to move, so why wasn't she grateful for his help?

He had begun to pull at the branch, so she grabbed another part and pulled as well, and together they dragged it to the hedge. It *would* have been too heavy for her to move alone. But she could have sawed it up into smaller pieces, couldn't she? She didn't *have* to have his help. It made her feel better, to think his assistance was something she allowed but didn't need.

"Thanks," she said. "This was very good of you."

"No problem." He dusted off his hands, rubbed at a spot at the base of his thumb.

"Did you get a sliver?"

"Nothing serious." He dropped his hands into his pockets, pulled his shoulders up a little. "Getting colder," he said. He looked down the street, tilting his head at the weary monologue of the barking machine. "Is it like that every day? That dog? Don't people find it annoying?"

"Oh, yes," she said. "It barks like that until the people come home from work. My neighbour on the other side, Mrs. Birdsell, went over to complain once but they were very rude to her, and we haven't done anything about it since."

Richard Menard's eyes narrowed, two deep lines embedding themselves between his brows. "Pretty damned inconsiderate," he said. "Maybe I should go over and have a talk with them, too."

"Great," Vicky said. "I'll tell Birdy we have an ally."

"Go ahead. I liked this neighbourhood because it seemed so quiet."

Not one you should move into with young children, then, Vicky thought, but she said, "Oh, it is. Except for that house. Pretty well everyone else is older and retired. They're friendly, but they mind their own business." Did that sound like a hint? Everything she was saying to him seemed wrong. She wiped at the moisture gathering on her face with the back of her glove, could see the same mist, the minuscule droplets, collecting on his cheeks, his eyebrows and lashes.

"That's good. Our last neighbourhood had some pretty tough characters. I'm glad to get Jason away from there."

They both looked over at where Jason had been playing on the front steps of his new house, but he was no longer there. Richard sighed. "I'd better go see what he's into now."

Vicky took a step back. "Well. Thanks again for the help."

His eyes snapped back to her, and he smiled. "Any time."

Vicky watched him walk away, then quickly, in case he turned around, crouched down and began gathering some of the bigger twigs. When she heard his door close, she dropped her armful by the hedge and went inside.

She ran the hot water over her hands until they no longer felt like two clubs of ice on her wrists. She washed the sweat and the dewy rain off her face, and then she sat on the toilet seat lid and pressed the bath towel against her cheeks.

She would have to be careful, not let the man think she wanted his help, not let herself think she owed him anything.

He was very attractive. It was a complication.

Something had leapt up in her as she stood watching his sharp profile, watching the way the muscles moved in his forearm while he cut the branch. Vicky dropped the towel slowly from her face, let it pile up in her lap.

It had happened often enough since Conrad's accident, that sudden acceleration of the pulses—when she was in the middle of a conversation about Whole Language with the principal at McCauley Junior Secondary; when she was just standing next to the furnace repairman, for god's sake; when Amanda's brother was visiting from San Diego. She had decided it was rather like the automatic choke in her car that got stuck sometimes, revving and using up a lot of gas in neutral. It was the passage of pheromones in the air; it was the body's simple language and her mind did not have to listen. She was still Conrad's wife. She had never felt as much loyalty to him as she did when she was faced with losing him.

The doorbell. She glanced out the living-room window, which gave her a partial view of her front step, but she couldn't see anyone. She hooked the chain on and opened the door.

It was the child from next door. Jason.

"Oh," she said. "Just a minute." She unlatched the chain and pulled open the door, thinking she would have preferred to see the Jehovah's Witnesses. The noise of the barking machine rushed in with the cold air.

The boy now was wearing a blue corduroy jacket several sizes too small for him; the cuffs reached halfway up his forearms. In his right hand he was holding the saw up to her. "You left this out in your yard. Dad said I should give it to you."

"Oh, yes, so I did, how good of you to bring it over, it would have rusted out there." Babbling, the phony cheeriness in her voice.

And then she noticed the cuts in the door frame. About half a dozen, some of them a quarter inch deep, just where he was now leaning the blade.

Her stomach tightened, went cold. She made herself reach for the saw. The second her hand closed on the handle he released it. He was smiling slightly, ingenuously. But she could sense his excitement, the tension in his body, the way it was leaning slightly to the side, poised to run.

"Did you do this?" She pointed to the cuts. Her hand was shaking a little.

"Maybe." His large blue eyes looked up at her. When he blinked he seemed to raise his bottom lids slightly, a kind of twitch.

"Why? Why would you want to do that?"

"I was just leaning the saw there while I was waiting for you. Maybe it slipped."

"The cuts are too deep for that."

"I told you. The saw must have slipped."

She had no idea how to deal with something like this, how to talk to children his age. "Maybe we should speak to your dad about it."

He blinked several times, harder, so that he seemed to be squinting. Then he shrugged, looked away with improbable casualness at a passing bicyclist in a long yellow raincoat.

What should she do, say, now? She mustn't overreact; he might do something worse.

She leaned over to set the saw down behind her. The child took a quick step back, stopped when he saw she was not moving towards him. Vicky crouched down so she could look him in the face. She took a deep breath, put on her teacher's voice.

"We won't tell your father, all right? But don't do anything like this again. Will you promise me?"

The boy glanced across at his house, where Vicky heard a sudden sound, like a door slamming. She looked over, too, but she couldn't see next door from where she was.

The boy took a step backward, then another, and another, until he was standing at the bottom of her three front steps.

"Maybe," he said. He shoved his hands into his jacket pockets, and then, in no hurry, not looking back, he walked away across her lawn, kicking a little at the ground as he went. The untied shoelace from his left runner twitched along behind him through the grass.

When she couldn't see him any longer, Vicky closed the door, quickly, and put the chain back on. She had to stop herself from rushing to her bedroom window, which faced west towards the Menard house, to see if he really was going home.

She would call Amanda. Amanda had subbed in elementary schools; she might know what was going on with this boy.

But there was no answer. Of course: she would still be at school, at Fraser Secondary, her second week there, smiling politely at Jesus Christ. The memory of what he had done to Vicky yesterday surged over her. What if he *had* blackballed her; what if she couldn't get any more work—

She wouldn't think about it, any of it, not Jesus Christ or work or money or the boy next door.

She dug out the vacuum cleaner and shoved it with vicious concentration around the living room, jabbing it into corners she had avoided for months, moving end tables and chairs to get at the puddles of dust around their legs.

In the study, really only the other small bedroom, she

pushed the blunt nose of the machine too aggressively into the bookcase, toppling a stack of Amanda Cross mysteries Amanda had given her during what she called her heroine addict phase. Vicky knelt to pick them up, then reached as well for a piece of paper fallen into the gap between the bookcase and the desk.

It was an old, yellowed crossword puzzle, torn from the daily paper, half completed.

It was Conrad's. He would work on a crossword to relax, and she would sometimes wander by and offer suggestions.

She picked up a pencil. 32 Down: *Little*. Five letters, second letter, "c." *Scant*, it must be. She wrote in the "s," moved her fingers slowly past the "c" that Conrad had written here over a year ago, and printed, *ant*.

A dark splotch appeared on the second empty square of 28 Across.

"'Scurf'? Come on, there's no such word." He poked his pencil at her arm.

"Yes, there is! Don't you know nothin'? Scurf is dandruff." She pulled the pencil from his fingers and wrote in "scurf." "See, it fits."

"Well, I'll be scurfed."

"Flake off."

Don't. Don't. Don't.

She let her head fall forward onto her arms, and she cried.

Finally she could stop. She wiped at her nose and eyes, and then she folded up the wet puzzle and dropped it into the garbage can beside the desk.

Grief is a kind of laziness, she had read once. It had made her angry then, the writer's insensitivity, but now the idea seemed oddly reassuring.

She was just taking out the macaroni for supper when

the phone rang, and it was Joyce Holly from Southridge Secondary asking Vicky to come in for her until the end of the week. Yes, yes, of course she could: her voice gushy with relief.

As she was driving to see Conrad that evening, she thought of everything she would have to tell him. There was the business of her father and his stupid socks—and his gun, good heavens, she mustn't forget that; and how she had fixed the back steps; and that disturbing boy. She would tell him about Richard Menard, too, but not, she thought, about the feelings he had stirred in her. Although she could. She wasn't ashamed. Or was she? If she wasn't, she should be able to tell Conrad. She wondered if he would have understood.

WEDNESDAY

"DRUMLIN."

They wrote it down.

"Medial moraine."

Geography 12 was her favourite course. The students were usually good, and the course itself was such a peaceful one—no wars, no human involvement at all, just the implacable life of the earth.

"Esker," she said, walking up the middle aisle to the front of the room.

Someone had opened the door and was gesturing at her. "Col," she said, going over.

It was one of the secretaries, a pony-tailed brunette with translucent skin and a smudge of lipstick on her teeth. "There's a phone call for you," she whispered. "It sounds urgent."

"Who is it?" Conrad, she thought, something's happened to Conrad.

"Your father."

Vicky let out the breath she'd been holding. "Did he say what was wrong?"

"No, he just wants to talk to you. He sounds pretty upset."

"Well, could you tell him I'll call him back at the end of the period? It's only ten more minutes. I'm in the middle of giving a quiz."

"Okay, sure." The secretary stepped back and closed the door, gently.

Her father. She felt a pang of guilt at her relief. But it could be something serious; he could have fallen and broken something. He must be desperate to have tracked her down at school; he'd never done that before. She glanced at her watch. Surely a few more minutes wouldn't matter.

The bell. She dashed around the room snatching papers from under still-scribbling pens, then pushed her way down the hallway to the general office. The secretary handed her the phone over the counter.

"Thanks." Vicky punched out the numbers.

It rang three times, four times. What should she do if he didn't answer—

"Yeah?"

"Dad! Are you okay?"

"Those damned Meals-on-Wheels people didn't come. I'm sitting here starving and they didn't come. Eleven-thirty, that woman told me, and sometimes she hasn't come until after twelve—"

"Is that why you called me? To say you haven't had *lunch*?"

"—and now look, it's after two and where is she? I got a number for her and nobody answers. What the hell good are they—"

"You call me at school, say it's urgent, get me out of my class—" She could hardly speak. The secretary was listening, a little collusive smile twitching her lips.

"How did you get this number, anyway?"

"I called the school board."

"And said it was an emergency, I suppose."

"So what? Now come over when you're done there and fix me something. Doesn't have to be fancy."

"You can open a can of something for yourself, for god's sake—"

"Someday you'll have crippled-up hands and you'll

know what it's like, even something like a can-opener—"

"All right, all *right!*"

The *nerve* of him, to call her here, because his *lunch* was late.

But after school there she was, driving over to his apartment even though Amanda was expecting her at the pub at four.

She knocked. When she heard him reply, she turned the handle, and the door opened. Not locked, not with the chain on: she'd told him a hundred times—

She froze. Directly across the room from where she stood her father sat in his wheelchair, holding the gun in both hands. It was pointing right at her.

"Oh. It's you." He set the gun on the windowsill behind him.

"What are you *doing* with that thing?" Her voice was so loud the woman in the apartment across the hall cracked open her door and peered at Vicky over her security chain.

Vicky came inside and slammed shut the door. This was the last straw.

"I didn't know it was you," he said. "The apartment across the street got its front doors kicked in last night. I have to be careful."

"Your door wasn't even locked!"

"I was waiting for those damned Meals-on-Wheels people."

"And if they'd come you'd have pointed your gun at them."

"I didn't know who it was! I said, 'Who is it?' and you didn't answer."

"I thought you said, 'Come in.'"

"I said, 'Who is it?' and you didn't answer."

"You tell me your hands are so bad you can't even open a can but you sit here with a gun—"

"It's not hard to fire a gun."

"I'm taking it out of here." She stepped around the coffee table, heading for the window.

He wheeled his chair around faster than she thought he could and snatched up the gun. "Don't you touch it! I know what I'm doing!"

She stopped, looking at him hunched in his chair, holding the gun close to his chest like some desperado. "If you don't give that to me I'm leaving."

"I know what I'm doing!"

"Then I'm leaving." She turned and strode to the door, her coat flying open and catching on the coffee table. She jerked it free.

"Aw, Vicky."

She stopped, didn't turn around. "Then give me the gun."

"Aw, Vicky. Come on."

"No. I'm leaving." She put her hand on the doorknob.

"Just open a can of beans for me before you go, then. That's all. Is that too much to ask? Just open a can or two. So I can have something to eat. I haven't had anything since breakfast. Come on. Is that too much to ask?"

So she gave in. God damn him. (And what if she hadn't given in, she was asking herself now, sitting in the police station; what if she had been as stubborn as he was and had kept saying, no, I won't do anything for you, no, unless you give me the gun?)

Vicky found a can of beans and another of creamed corn in his cupboard, and she dumped them into pots and warmed them up. Her father sat watching her, holding his gun in his lap. When the corn began to bubble, Vicky poured it and the beans onto a plate and set it on the counter beside the sink. She poured him a glass of milk, too, from the surprisingly well-stocked refrigerator, restraining herself from asking him to identify the blobs that looked like lumps of green petroleum jelly in a saucer on the top rack. She set the milk on the counter, picked up her purse, and walked to the door.

She was just closing it behind her when her father said, "Wait."

She turned and saw him wheeling toward her with a string bag of oranges in his lap.

"Take these," he said. "Leo bought a whole bunch. I don't want them. I can't peel them and anyway they just squirt juice up my nose."

"I don't want them, either."

"They'll just go to waste."

"All right." She sighed, picked up the bag by the metal clamp at the top of the strings. She never seemed able to win these last-minute skirmishes at the door.

She had just taken a few steps down the hall when the elevator door opened and Leo stepped out. He was wearing a huge olive-green parka with the fur-lined hood up. When he saw her he pushed it back, where it clung to the back of his neck like some animal with its hair on end. Vicky stood, trapped, clutching her guilty oranges.

"Been to see your dad, eh?"

"Yeah. Big crisis. His Meals-on-Wheels people were late so he phoned me at work to come over and save him."

Leo looked down at his feet as though she had reprimanded him. "Maybe he called me, too. If I'd been home I coulda come over and made him something."

"Oh, Leo," she said, "you don't need to do that. He can do things for himself."

"You just call me if you need me. You and your dad both."

"Well ... thanks," she said awkwardly. Behind Leo the elevator doors closed; Vicky could hear the lift lumber away.

"Your dad says you should have a gun," Leo said. "Living alone and all. I can get you one. From the States. 45's."

45's. It took her a moment to realize he was not, in his usual fractured way, suddenly talking about old records.

"No, Leo, really, I don't want a gun. You shouldn't have one, either. You don't have a licence, do you?"

"Don't need one," he said slyly.

It would be worse than trying to argue with her father. "Well," she said. "Thanks for the oranges." She held them up as though he could possibly have missed seeing them. "Dad couldn't eat them all and they looked so good we hated to let them go to waste."

He grinned, seemed actually to raise himself on tiptoe for a moment. "Yeah. They were two-for-one. Pretty nice deal. And no toothpaste."

"No toothpaste, eh?" Help. She began edging past him to the stairs.

"An orange a day keeps the doctor away."

She had to laugh. Maybe he had even intended to make a joke. Leo's mind worked in strange and mysterious ways.

When she pulled into the parking lot at the pub, Amanda's green 1960 Chevy was already there. Amanda had bought it twenty years ago when the car was cheap and tacky, and she'd kept it long enough for it to have become valuable and tacky. She had named it "fins-*de-siècle*."

Vicky pulled open the heavy door of the pub, detonating a charge of rock music and cigarette smoke. The bar was large but able to feign coziness with poor lighting and a few booths strewn against the walls. The place had a nautical theme, with pictures of ships and sailors on the walls and several anchors embedded in the floor where people were most prone to stumble over them. Vicky was meeting

Amanda here today only because it was equidistant from their schools. Bars were places Vicky preferred to stay out of. She knew too well their dangers, their temptations.

"About time!" Amanda shouted, making the people at the next table stop talking to stare at them both.

"I'm sorry, I'm sorry." Vicky dropped into a chair. Amanda had two empty glasses in front of her and was starting on a third, but Vicky knew this was not necessarily evidence of the length of time she had been waiting. The speed of her drinking could be formidable if she was depressed.

"And happy birthday," Vicky said. Amanda was thirty-eight today. Vicky was two years older.

"Yeah," Amanda said dolorously. "Happy birthday. I used that in English 12 as an example of oxymoron." She lifted her arm to wave at the waitress, almost slapping a passing man in the stomach. "A ginger ale for my friend," she shouted. "And another keg for me."

Vicky gestured at the empty glasses. "This looks very celebratory."

"Celebratory, fuck. I just wanted something to pick me up. Besides pallbearers."

"You *are* in a good mood."

"I'm in a rotten mood. Of course, when you're in a rotten mood for thirty-eight years they call it your personality." She sighed lugubriously. "I got a gift from my sister in the mail yesterday. A travel alarm, and she wrote on its face in red felt pen: *your biological clock*. Bitch."

"Oh, I'm sure she just meant to make you laugh." But Vicky was thinking, yes, that's pretty nasty all right. The sort of thing her father would give her if he were clever enough.

"Yeah, well. I guess I have to face it. Age has withered my infinite variety."

"You're not getting older; you're getting bitter."

"Huh. The school board could use that one for their Hallmark line of teacher evaluations."

"Speaking of which, how has Jesus Christ been shaping up?"

Amanda poked her forefinger into her mouth and made a retching sound. "He's been walking up and down the hallways during classes writing on a clipboard. Compiling secret files on us all for the Last Judgement or something." The waitress brought their drinks. "Really, the man is so anal-retentive the shit in his bowel's as old as he is."

Vicky laughed, took a sip of her ginger ale.

"Damn." Amanda had spilled a little beer on herself. "I hope this sweater can be washed," she said, rubbing at the spot.

"That's new, isn't it?" The sweater was elaborately beaded, attractive but pushing towards excess. Amanda tended to swing from wild materialism to hoarding, the latter in preparation for a barbaric future in which only the rich would survive. Amanda had, Vicky thought, a kind of financial bulimia.

"Yeah." Amanda stroked the beadwork. "It cost the earth. It'll be just water and beans for the next month, I can tell you."

"Beans."

"Beans?"

So Vicky had to explain. She had never really told Amanda about her father, just that he was there, a generic sort of parent, getting older and needing attention.

"He really has a *gun*? What are you going to do?"

"I don't know. He's driving me crazy. I keep telling myself I won't put up with him any more, but next day there I am again. I just feel kind of ... stuck with him."

"Oh, well. He's your father."

"Sort of."

"What do you mean, 'sort of'?"

"He's not my real father."

She hadn't intended to tell Amanda that. Vicky had never told anyone. Not even Conrad.

What her mother had given her, in an envelope, wrapped in tissue, on her seventeenth birthday, and what she kept pressed between pages 22 and 23 of her high school yearbook, was a picture of a gawky white youth with red hair, wearing a wrinkled blue suit jacket and black slacks. He had been killed in a car accident, and Vicky's mother, pregnant and terrified, had married Arthur O'Rourke a month and a half later.

"Wouldn't he have known?" Amanda was leaning across the table, sucking the story in. "Or at least guessed?"

Vicky shook her head. "I considered that. But I don't think so. He was too ..." She drummed her fingers on the table, looking for the right word. "... limited, somehow, not to have let it slip if he knew. The only times he would say anything good about me was when he thought it reflected on him, because I was *his, his* genetic offspring."

Amanda leaned back, pressed her palms together, and balanced her chin on her fingertips. Vicky recognized the posture: Amanda was going to Analyze The Situation. Why had she told her any of this? She poked her straw gloomily at the sliver of ice in the bottom of her glass.

"Maybe that was his only way of telling you he was proud of you. Maybe you're being too hard on him."

"You don't know anything about it."

Mind your own business. Vicky hadn't meant it like that, but she didn't know what else to say now.

Amanda dropped her hands onto the table, folded them together, and leaned forward a little. "Did you ever wonder," she said, "why the two men in your life are, shall we say, manqué—you know, men-with-something-missing?"

Vicky stared at her. "What do you mean by that?"

"Both Conrad and your father are invalids, neither of them offering you much but frustration, yet you seem to be devoted to their caretaking. Just an observation."

"That's not fair." It was one of Amanda's little defensive tricks, to make some personal comment she would profess was innocent when she meant to be hurtful. Vicky pushed her chair back, reached behind her and pulled her coat across her arm. "I have to go," she said stiffly.

"Wait. What's the matter? You don't have to go yet." Amanda, Vicky was gratified to see, seemed genuinely dismayed.

"I have to go."

"Are you mad at me? I'm sorry—I know I can be too outspoken sometimes."

"You? Outspoken? By whom?"

Amanda laughed. "Now, Vicky—"

"Really, I have to go." She turned and walked quickly away, trying not to hear what Amanda was calling after her. A drunk stuck out his leg in front of her, burped, "Hey, chickie." She stepped over it without breaking her stride.

There was definitely snow in the rain now. She sat shivering in her car waiting for it to warm, watching the mushy blotches hit the windshield and run down, like partly coagulated egg white.

She should have stayed and talked it out with Amanda. It was her birthday, for goodness' sake. Vicky had been walking too angrily out of too many rooms lately.

Men manqué. What hurt most was the way Amanda had lumped Conrad and her father together, as though they belonged in the same category. She must have known how that would make Vicky feel.

But that was Amanda. Vicky sighed. She would refuse

to speak to her for a few days, which she knew made Amanda crazy, and then they would go on as though nothing had happened. They were childish and immature, of course they were. Maybe they were friends manqué.

Well, they had survived harsher arguments than this one about Vicky's relationships to men. About five months ago Amanda had accused Vicky of feeling superior because she had a husband. Vicky hadn't believed she was serious.

"How very 1955 of you, Amanda," she'd said.

"I mean it, Vicky. Before Conrad's accident you hardly ever bothered with me. That time we were both subbing for a week at Cloverdale I asked you twice to come for a coffee or something after school. You kept saying no, Conrad was expecting you home."

"But that doesn't—"

"And even now I'm just a second choice. You'll do things with me only because your man isn't around. 1955? Yeah, okay. 1955."

"Jesus, Amanda. I'm not married to you."

"Precisely."

And they had gone on, saying crueler things, accusations of selfishness and possessiveness. But what Vicky felt, finally, was less anger than shame. Because she knew Amanda was right. Not about Vicky feeling superior, but about most of the rest of it. She knew she had felt a need to make it up to Conrad for the years she hadn't appreciated him, the years she had yearned for the hard glitter of passion and independence.

She rubbed a hole in the fog on her windshield and headed for home. The snow was sticking to the road now, and the car started to slide when she braked. What if it was worse tomorrow? She *had* to get to school; she was taking home student exercise books and one of the texts, and not going back when she had more than a one-day assignment meant she lost the chance, however remote, of a second week and higher pay. Although, she thought, glancing at the pile of marking on the seat beside her, the second day was harder than the second week. If she were god she would make subs human on the second day.

As she pulled into her driveway she saw Birdy setting her garbage out. Birdy trotted quickly around her hedge to cut Vicky off before she could escape inside.

"I met your new neighbour," she said, in a whisper they could hear in Blaine. She gave a sly look next door. "Richard. We had a nice little talk. He's from the States somewhere, Seattle, I think. And he's a part-time teacher, just like you. An art teacher." She shuffled closer. "And you know what else? He went over and made those people do something about that barking machine! Not a peep out of it all day. Isn't that amazing?"

"It sure is," Vicky said, impressed.

"Well, a man that handsome and efficient can put his shoes under my bed any time." Birdy nudged Vicky's purse with her elbow. "He was asking all about you."

"He was, was he? And what did you tell him?"

"Oh, just that you were one hot tomato."

"Birdy!"

Birdy snorted. "You get to be my age you learn you can't waste time. You can't wait forever."

"Sometimes we aren't the ones who make those choices," Vicky said, a bit stiffly. She had never quite learned how to handle Birdy's blunt pragmatism, developed from years of co-owning a local auto dealership.

"Sure, sure," Birdy said. She rubbed fiercely at her upper arms, as though she were trying to start a fire from the friction, and trotted back around her hedge. "So don't do anything I couldn't do," she called over her shoulder.

Vicky waved and started up her back steps, pleased to

feel them firm under her weight.

Her foot stopped in midair above the second step from the top. She could feel her heart begin to race.

In front of her door were a toy tractor, about the size of her fist, and a stuffed animal, slightly larger. Both seemed to have been carefully placed, facing the door, their backs to her, as though waiting to enter. Vicky's hand tightened on the railing. Jason: he must have left them, and purposefully, not because he just forgot. He wanted her to know he had been here, on her back porch.

Suddenly she was sure he was watching. She could literally feel the hairs rise on the back of her neck. She forced herself not to turn around, not to look across at the three windows of his house overlooking her back yard.

She stepped up to the landing, inserted the key into the lock. With her right foot she pushed the toys to the side, slowly, to make it clear she did not want to damage them, but also, she hoped, with enough casualness to show she had no time to bother with them. When she was inside she leaned back against the closed door in relief.

He's just a child, she told herself, just a child. There's nothing sinister in what he's done: odd, maybe, but not sinister. She went into the living room, turned up the thermostat, listened to her messages. There were requests from two teachers asking her to sub for them tomorrow, and it gave her some satisfaction to phone back and say no, she was sorry, she was already booked.

"I'm one hot tomato," she said to her cat, who crawled out from under the sofa and sat looking at her with his left eye still closed. "Come here," she said, leaning down and patting the carpet. Of course he didn't move.

When Ernest, Conrad's cousin, had first seen him, he had winked and said, "You realize they say that when couples get a pet it's a trial run before having children."

Vicky had laughed. "Don't be silly," she'd said.

The cat lay down now on his back with his legs curled in the air, looking at her suggestively. It was supposed to be a posture of trust, but after all this time she didn't believe it. It was the posture of a Venus fly-trap.

"You don't fool me," she said. The cat began to writhe persuasively.

She really should have a name for him. But Conrad had said it was anthropomorphic to name animals, and since it had taken her weeks to talk him into getting a cat in the first place, him arguing that with half the world starving it was immoral to feed an animal whose only function was to lick its genitals to entertain them, she didn't insist. But she was amused to see Conrad become even more fond of the cat than she was, buying him silly toys, letting him sleep on their bed—

Don't remember. Don't. Don't.

She made herself an omelette for supper, eating little chunks from the pan as it cooked, eyeing the pile of Geography quizzes. A teacher had said to her once, "You subs are so lucky, you don't have to do any homework." Vicky had smiled and said something polite.

She picked up the first paper. Hell, she thought, would be a series of rooms filled with unmarked papers; she would finish in one room only to be thrown into the next. Like all the fairy tales of maidens given huge, impossible, boring tasks. At least the men in fairy tales, she mused, circling for about the thousandth time in her life a spelling of "government" without the "n," were, for their tests of character, given adventures, quests, voyages, dragons to slay. The maidens were given drudgery, confinement, sleep, a long wait for rescue.

There was a knock at the back door.

That boy. Jason. Who else would come to her back

door? She sat, unmoving: maybe he would go away. Another knock, louder. The lights were on, and the radio; her car was in the drive; she couldn't pretend she wasn't home.

When she opened the door, warily, wishing she'd had a chain put on the back door as she had on the front, it wasn't the boy who stood there, but his father. Richard.

"Vicky," he said, as though they were friends, as though he had said her name a hundred times. The light from the kitchen lay itself in odd angles across his face, drawing a sharp triangle from his right ear down, across his neck to his shirt collar. Flakes of snow were clinging to his hair.

"Yes," she said. She had wanted to make the word harder, interrogative, but it came out sounding acquiescent. But she *wasn't* glad to see him; she was relieved it wasn't the boy, that was all. Her fingers were pressing so hard on the door frame it felt as though she were driving her nails back into the quick.

He must have come for the toys. But when she looked down they were gone, and he wasn't holding them. So the boy must have sneaked over while she was having supper, and gathered them up—

"—to bother you," Richard was saying. "I know it's late. But I'm in a bit of a fix. I was trying to get the stove set up and the damned thing fell on me and I've cut my hand. I think it needs some stitches, so, oh, I know this is a real imposition, but could you drive me to the hospital? I don't think I can drive myself, and I don't know how long a cab would take—"

He kept talking, but Vicky had stopped listening, could only stare at his left hand, around which he had wrapped a dishtowel but from which blood was slowly seeping, dropping now in two, three, thick dark drops onto her doormat.

She had taken a first-aid course once. All she could

remember was that she wasn't supposed to panic.

"I'll get my car keys," she said. "Stay right here."

She rushed upstairs and grabbed her purse and coat, and jerked a towel from the bathroom as she passed. Richard had already started back down the outside stairs, holding his hand over the railing so he wouldn't drip onto her steps. She shoved the towel at him, realized he wasn't able to take it without letting go of the dishtowel, so, clumsily, trying to make her way past him and down the steps, she took hold of his hand and wrapped the towel around both it and the dishtowel.

He was telling her again how it had happened, something about the metal edge at the bottom of the stove, but she was barely listening. She heard her voice say something, too, something about the car, and then she was unlocking the doors, opening his, getting in herself and starting the motor.

"This is awfully good of you," he said, leaning back and closing his eyes. His face in the dim light looked pale, ghostly.

"What about Jason?" she asked. "Will he be all right alone?"

"He'll be okay. He was in the middle of some television program I couldn't pry him away from."

The hospital was only a few miles from her house. She had driven to it so often before Conrad was transferred to the extended care unit that knowledge of the quickest route seemed to be preserved in her hands, in the car itself. Stop here, turn right there, cut down the alley to avoid the wait on Sixteenth—

"It'll be okay," she said, for at least the third time. "There's Emergency."

"Such a stupid thing to do. I should have been more careful."

"At least it's your left hand." She remembered his right, sawing the branch.

"Small mercies," he said. She could hear his breathing, uneven, pulling the air in through clenched teeth.

There was nothing as effective as bleeding onto the nice clean floor in Emergency to get attention, Vicky thought, as a doctor hurried over, saying in his practised paternal way, "Well, well, what have we here?" The nurse took Richard's elbow and ushered him away into one of the cubicles.

Vicky stood, halfway between the doors and the admitting desk, and wondered what she should do now. It had all happened so fast: it must be barely ten minutes since she'd heard the knock on the door, and now here she was in Emergency, with a man she had just met yesterday.

She had brought him here: surely that was all that was necessary. It might even look odd if she hung around, waiting. She turned to go.

"Just a minute." The nurse was back at her station, and Vicky couldn't pretend she didn't know that peremptory voice was directed at her.

"Yes?" She turned, aware that the two women sitting in the waiting room had looked up from their magazines and were watching her. She walked back to the admitting desk.

The nurse was a solid, rectangular-shaped woman; the belt that went around the middle of her uniform encircled the idea more than the reality of a waist. "We need some information on … is it your husband?"

"No," Vicky said stiffly. "My neighbour."

"Well, tell us what you know, then. His name, anyway."

"He just moved in yesterday. I don't know anything about him." Why was she so defensive? It wasn't as though he had been arrested and she was an accomplice.

The nurse looked at her with obvious skepticism.

"Well, okay. I suppose I can get it from him."

"Will it, will he, be long? I mean—I don't know whether I should wait—"

"Half an hour, maybe. You should wait. He'll be on some painkillers and we're not supposed to release him unless someone can assume responsibility for getting him home."

Great. Wonderful. Assume Responsibility. Another man manqué. She dropped herself onto one of the inhospitable chairs in the waiting room. She remembered her anxiety about Richard helping her with the tree, her fear of owing him something; but it might be just as dangerous to have him feel he owed her something.

She sighed, picked up a magazine. The woman across from her glanced up, smiled tiredly. Her eyes were red, the skin around them puffy. She reminded Vicky suddenly of herself sitting here a year ago, dazed and exhausted, waiting through the night for news, any news, and how at last when the doctor had told her, gently, she had nodded and stood up and driven home, and at eight o'clock had gotten back into her car and gone to work.

She turned a page in the magazine, another, another, so hard it tore a gash into the forehead of Madonna on page 97.

She shouldn't be here. She should be home marking Geography quizzes. Now by the time she got them done it would be too late to go see Conrad.

Then there was the boy. Was he really okay? He shouldn't be left for long. Surely he would be worried. No matter how compelling his TV program, the last he'd seen of his father he was dripping blood and stumbling out the door.

Vicky closed the magazine. Half an hour, the nurse had said: it must be that by now.

And then there he was, coming out from behind the admitting desk, his hand tidily bandaged. He was, she noticed for the first time, wearing dark blue rugby pants and a faded beige sweatshirt with a smeary red stain on the left sleeve. The nurse was talking to him and writing things on a clipboard, but he was paying her little attention. His eyes were scanning the room, until they found Vicky. He waved, and headed over. She went to meet him. She was aware of the woman across from her watching them, and again she could feel herself sitting there, while others got up and left with those they were waiting for, sitting there all night, waiting, for the husband who would not come back.

"I'm glad you're still here," Richard said, smiling. He had the most handsome teeth.

"It wasn't very long." She wasn't going to tell him she had Assumed Responsibility. "How's your hand?"

He lifted it, flexed the fingers slightly. "Not bad. Three stitches. I was lucky I didn't cut any nerves."

They went out to the car, which, Vicky was startled to see, she had left in an ambulance zone.

"Did they give you anything? Tranquilizers or something?" Vicky turned onto Sixteenth, the car sliding a little in the snow.

"A pill of some kind. I do feel rather tranquil, now that you mention it." He sighed and leaned back, holding his bandaged hand up against his chest. "Oh, shit," he said, sitting back up.

"What?"

"I forgot your towel. They'll probably just throw it away."

"It doesn't matter. It was an old one, anyway." The towel had been a wedding gift, part of a set. *It doesn't matter.* Her lie was a physical cramp in her chest.

She accelerated into their alley faster than she should

have, and the car skidded almost into the fence of the corner house. Richard braced his free hand on the dashboard, but he didn't say anything. She let the car roll to a stop at his driveway.

"You can walk from here, I hope," she said. "If I pull into your driveway I might not be able to back out."

"This is just fine." He released his seat belt, opened the door. "Ah, I wonder if I could ask you just one more favour." He fiddled with his seat belt strap, letting it retract, pulling it out a few inches, letting it retract. "Please say no if you're too busy. But when the stove fell it blocked the refrigerator door, and I'm wondering if you could help me push it out of the way. It's just that I'll need to get into the fridge to make Jason's lunch for tomorrow...."

So of course she had to agree.

She followed him nervously into the house. She had been inside once when the McClintocks lived here, but now, in the dark, it felt strange, unfamiliar. The house was larger and newer than hers, which was so old city hall had no record of its year of construction, but the plans of the two houses were similar: a back staircase leading to a small porch which opened onto the kitchen, a combined living room and dining room off to the right and the bedrooms and bathroom to the left.

The kitchen, when she entered, made her think an earthquake had hit while they were out, knocking open cupboard doors and spilling the contents onto the counters, into the boxes piled everywhere.

"It's such a mess. Sorry."

"The day after a move," she said. "I know."

The stove lay on its side in front of the refrigerator, two of the burners knocked loose and lying several feet away. A trail of blood drops led from the side of the stove to the sink. She shuddered.

From the living room she heard the shrill noise of the television, so she assumed the boy was there. She expected him to come out and see what was happening, but he didn't.

Richard went to the doorway and said, "Jason? Everything okay?"

The boy made a reply she couldn't hear, and Richard came back into the kitchen, stood looking down at the stove. "If we move it back towards that wall," he said, pointing, "just a few feet, it should be okay."

"All right." She bent down and began to push. Richard knelt beside her and began shoving with his shoulder and free hand, and slowly the stove scraped across the floor, leaving a dark scratch in the tile, until there was enough room for the refrigerator door to open.

They stood up, clumsily, bumping into the strewn boxes to avoid bumping into each other. Vicky wiped her hands on her pants, dismayed to see a greasy black smear appear on her right thigh.

"Aren't you going to set it up?" The boy was standing in the entrance to the living room looking at the stove critically. He was wearing a pair of wrinkly pajamas with spaceships on them and holding a bowl of potato chips. He took one out, bit into it noisily. Some of it crumbled and fell to the floor.

"No," Richard said, turning to him. "I'll have someone come in tomorrow and install it."

The boy took out another chip, gestured with it at Richard's bandaged hand. "She put that on?" He pointed the chip at Vicky, not looking at her.

"No. She took me to the hospital. You know that."

Jason shrugged, bit into the chip.

"You should be in bed by now." Richard took a step towards him. The boy took a step back.

"You haven't put the sheets on it yet."

"All *right*! I will."

Vicky took a step back, too, like the boy. Her heel hit the stove, and she stumbled back, grabbing the kitchen counter for support. By the time she regained her balance, she was in the doorway to the porch, and, taking advantage of her location, she took another step into it. It would be hard to miss the fact that she was leaving.

Richard turned to her. He looked exhausted. When he smiled she could tell it took an effort. "Thanks for everything, Vicky. I don't know what I'd have done without you."

"You'd have managed," Vicky said, stepping outside, into the clean snowy air.

As she trudged gratefully up her own back steps, the cat bounded out from underneath them, startling her, and leaped up the stairs in front of her. She thought she'd left him inside, but he must have gone out when she had, in all the excitement. As she put her key into the lock, she realized she hadn't locked the door behind her when she left, either. Well, in the state she was in she should be glad she'd even closed it.

It wasn't until she was in the dining room, setting her purse onto the bookcase where she always kept it, that she knew somebody had been in the house.

She stayed completely still, her hand frozen on the strap of her purse. On the table in front of her, the Geography quizzes were strewn across the table, as though a wind had raked over them. Two of her books had been pulled from the bookcase and were lying, open, pages squashed down into the carpet in the middle of the living-room floor. The blue vase from her buffet was sitting upright on the sofa.

She knew she should run out of the house and call the police, that the intruder could still be here. But she stayed where she was, still, for a long time. The cat came into the living room, headed straight for the books and sniffed them suspiciously. Then he sat down and began grooming himself. It was his apparent unconcern that finally made her let go of her purse and walk slowly through the living room, looking for what else had been moved.

Whoever had done it was gone now, she was reasonably certain of that. And with each step she became more sure of who it had been.

Nothing else in the living room seemed out of place, although she didn't think she'd left the phone book open on the coffee table like that. The bathroom and bedroom seemed untouched. She sat on the bed for a moment, gingerly, looking around, reassuring her eyes with familiar objects in their familiar places.

But in the study she found something else. The fern that had been sitting on the little stool by the window was lying on the floor, its dirt spilling out onto the carpet. She scooped up as much as she could and put it back into the pot. But no fronds had been broken, and the dirt left on the carpet could be vacuumed up easily enough. It was as though the pot had not been dumped from its perch but lifted down and placed on its side on the floor. She looked around at the rest of her study, at the computer and disks, the antique clock Ernest had given them, the soapdish full of coins on the file cabinet. This was not ordinary vandalism; this was not theft. But what *was* it, then? A message? A warning?

She went back into the living room, sat down on the sofa. She should call the police now, she supposed, but she knew she wasn't going to do it. She couldn't prove it was Jason. Even if she could, would phoning the police be the best thing to do? And she *had* left her door unlocked; she was partly to blame. At best, the police would talk to

Richard about it, and it would be better if she tried that first herself. She had given the boy a second chance after the saw business, and it obviously hadn't worked, so she had to do what she said she would: talk to his father.

Why did the McClintocks have to move? As though her life weren't difficult enough as it was. She leaned back and closed her eyes.

On the inside of her eyelids, like some delayed after-image, she saw Richard standing at her door, the light from her kitchen laying itself with delicate shadows along his cheek.

She sat up abruptly. The cat stopped licking himself and looked at her, his rear leg propped up at an obtuse angle.

"Don't ask me," Vicky said. "I have no idea."

She had to mark the Geography quizzes. She got up, closed the phone book and put it away on the shelf under the phone. It would be several months before she would open it to that page again, and she would see, circled in the red pencil that now lay on her kitchen table, the name *Christine Menard.*

THURSDAY

"YOU CAN'T IMAGINE how creepy it felt, coming into the house and finding things lying around like that."

Vicky lifted the last spoonful of tapioca pudding to Conrad's lips. He seemed to lean his head forward a little in anticipation.

"Oh, maybe I'm overreacting. He probably won't do it again. Remember when we talked about getting new dead-bolts and you said more people want to break out of homes than into them?"

She tried the glass of orange juice. He puckered his lips and let her pour some into his mouth.

"Tomorrow's my last day at Hillcrest. Joyce will be back Monday." Vicky sighed. "At noon the principal caught me as I was coming down to the staff room and, Mr. Ingenuous, he says, 'I was wondering if you'd like to coach the girls' volleyball team over lunch. Joyce enjoys doing it. But you don't have to.' I liked that *you don't have to.* As though I could really refuse."

She wiped a little trail of orange juice from Conrad's chin. His hands curled into soft fists, the thumbs moving back and forth, pulling the fabric of his pants into soft pleats.

"Not that being a suck is paying off. Hillcrest just hired three new teachers, and I'd applied for the Socials position, of course, but the man who got it was right out of university. The principal introduced the new teachers in the staff room in the morning, and when he came to me he said,

'She's just subbing today,' not even saying my name. It makes me so mad. I have to sub to stay in the system, but the longer I do it the more they think, if she's any good, why is she a sub?"

She walked over to the window, looked out at the white streets, the wet snow bending the willows in the front grounds to the earth. Anger, useless anger. Anger turned inward equals depression; anger turned outward equals ... what? Beating up a student? She stood there for several minutes, and then she went back to her chair. There was a smell in the room of fresh wax or polish, with perhaps a hint of urine (the same smell, almost exactly, as there was here, in the police station, where she and Amanda sat waiting).

Conrad stared across the room, at the painting of the ocean on the far wall. Vicky looked at it, too, at the way it showed the white waves folding onto the beach, the way it stopped time. The artist had held up his hand and commanded the ocean to stop, and it did.

"I wish I knew what to do about Dad," Vicky said. "That gun business. If I report him I'll get old Leo in trouble, too, and Leo's the only friend he has."

"Sky," said Conrad suddenly, his voice raspy.

"Sky," Vicky said. "Yes. Sky."

She sat watching him for a while, noticing how his hair curled around his right ear. His hair had grown back so thickly it had amazed her. She remembered sitting here, once, and thinking that it must be feeding on the dead parts of his brain, and it had taken her weeks to force the repellent image from her mind.

She reached up now, ran her fingers, slowly, through his hair, from the forehead to the crown to the back of his neck. He sat still, not resisting.

•

By the time she got home it had stopped snowing, but it was so cold the car heater hadn't managed to warm her up. She had given away all her warm Edmonton clothes when she moved here, believing people who told her the West Coast didn't have winter, and she couldn't afford to buy anything new. Money: she was sick of worrying about money. She could sell the house, but it was old and mortgaged, and she would lose her only security. Besides, the house was all she had left of her life with Conrad. Maybe she was just making excuses not to sell. But what were excuses, anyway—just reasons with emotions attached.

As she hurried across the brittle lawn to the back door, she was overtaken by a sudden dread: Jason could be watching her. What nasty surprise might she find from him today? She unlocked her door cautiously, as though she expected something to explode.

But inside, although she looked nervously in every room, she found nothing disquieting, and out her front windows she saw only the untouched snow covering her yard, lying along the branches of her elm like a whole duplicate white tree. She watched the children at the house on the corner building a snowman.

She and Conrad had decided not to have children. It didn't mean she hadn't wanted them. She pulled closed the curtains.

After supper she washed her hair, then watched *Jeopardy*, shouting the occasional correct answer to impress the cat, who had jumped into her lap and was kneading at her chest. Vicky had heard someone say once that a cat could be neither hypocritical nor sincere. She suspected hers could be both, usually simultaneously. She dabbled her fingers in his fur, yawned, flipped to a drama about lawyers. They should make a show about subs, she thought: like doctors and lawyers and police and mercenaries, the picaresque hero could have a new adventure, new problems, new people to save or destroy every week. She tried another channel, something with "Murder" in the title, but after the first five minutes she could tell from the expensive houses, clothes, cars, and faces that nothing that happened to the characters would be bad enough.

Her head drifted back against the sofa.

The doorbell woke her, and she sat up with a start. She pushed vaguely at her hair, which had begun to dry with that squashed-up-against-a-sofa look, turned off the TV, and went to the door.

It was Richard. She peered at him, her mind sluggish. For some reason it seemed wrong for him to be here, rather than at the back door, where he had come before.

He was holding something out to her, in both hands. It was a towel, with a red rose sitting on top. Oh, god, she thought, her brain kicking in at last. A rose. For the towel she wouldn't have to ask him in, but for the rose—

"It's to replace yours," he was saying. "I hope it's okay."

She slid her hands underneath the towel, brushing his; she pulled back quickly. The towel, she could tell, was about twice the size of the one she had given him.

"You really needn't have," she said. "And what a lovely rose." She lifted it to her nose. It had no scent at all.

"I hope it didn't get frostbite coming over here," Richard said. "It sure is bloody cold." He was wearing only a flannel shirt, its cuffs rolled back one turn up his forearms, and loose-waisted black cotton slacks fastened with wide grey suspenders.

"Would you like to come in?" She stepped aside a few unconvincing inches.

"Oh. Well, just for a minute, maybe." He rubbed his hands together, breathed into them.

Vicky backed away, let him enter.

"Sorry it's so late," he said, glancing around her living room. "I was over earlier. But you were out."

"I was at the hospital visiting my husband."

"Yes, of course. Mrs. Birdsell told me what happened."

Birdy and her big mouth. Vicky set the towel on the coffee table, picked up the rose. "I'd better put this in water."

She picked up the blue vase, reminding herself that yesterday she had found it sitting on her sofa. I should be glad he's here, she told herself; I've no excuse now not to tell him about Jason. She went into the kitchen, filled the vase, inserted the flower, and then, holding it out in front of her like something ceremonial, she took it into the living room, set it on the coffee table.

"How's your hand?" she asked.

"Fine. I hardly notice it."

"That's good. Sit down." She was hoping he would refuse.

"I shouldn't stay. I know you're busy." But he lowered himself into the armchair opposite the sofa. At least, Vicky noticed, he only perched on the edge, his back straight.

She sat on the sofa, stroked the towel. "It's really lovely," she said. "Thank you."

"The least I could do."

She had to tell him about Jason. But maybe she could just let it go, maybe later— The cuts in the door frame. The blue vase sitting on the sofa. The upturned plant.

"How's Jason adjusting to the move? Is he in his new school already?"

"He's okay," Richard said, but there was an edge to his voice. He pulled slightly at the bandage on his left palm, flexing the fingers of his injured hand. "His new school seems all right. He's a little ahead in the curriculum, so that's an advantage."

Vicky fiddled with the corner of the towel. She had to tell him. She had ignored the first things the boy did, and it hadn't made him stop. She'd seen enough horror movies to know how it could go on, getting worse and worse, one day she'd come home and find her cat stapled to her back door—

"I, uh, I think Jason might have been in my house yesterday. When I took you to the hospital. Someone was here, you see, and I think it might have been him. Because earlier he left some of his toys by the back door, or someone left some toys there, and I think it was probably him—oh I know it all sounds very vague—" she could hear her voice accelerating, as though speed could make it sound more logical "—but that first day when he brought my saw back he made some little cuts in my door frame, and it's nothing I'm really upset about or anything, but I think maybe you should know, so you could talk to him, tell him he shouldn't be doing that sort of thing." She stopped, hating the way she had sounded, unsure and dismissive.

Richard leaned forward, setting his forearms on his thighs and clenching his hands together. Vicky was sure he could hear her heart across the room, going bang, bang, bang, like a fist knocking at her ribs.

"God," he said finally. Then he looked at her, sighed, straightened. "I'm so sorry, Vicky. I had no idea. But it's not the first time he's done something like this. Acting out, they call it, right? He has a twin sister, you see, and my ex-wife's got custody of her, and I've got Jason, except that Jason is pretty unhappy about this. He'd rather be with his mother."

"I see," Vicky said. At least he believed her; at least he hadn't gotten hostile or defensive.

Richard drummed the fingers of his right hand on the arm of his chair. "My ex was—" He hesitated. "Well, neither of us behaved very well. Jason hasn't had an easy time of it. And he's, well, a difficult kid. When we separated she simply refused to take him, and I have the happy job of trying not to let him know that. So he blames me for not letting him live with her, when the truth *is* that she doesn't want him. She just wants Lisa."

"Oh, I didn't realize—"

"Well, it's bloody time she took some responsibility for Jason. She can have him this weekend at least, longer if I can swing it. I can take Lisa. There won't be any problem with Lisa."

"I didn't mean—that is, please don't think you have to punish Jason because of what I said. I just thought you should talk to him."

"It's not a punishment. It's exactly what he wants, to be with his mother."

"But if she doesn't want him—"

"She's got to work this out with him. It's the best way to go. Really."

It had all turned into something complicated and dramatic. Now she was responsible for rearranging a whole family. She felt a leap of sympathy for the boy, caught in his parents' problems.

And Richard, what did she feel for him? Sympathy, too? And what else? What alarming else? She tried to make herself think of it as just her body's automatic response to stimulus, something atavistic, programming for survival, nothing really even to do with her. Yes, she told herself: I am sexually attracted to him, but it means nothing; he's like the rose I instinctively tried to smell, a reflex.

"Well," she said. "I hope things will get easier for Jason."

Richard passed his hand over his face. "Oh, they will. He's not a bad kid. I'm just sorry he's started off so badly with you. But I promise, it won't happen again."

"I appreciate your taking this seriously. I was a little afraid to bring it up, I mean, you just move in and already you're getting a complaint from a neighbour."

He smiled. "Well, I'm glad you did tell me. Instead of calling the police and having us arrested or something."

Vicky laughed. It occurred to her that she should have offered him something to drink when he came in, a coffee or glass of wine or something. But it was too late now. She didn't want to give him any encouragement to stay, not after this long.

He was looking around at the room, his eyes lingering on her bookcases lining the far wall, on the dining room table strewn with her schoolwork. "You're a teacher?" he asked.

She nodded. "Although I do also have an MA in film theory." Brag, brag. "I was going to go for my PhD but my funding disappeared, and I thought, okay, be realistic, film theory won't exactly pay the bills, so I made a last-minute switch to Education, where I could get a scholarship."

She didn't tell him how angry Conrad had been when she'd told him what she'd done. Stubborn, he had cried at her over the phone, you're so damned stubborn—you know I'd have given you the money; and, yes, I know, she had answered, stubbornly, but this makes more sense.

"So, yes," she continued, pushing the memory away, "I'm a teacher. A substitute teacher. Or, to use the latest euphemism, an on-call teacher."

"Ah, I see. That would make you an on-callogist."

Vicky laughed, surprised. A sense of humour: he was more dangerous than she'd thought.

"And you teach, too?" she asked. "I think that's what my neighbour said," she added lamely. So now he would know they had been gossiping about him.

"Well, yes." He looked away from her. "Although really

I'm an artist." He pulled a little at the side of his shirt, which, Vicky could see now that he drew her attention to it, had smears of green paint on it. "But I do teach, too. At the college in Vancouver. Part-time, like you."

"Subbing isn't necessarily part-time," she couldn't resist saying. "Just the salary is."

He laughed, leaned back in the chair, hooked the ankle of his right leg over the knee of his left. She could see several inches of bare leg above the top of his sock, and she looked quickly away.

"I know what you mean," he said.

"It's always a stretch. If we didn't have savings I couldn't make it. And I can't count on getting called every day."

"About how many days a week *do* you get called?"

"It varies. Of course it doesn't help that the vice-principal at the largest school in the district seems to have made it his personal mission to keep me out of his school."

"Really? How come?"

Why had she told him that? "Oh ... I'm an affront to his religion, I think. How many days a week do you work?"

"Three, four sometimes. And it's a stretch, too, as you say."

"It costs a lot to live in lotus land."

"Lotus land? It's warmer today in Whitehorse." He smiled. "Well. I've kept you long enough." He stood up. "Jason has probably set fire to his bedroom by now."

"Only because he's cold, I hope," Vicky said lightly.

But when she held the door open for Richard she had to resist pointing to the cuts on the door frame. The cold air rushed in, raising goose bumps on her arms. Across the street the house on the corner had its outside lights on, and she could see the remains of the snowman the children had built. It looked as though it had been kicked at, the head pushed off. It occurred to her Jason might have done it.

"Thanks again for the towel and the rose. It really wasn't necessary."

He ran his hand lightly up and down the edge of the door. "It's the least I could do."

And then, quickly, before she could react, he leaned over and kissed her on the mouth. She pulled back, stumbling into the hall table. She stared at him, dumbly.

"I'm sorry," he mumbled. "I had no right to do that." He turned abruptly and went out, leaving the door open.

Vicky stood behind the door for several moments, hearing the soft crunch of his shoes as he went down the front walk. Then she raised one arm and pushed at the door, slowly, then harder, leaning her whole body against it until she heard the snap of the lock. She fumbled the chain in place.

She was shaking. She began pacing up and down her living room, hugging herself as though she were still cold. He had been presumptuous, of course he had, but why hadn't she said anything; why had she just stood there staring at him, letting him think it might have been okay?

She dropped herself onto the sofa. The cat crawled out from underneath it and sniffed at the chair in which Richard had been sitting, then rubbed his head on the front corners, marking his property, reclaiming his territory from the intruder. In front of Vicky the red rose on the coffee table was responding to the water, opening.

Well, he did seem genuinely sorry, she thought. Perhaps he had simply felt what she had, an impulse his body acted on before his mind had a chance to stop it. She wasn't sure if this explanation made her feel better or not. In any case, she mustn't let it go any farther. She wasn't free to become involved with anyone, no matter how attractive he was.

And he was attractive. Oh god yes he was. She leaned her head back, closed her eyes. He had put his hand on her arm when he'd kissed her and she could still feel its heat. Her whole body felt charged, speedy, the way it would after a roller-coaster ride, and she could tell herself it was just the same adrenaline high after an escape from danger but people got to like it and need it, didn't they, they'd want the danger again and again.

FRIDAY

VICKY WAS JOSTLED into the staff room by a gaggle of Grade 10's flapping to the cafeteria. She sat at a table with the two other Socials teachers and a sad-looking middle-aged man subbing in Science and trying hard now to fake interest in the conversation about book orders.

Then one of the teachers, a short chunky woman, said, "You hear about Peter Clemchuck? He teaches at Oakdale."

"No, what?" said the other, jabbing her straw through the foil circle of her apple-juice container. The veins in her hands were so prominent they seemed almost to be growing outside her skin.

The first teacher glanced conspiratorially at Vicky and the Science teacher, lowered her voice and said, "The fire alarm went off just after school let out, and when the fire department came racing in they found Peter had dumped all his new curriculum guides from the ministry, and the Year 2000 stuff, and the Instructional Resource Packages, all of it into a couple of wastebaskets and set it on fire."

"No!" exclaimed the other teacher, letting the juice she had been sucking up her straw drop back into the container.

"Really! I'm not kidding."

The two of them began to laugh, and then the Science teacher joined in, and Vicky made herself laugh, too, so that one of the teachers at the next table looked at them all and made some comment about hysterical historians.

And it *was* funny, wasn't it, Vicky told herself, laughing, trying not to think of what might have made Peter Clemchuck succumb to this bewitchment by the irrational and of what would happen to him now—something disciplinary, a suspension probably. Trying not think of herself, screaming and slamming the textbook at Jeremy Mill, and of the teachers who must have sat around the staff rooms the next day saying, "No!" and "Really!"

She excused herself and sat on a couch in the corner to mark the Grade 11 map assignments. Right, wrong, wrong, and good heavens did this kid really put the Central American countries in Africa? She didn't get done by the time the bell rang; it meant she'd have to stay after school.

But in the Geography 12 class, she was guiltily pleased to discover, half the students had permission to be at band practice, so she let the others work independently and finished her marking, with time left over for her obligatory snoop through Joyce Holly's desk. The most interesting thing she found was an empty bottle of Prozac. She put it back, gently. She really must stop this, she thought, really she must.

Her next class, another Socials 11, meant galloping again through the NAFTA implications for Quebec. This could, she thought sadly, be interesting, but she saw on the faces before her only the same bored weariness she hoped they could not see on hers. She sped on. The desks in the room seemed increasingly to be chaffing the thighs of their occupants.

The bell, at last, the Pavlovian bell. Most of the students ran from the room, shouting after their friends, dripping behind them papers that other friends retrieved, brushing past Vicky as though she were a chair, a desk, a part of the room. Would it really have been any easier for Joyce Holly? Perhaps she was remembering a fiction, that a permanent job was so much better.

Well, fiif, as Amanda would say: fuck it; it's Friday.

The parking lot glittered with patches of ice, as though a huge pane of glass had shattered above. Some of the students were trying to hit them on purpose, to make their cars spin out and lurch sideways, like horses kept tethered too long and now bucking excitedly at release. When Vicky reached her own car, she found a notice under her windshield wiper.

> *You have parked in the TEACHERS ONLY lot.*
> *We have noted your licence and if you*
> *park here again your car will be towed.*
>
> — *THE ADMINISTRATION*

Damn them. She had registered her number at the general office, the way she was supposed to.

She was still angry when she arrived at her father's apartment and dragged the vacuum cleaner out of the back seat, cursing as the cord tangled in the seat belt. Her father had called her last night: you said you would come, when are you coming, the place needs to be vacuumed, is that too much to ask? Allrightallrightallright. As she jerked the cord free she thought she'd like to wrap it around his neck. The bag, looking like a diseased lung, bumped the front seat and sent a puff of dust into her face.

She tiptoed past Leo's door, but at her father's she made a point of knocking loudly and saying her name and when he said, "Come in," she shouted, "Have you put your gun away?" She could imagine the woman across the hall gasping, looking through her peephole—well, she had a right to know her neighbour was demented. Armed and demented.

The door was locked this time, so she used the key. She nudged the door open with the vacuum cleaner and said loudly, "Don't shoot."

"All *right*," her father said irritably. He was sitting on the sofa, with a blanket over his legs. Vicky wondered if he had his gun under there.

"Your Meals-on-Wheels person come today?"

"Yeah," he grunted. "Half an hour late." He jabbed his finger in his ear and jiggled it, as though he were scratching his brain.

Vicky plugged in the cord and turned on the machine, telling herself, as she had dozens of times, that she could just refuse to believe he couldn't do this for himself.

When she was finished, she tried to anticipate how he would tell her he was glad the job was done without actually thanking her.

"I sure don't know how this place gets to be so goddamned dirty," he said.

"You live here, it gets dirty." She sounded harsher than she had intended, putting the emphasis on *you.*

But he only grunted. "Look at that bank statement on the kitchen table, by the way. I added it up half a dozen times and I don't get the same total they have."

Vicky picked it up, curiously. He had never let her see his financial records. But the balance on this statement was only a few thousand dollars; she knew he must have more than that. "I don't see any deposits here," she said. "Where are your old age and disability pensions?"

"Never mind about them. They go right into the savings account. This is the one that doesn't balance."

Vicky sighed, picked up her father's chequebook. "Where's your calculator?"

"Calculator!" he snorted. "There's only a dozen cheques."

"I can't do this without a calculator."

"You can't add up twelve goddamned numbers? What's wrong with you? I can add up twelve numbers in my head."

"Then do it yourself."

"You can't add up twelve lousy numbers. No wonder nobody wants to trust women with money."

"Oh, for heaven's sake."

"Your mother was just as bad. Give her two numbers and she'd faint. 'Oh, I was never any good at arithmetic.'"

Vicky shoved her chair back and began coiling the vacuum cleaner cord around the hooks on the handle. She pressed her lips together tightly, keeping the words in.

"Are you gonna do my chequebook then or not?"

"Not."

"Well, don't be in such a huff. Bring your calculator next time, if you need the damn thing."

Driving home, Vicky could still hear his voice, the cruel falsetto. *Oh, I was never any good at arithmetic.* Had he ever loved her mother? Had he ever loved Vicky? If he had, could he have left them? *Better off without me.* The one time she had directly confronted him with what he'd done he'd shrugged and said, "What good was I to you? What good's a man who can't work?" And the answer had been both so obvious and so impossible to explain that she had said nothing, had let him get away with it.

A guy in a boom car vibrating the whole street pulled up beside her at the lights and grinned at her. It made her remember suddenly where she was going: next door to Richard Menard, who had kissed her last night and how was she going to face him again? She pushed the memory away, concentrated on the lights. Red. Green.

When she got home and played back her messages, the first one was one from Amanda. "Call me, bitch," it said.

Vicky smiled. They were supposed to be mad at each other, she knew, but she couldn't exactly remember why. It was usually the way their arguments resolved themselves.

The second message was more of a surprise. It was from

Conrad's cousin, Ernest.

"Hi, Vicky," he said. "Hope everything's going okay. Look, I'm sorry to bother you but I'm hoping you can find the technical German dictionary Conrad borrowed from me before he, well, before the accident. I'd get myself another one except that they aren't available here, and I need it rather badly. Could I drop by tomorrow and pick it up? Call me if that's not okay."

Trust him to get in touch only when he wanted something, Vicky thought sourly. At one time it was all Conrad this and Conrad that; it was promises to make him a partner in his company; it was invitations to dinner; it was here're the keys to the condo at Whistler.

Call me if that's *not* okay, he'd said. As though she would have nothing better to do with her weekends than wait for him to drop by. She found the dictionary, was tempted to call Ernest and say she was leaving it outside her front door, but with Jason around she decided she had better not.

She phoned Amanda instead, got her machine. "I got your message, slut," Vicky said. "Where the hell are you?"

She had just hung up when she heard a faint knock at the front door. She sat still, listened for it to repeat. Nothing. She tiptoed to the door, looked through the peephole. At first she saw only the empty stretch of her front walk, but then she noticed a movement at the bottom of her vision. A child was standing on the steps.

It must be Jason. A shiver went through her.

She backed slowly from the door, holding her breath. Then the doorbell sounded, so loud it made it her jump. She let her breath out. He knew she was here. There was no point pretending.

She opened the door.

The child standing before her wasn't Jason. It was a girl,

in a frilly, blue dress. But she looked so incredibly like Jason that Vicky knew this must be the twin Richard had spoken of. She had the boy's height and stature, the same round face and large thick-lashed eyes, the perfectly shaped little mouth. Her hair was blond, too, like his, but curly and shoulder-length, with two rectangular and garishly purple barrettes on either side. And the smile, a shy, uncertain child's smile, was unlike anything she had seen on Jason's closed face.

"Why—hello," Vicky said. She felt shy and uncertain herself. What was the girl doing here? Had Richard sent her? Should she ask her to come in?

"My dad said I should give you this." The girl held out a towel she had folded over her left arm. Her eyes squinted up at Vicky.

Confused, Vicky only stared at it. It looked like the towel she had wrapped around Richard's bleeding hand. But he had already replaced it, yesterday.

"My dad said to tell you he got it back from the hospital after all," she said, a little plaintively. Her smile had faded in the face of Vicky's silence. "And that he got it washed out okay. You're supposed to take it."

"Yes, of course," Vicky said at last, making herself pull the towel from the girl's arm. It unfolded, spilling from her fingers to brush the steps. She gathered it clumsily back up. She could see the goose bumps on the girl's arms: she was wearing nothing over her thin dress, some nylon-cotton blend a size too small for her.

"You must be cold," she said. "Come in and warm up." She stepped back from the door, reluctantly. But she couldn't just send the child away, even if it was only next door. Maybe Richard had planned it this way; ignoring the weather had gotten *him* invited in, after all. Why hadn't *he* returned the towel? Yet she was just as glad he hadn't.

Perhaps it was the discreet thing, really, not to use this as an excuse to come over.

The girl hesitated on the doorstep, but then, smiling nervously, she stepped inside. "It *is* cold," she said.

"Too cold to be outside without a coat." The girl looked down at her feet, the clean white runners with pink, carefully tied laces, the socks puddling around her thin ankles, and Vicky realized her comment must have seemed like a reprimand. "I mean, your father should have given you a coat." This didn't sound any better. "Come into the living room." Her voice was a little desperate. "I'll make you a cup of hot chocolate. Would you like that?"

"Yes, please," the girl said. She came into the room, sat down carefully on the edge of the sofa. She pressed her legs neatly together and squeezed her hands into each other on her lap, not bending her elbows, so that it raised her shoulders level with her ears. She looked like a beautiful doll someone had packed into too small a box.

"And what's your name, then?" Vicky asked, standing awkwardly looking down at her.

"Lisa."

"Lisa. What a pretty name. My name is Vicky. Well. You just wait here and I'll get you your hot chocolate."

She went into the kitchen, mixed up a cupful, shoved it into the microwave. She watched the seconds ticking off on the timer, wishing she hadn't gotten herself into this. Now she would have to wait until the girl drank it. She had no idea how to talk to someone that age.

When she brought the cup back into the living room Lisa was still sitting as Vicky had left her, stiff and polite on the sofa, hands shoved together into the folds of her dress. She took the cup, said, "Thank you," had a sip, another, then set it carefully, with both hands, on the coffee table.

Vicky sat down in the chair opposite the girl, whose

posture had relaxed a little. She began looking around the room, drumming her feet lightly against the bottom of the sofa. A brown scab stuck like a dead elm leaf on her right knee.

"This is a nice house," she pronounced. "Nicer than Dad's."

"Thank you. But your dad just moved in. Once he gets everything straightened out it will look better than this."

Lisa looked around again, thoughtfully. "Mom's house is nicer than this, though."

"Oh. It probably is." Absurdly, she felt hurt at the blunt comparison. She had to remind herself the child was just reporting things as she saw them. "And where does your mom live, then?"

The girl stopped drumming her feet, shoved her hands back into her lap. "Burnaby."

"Burnaby. It's nice there."

"I've got my puppy there."

"A puppy! That must be fun! What's its name?"

"Leroy."

"Leroy. That's an interesting name. Does he like it?"

Lisa giggled. "He's just a *puppy*. He doesn't know if he likes it."

Vicky laughed. The kid was no slouch.

"Jason doesn't like him."

"Oh? Why not?"

"I don't know. He just doesn't."

"Well, so long as you like him."

Lisa began drumming her feet again against the sofa. "Yes," she said, decisively. "I like him." She reached for her hot chocolate, took a long drink.

"Is Jason with your mom now?" She was prying, but she wanted to know.

Lisa shrugged. "I don't know. I suppose so," she said,

sounding suddenly petulant, annoyed.

Perhaps her indifference to her brother's whereabouts shouldn't be surprising, Vicky thought. If they were each living with different parents they probably rarely saw each other. Still, the girl's response bothered her a little. Vicky wondered if she might have learned her dismissive attitude to Jason from her mother. Could the woman really care as little about him as Richard said?

"Do you miss Jason?" Snoop, snoop. "I mean, since you're twins you must have gotten pretty used to being around each other."

Lisa seemed to think about it for a minute. "Jason can be really mean sometimes," she said, reaching for her cup again. "It's nice being just my mom and me."

"I never had any brothers or sisters," Vicky said. "I suppose I always thought it would be fun not to be an only child."

"It's fun sometimes, when Jason isn't being mean."

"What does he do when he's being mean?"

Lisa set the cup down, shifted herself in her seat, blinked several times in the same squinty way Jason had, reminding Vicky again of how much they resembled each other. "He hits me."

"That *is* mean," Vicky said, wondering if she was wading in beyond her depth. "Do you tell your mother?"

Lisa nodded. "She gets mad at him," she said with obvious satisfaction.

Vicky had to laugh. "Poor Jason."

Before she could decide what to say next, someone began pounding at the door. It had to be Amanda—no one else would come by unannounced on fiif day and then bang like that with the doorbell in plain sight.

"Open the pod bay doors, Hal!"

Lisa jumped up. "I have to go. Dad said I shouldn't stay

long."

Shouldn't stay long. It suggested he might have told her to stay for a while, though.

"It's all right," Vicky said. "It's just my friend Amanda. You can say hello to her and then go home."

She opened the door and Amanda swept in, talking even before Vicky got the door open. "So fucking cold out there, the wipers froze onto my windshield and now one of them won't work at all, I mean, do I need this—" She saw Lisa, stopped abruptly, her arm halfway out of the sleeve of her coat. "I didn't know you had company."

"This is the neighbour's girl. They just moved in next door. Amanda, this is Lisa. Lisa, this is my friend Amanda." She felt absurd, making the introductions. Was it what one did with children?

"Hiya," said Amanda, pulling her jacket the rest of the way off and tossing it in the direction of the closet. She was wearing a crinkly blue silk blouse with sweatpants and short pink socks that had small puffy balls sewn onto the backs to prevent them from being sucked into her runners.

"Hello," said Lisa.

"Lisa was just going home," Vicky said. She stood back from the open door, and the child moved over to it, in small steps, flicking her eyes from Vicky to Amanda, as though she had to keep them in sight. When she reached the sill, she bolted over it and down the icy steps so fast Vicky winced.

"Goodbye," Vicky called after her.

"So," she heard Amanda's voice from the living room, "since when are you into entertaining the neighbour kids?"

"Her father had an accident and I lent him a towel. She just came over to return it." It was too complicated a story to go into. Besides, what would she say? Richard, Jason, Lisa—they were just there, suddenly, next door, leaning over into her life.

She dropped onto the sofa across from Amanda, who had spotted the tail of the cat protruding from under her chair and was trying to drag him out by the hind legs. Vicky grimaced as she heard him growl, but for some reason Amanda could get away with handling him like a bag of empty fur.

"Come here, you sexy boy." Amanda made lewd kissing sounds at him. "I've decided to look for love in all the wrong places."

The cat put his ears back at this news but didn't jump down from her lap.

"He's been neutered, Amanda."

"*Plus c'est la même chose.*" Amanda sighed. "Oh, here's one you'll both like: what did the man say when he came home and found his wife in bed with his best friend?"

"What?"

"Bad dog! Bad dog!"

"Amanda. You're the one who should be neutered."

"Thank you. Speaking of being tutored—"

"*Neut*ered."

"—look what I've done." Amanda dabbled her fingers in her overstuffed purse and withdrew a sheet of paper. "It's just a notice I put up yesterday, but would you believe I've already had two calls, and I've an appointment with one of the kids tomorrow."

Vicky skimmed through the page. "They'll really pay this much for tutoring?"

"These are rich kids, Vicky. Their parents are used to buying them whatever they need. That mean old teacher not giving them A's? Well, they can buy a personalized teacher who'll show them how to get that A. Look, if I find any who want tutoring in Socials or English, why don't I send them to you?"

"Well ... sure. Why not?"

"We're cutting edge here, you know. Soon the whole education system will be privatized and this is the only work teachers will have." Amanda was petting the cat on her lap so hard he was sinking down between her thighs. "Oh, I brought you something else, I almost forgot." She felt around inside her purse and lifted out a tinfoil-wrapped package. The cat expressed immediate interest. "Someone at school had a birthday and there was a whole bargeful of this."

"Brownies!" Vicky exclaimed, unwrapping the pieces. "Yum."

"You've gotten so skinny lately you can eat chocolate." Amanda sighed. "I think I'll start telling people I'm not fat, I'm metastasizing. You get sympathy for that."

Vicky laughed, then caught herself and said severely, "Why am I laughing? It's not funny, women wishing themselves sick just to be thin."

"And women wish themselves thin to please men. Ergo—this is a syllogism, pay attention—women who want to please men are sick."

"Oh, Amanda. I'm glad you came over."

"Well, fuck you, too," Amanda said, pleased.

.

Nurse Ratched poked her head in at nine-thirty. "Time to go," she said.

Vicky started awake, looked around in confusion. She had fallen asleep in her chair. "Yes," she murmured. "All right."

Conrad sat in the chair beside her, his head drooping to the side. Perhaps he had been asleep, too, although now his eyes were open, focused more or less on the bottle of hand lotion she had brought and which must have fallen to the floor by his bed. Vicky picked it up, watching him in case his eyes would follow it, but they remained on the floor. He was rarely alert this time of day. In Alzheimer's patients, she remembered, the fading in the evening was called "sun-downing."

"I had the strangest dream," she said to Conrad. "It was Ernest in the hospital here, not you. And we'd had to adopt his children. There were a lot of them, four or five, and they were very small, the size of cats. Isn't that strange? Little cats, all these little cats."

SATURDAY

She was aware of someone watching her. Quickly, she looked down. It was Richard.

Her first reaction was relief, that it wasn't Jason, reaching out to shake her from the rickety ladder like a squirrel from a tree. But then she thought of when she had last seen Richard.

"You startled me," she said, trying to keep her voice even.

She turned back to the eavestrough, began pressing the piece of linoleum across the two-inch hole. She was aware of how she must look, of her sweatpants with the seat worn thin and Conrad's old suede coat and thick knitted scarf whose stitches were so tight it had been like wrapping a piece of chain mail around her neck. Her hair was glued to her head by the drizzle.

"Sorry," Richard said. "I just wondered if you wanted some help. I'm an old gutter man from way back."

"It's okay." The linoleum wasn't going to work. The water was already starting to run underneath. She had considered trying to nail it down, but the whole section of gutter was rotting and she was afraid a nail would just knock out another chunk.

There was obviously no point staying up here. Clumsily, feeling Richard's eyes on her, she began to climb down. The side of the ladder swayed as she moved from rung to rung, and then she felt it steady as Richard braced it with a hand on each side. But she could see what would happen—she would be backing right into his arms. She could feel sweat starting to pulse in her armpits.

But when she got to the last few rungs, he stepped back. By the time she turned to face him, he wasn't even looking at her; he was squinting up at the eavestrough.

"That's redwood, you know. The whole eavestrough is redwood. Amazing how long it's lasted. All one piece, too, see? A shame to tear it down. But you can just replace this bit—" he waved his arm from the west end of her house to a few feet beyond the hole "—and attach a plastic gutter to the redwood that's still in good shape."

Vicky listened and nodded, looking at where he pointed, brushing the water out of her eyebrows. She was grateful for his advice, but she found herself swallowing querulous responses: what do *I* know about plastic gutters; one section or the whole damned house, it will still cost more than I can afford; I can't tear down twenty feet of redwood by myself. She sighed.

Perhaps Richard heard her, because he glanced at her. The rain was running down his cheeks, dripping onto the collar of his yellow raincoat. "It's not really a big job," he said. "A handyman could do it in an hour."

"I suppose so," said Vicky vaguely. Would it be too rude to say she had to go in?

"Look," Richard said. "I know this guy who does good work—he built a shed for a friend of mine that's good enough to live in. He could at least give you an estimate."

"Yeah, that would be great." She tried to sound enthusiastic.

"Let me write down his name for you, then. I can't remember his address exactly, but you can look him up in the book."

"All right," she said. So now she would have to ask him in. She could feel the sweat again in her armpits.

Okay—she would go in first, snatch the pen and pad of paper off the top of the refrigerator and make him use the kitchen counter to write down the information. She heard him coming up the steps behind her, the soft squish of running shoes on wet boards. She resisted the urge to turn and face him, to say something, anything, to make him stop.

Inside, he bent to untie his shoelaces. "Oh, don't worry about your shoes," Vicky said. "My floor doesn't care."

"They're pretty dirty," Richard said. "No problem."

He pulled them off. Vicky watched in dismay as she saw the laces on his right runner tighten into a knot. It would take him forever to undo when he left. He set the runners neatly beside the door. *He can put his shoes under my bed any time.* Birdy had said that. What a thing to remember now.

She shrugged off her jacket and kicked off her boots and ran up the last few steps into the kitchen. She grabbed the notepad from the fridge. The pen, where was the goddamned pen? By the time she found it Richard had not only come into the kitchen, he had taken off his coat and draped it across the stair railing.

As she handed him the paper, she saw the pen rolling slowly to the edge of the counter. She reached out to grab it the same time Richard did, and her hand clamped onto the back of his. She jerked away.

Richard laughed, a bit nervously, she thought, hoped. "You feel like a piece of ice," he said.

She shoved her hands into the pockets of her sweatpants. "I should have worn gloves, I guess."

"Anyway. The guy's name is John Penner." He wrote it down, pressing hard on the pen, making large loops on the capitals. The paper crinkled from the dampness of his wrist. She fixed her gaze on his long fingers, the nails cut evenly and straight across, no trace even of one reassuring hangnail. "And he lives somewhere in South Surrey. I'd recognize the address if I saw it. Got a phone book?"

"In the other room."

He followed her into the living room. She was just reaching for the phone book when the doorbell sounded.

"Probably just the local JW's come to save my soul," she said, going to answer. Maybe she could invite them in; they could talk about the sins of the flesh.

It was Ernest. She had completely forgotten he would be coming today.

"Hi," he said.

He was a short, balding, ruddy-faced man in his forties, with thick-lensed glasses and a smile that never seemed able to pull his mouth into anything more than a straight line but that compensated by activating a dimple in his cheek.

"Hello, Ernest. Nice to see you again."

"Yeah, sure is. You found it, I see." He gestured at the dictionary she'd set on the little table by the door.

"Yes." She picked it up. "Come in. I'll make coffee." Please, she wanted to say, please, but she didn't, couldn't make herself sound that needy, no matter how much she wanted him, wanted anyone, to come in right now. (But she should have, she thought now, watching two young constables walk past her, laughing at something they were reading on a clipboard; she should have swallowed her pride and insisted, pleaded, begged.)

"No, no, I have to go. Thanks anyway. And I see you have company."

His eyes had moved to somewhere behind her. Vicky made herself not turn around to look.

"It's only my neighbour. He dropped by to give me some advice about repairing the eavestrough." She was explaining too much, sounding guilty. "Conrad kept meaning to do it but we never got around to it."

She was pleased to see Ernest's eyes drop at the mention of Conrad's name. He nodded, shifted his feet a little.

"Have you been in to see him lately?" Vicky tried to make the question seem casual, ingenuous.

"Not for a while," Ernest said, raising his eyes to the dictionary in Vicky's hands.

"I try to go every day," Vicky said, the dictionary a hostage she was unready to surrender.

"I called the nursing home about a week ago. They said there was no change."

That surprised her. "No, there hasn't been," she said. She handed him the dictionary.

"Well. Where there's life there's hope, I guess."

"So they say. Tell Helen and the kids I said hello."

"Yes, yes, I will. Take care of yourself now."

She stood at the door longer than she needed to, watching him go. When she went back into the living room Richard was standing by the coffee table with his hands in his pockets, examining a framed Greenpeace poster of whales she had on the wall.

"Sorry for the interruption," she said. She sat on the sofa, picked up the phone book. "All right. Penner," she said briskly.

But when she found the columns of Penners, she groaned. "There are three Johns, and four J. Penners, all in Surrey. Any idea which one we want?"

"He's in the south end somewhere. Let me see."

He slid in between the sofa and the coffee table and sat down. Beside her. The phone stand and wall blocked her on her right side, and the only way to get out would be to leap over the coffee table or over him. The phone book weighed her down like a pile of bricks in her lap.

As Richard reached for the directory, he caught sight of her towel still folded across the back of the sofa, and his hand moved up instead, set itself on top of the towel. Vicky felt herself leaning away.

His forearms were bare. She could see the muscles and tendons in long smooth lines under the skin, the intricate linkages of blue veins in his wrist.

"You got the towel, I see," he said.

"Yes. Thanks so much. You needn't have bothered. You already gave me a better one."

"The hospital called and asked if I wanted it back. They even laundered it. Although that was likely just a mistake."

"It's probably cleaner than when I gave it to you."

"And you met Lisa."

"Lisa. Of course, yes. We had a pleasant little visit." She felt like reaching up and brushing at her face, wiping away his gaze.

"She *is* a nice kid, isn't she? I wish Jason could be more like her."

"She seems very mature. Very ... well-adjusted. She should be a good influence on Jason."

"It doesn't seem to work that way. Besides, they don't see much of each other."

"Is Jason with his mother for the weekend, then?"

"Yeah." His arm slid down from the back of the sofa and came to rest between them. "I wish I had more patience with him."

Seeing the arm no longer hovering behind her made Vicky allow a benign smile. "I suppose he's just angry because things have changed and he has no control over them."

"I know the feeling," Richard sighed.

"I do, too," Vicky said, and then wished she hadn't. "But he'll be all right," she added quickly. "He just needs time."

"Yeah, well, let me know if you see him behaving badly again." He reached for the phone book. "Okay—let's see if I can find the right John Penner."

He slid closer to Vicky, settled one side of the phone book on his knee while the other half remained on hers. She felt his leg brushing hers.

"Okay." Richard ran his finger down the column. "Nineteenth Avenue. That sounds about right." He tapped the other two John Penners. "These are North Surrey."

Vicky was squeezing her legs against the far side of the sofa so hard they ached, but even so she could feel the slight pressure of Richard's leg against her left thigh. He reached for a pencil on the coffee table. Vicky could see threads pulling loose from the sleeve in the armhole of his shirt. She had the absurd impulse to poke her finger at it. Richard circled the name he had chosen.

"There are still the J. Penners," Vicky said.

Richard bounced the pencil on the page, leaving a small cluster of dots in the middle of the next column. "It's usually just women who list with an initial. You know, to discourage crank calls."

"My husband listed us under 'C. Bauer.'" *My husband.* Yes.

"Anyway, I'm sure it's the John Penner on Nineteenth."

"Well, thanks," Vicky said. "I'll give him a call when I'm ready to get something done."

She reached over to close the phone book, hoping he would take it as a cue to slide away from her, letting her out.

Instead, he put his hand on her forearm, and, even as she looked up at him, protests forming in her throat, he was leaning towards her, his face already too close for focus, and then his left hand had reached over and taken her other arm, and he was kissing her on the mouth.

Her mind was empty, completely empty. Someone was kissing her: she felt her whole body being pulled towards him, like a dream of falling, the hard grip of gravity. Her hands went up, awkward dream wings trying to beat herself to safety, but they sank on his shoulders. She began kissing him back.

His hands slid along her arms to her shoulders, then down along her sides, to her breasts. She felt her skin warm under his touch, her heart pumping her blood, quickening, through her.

And suddenly she was aware, understanding her body's simple desires and her need to resist them.

She pulled herself back, turned her face aside. "No, Richard," she said. "I can't. I'm sorry."

"Why not?" She could feel his breath, humid and jerky, spilling against her cheek, his thumbs pressing lightly into her breasts.

"I'm sorry," she said. "A part of me wants to, but I can't."

"Listen to the part of you that wants to."

She began to laugh, stupidly, wildly. In disbelief, she saw a drop of spittle fly out of her mouth and hit him on the ear. "Richard, please. Let me go."

"All right." He dropped his hands but didn't turn away from her.

"I'm sorry," she said.

"It's okay."

"I mean, it's just ... I'm married."

"You don't have to explain."

"I do. It's not that, well, that I don't find you attractive...." She couldn't continue, had to stop herself from bursting again into mad laughter at the old girlhood phrasing.

"I know what kind of a hospital your husband is in,

Vicky," he said softly. "Nobody can expect you to stop your own life."

"It's nothing to do with what anyone expects. I feel married, that's all."

"You won't be abandoning him."

"I know. I just ... can't." Her throat tightened.

He put his arms around her, pulled her to him, pressing her face into his shoulder. She swallowed, fought against tears. He ran his hand slowly down her back.

"It's all right," he said. "It's all right."

He held her like that for several moments, his hands moving rhythmically up and down her back. She sat limply, struggling to trust her voice into words.

He began kissing her hair. One hand moved up her back to cup her head. His lips moved to her ear, her neck. She could feel his arousal, the tightening of his body against hers, his breath on her throat.

"Richard, no. Please. Don't."

She pressed her left hand awkwardly between them, against his chest, and with her right reached to the back of her head, pushing his hand away. It was his injured hand; she could feel the bandage.

He dropped his hand, abruptly, but she was still pulling away and the unexpected release toppled her over backwards. Richard, off-balance, trying to protect his injured hand, fell heavily on top of her. She tried to slide or roll away from under him, but although her right leg was free she succeeded only in banging her knee on the coffee table. Her left arm was wedged into the gap between the back of the sofa and the sofa cushion, and her other arm was half-pinned beneath her.

Richard began to laugh. She could feel the vibrations of his chest pass into her.

"Richard. This isn't funny. Let me up."

He leaned down, began kissing her neck. She could feel his erection pressing against her thigh. With his right hand he started to unbutton her blouse. She wasn't wearing a bra; she could feel his fingers on her breasts.

She closed her eyes. She could just let it happen, just give in.

She took a deep breath. No, damn him, she *wouldn't*. When she spoke she made her voice be loud, angry. There was fear in it, too, but she hoped he wouldn't hear that.

"I mean it, Richard. Stop this. Right now."

His fingers on her blouse went still. She made herself open her eyes, stare into his, fiercely.

Abruptly, he pushed himself away from her, sat back. Vicky twisted herself quickly to a sitting position, then stood up, facing him. He sat rigidly, not looking at her. She began to redo the buttons he had opened on her blouse, her fingers clumsy, shaking, not finding the right holes, but she didn't look down, kept her eyes on Richard, as though that were necessary to keep him from moving.

She stepped over the coffee table, gritting her teeth as she jarred onto a corner the knee she had bumped on it earlier. She detoured around Richard, warily, and went to the door, opened it.

After what seemed like a long time, neither of them saying a word, he got up and walked out through the open door.

SUNDAY

*A*MANDA TOOK her for lunch.

"Jesus, Vicky. It sounds as though he almost raped you."

Vicky winced. Maybe it had been a mistake to tell Amanda. But she'd had to tell someone.

She poked at her spinach salad. The leaf that caught on one of the tines of her fork seemed too large to fit into her mouth. She fixed her eyes on the knuckle of her thumb, noticing the way one of the lines went only half way across and then veered up at a right angle. She had had a cut there once, she remembered, so the wrinkle had made a detour. How clever of it; how adaptable.

"Vicky—come on. Talk to me."

She made herself look up. Her eyes hurt, felt the way they did in the sunlight after the optometrist put in the drops to dilate the pupils. Amanda was wearing a new blue blouse of some polished, glossy fabric; Vicky had to squint against the glare.

"I don't think he'd have gone that far," Vicky said. "I mean, obviously he *didn't* go that far."

"Well, it seems to me he was pretty close to it, that he just kept pushing you. No plus no does not equal yes. No does not mean punch her in the face."

"Oh, Amanda, it wasn't anything like that. He wasn't violent or particularly threatening."

"'Particularly.'"

"I mean, I don't think he *meant* to be threatening, maybe that's more to the point."

"And your perceptions don't matter?" Amanda demanded.

Vicky was getting a headache. "I don't want to think about it."

"Yeah, well." Amanda sighed. "This whole sex business. As Evelyn Waugh said, 'For physical pleasure I'd sooner go to my dentist any day.'"

Vicky grimaced a smile at her. "I'm too old to understand these games about sex. This is the sort of thing teenage girls worry about, not people my age."

Amanda snorted. "'People my age.' If you're alive and female you have to worry about it. Forget about 'alive,' actually. There's this lawsuit in the States against a whole chain of funeral homes—"

"Jesus, Amanda."

"Okay, okay, sorry."

They were silent for a while, poking at their food. "The person I think I'm *most* angry at is myself," Vicky said finally. "Because I encouraged him, because I responded to him at first."

"'At first.' Okay. But you have the right to change your mind, just like men do."

"Then there was a point where I was thinking, what the hell, I should just let it happen, would it be so bad, just to give in?"

"Giving in is hardly the same as enthusiastically participating, Vicky. But, yeah, we do it all the time. Show me a woman who hasn't had sex at least one time in her life when she didn't really want it and I'll show you a virgin."

"Have *you* had sex when you didn't really want to?"

"Of course. And don't tell me you haven't."

"But I *haven't*," Vicky said. "With Conrad it was ..." And then she began to think, well, except for that time when, and that time he, and soon her head was aching with the exceptions.

"Oh, *god*," she said. The word was so loud in the midst of their low-voiced conversation that Amanda jumped. "All I want is for him to leave me alone. And here he is living right next door. I can't even tell myself it's an isolated incident, it's over, I won't have to see him again."

"Well, make some rules and stick by them. Get control of the situation."

"Maybe it's too late. Maybe it's already out of control."

The waitress, a chirpy young redhead, came by with the coffee pot.

"Yes, please," Amanda said, before the waitress could ask. When she reached over to take away Amanda's plate, which had only two greasy French fries left, Amanda stopped her. "I need the fat," she told her. "It's brain food. The brain consists entirely of fat, you see. If you diet too much the brain is the first to go."

"So being called a fathead is a compliment?"

Amanda looked up, surprised. She wasn't used to people trumping her aces. The waitress grinned, walked away.

Vicky had been watching a woman sitting at a table by the door. The woman had wiped clean her fork, spoon, and knife on her napkin, and now she opened her purse and dropped the cutlery inside. Vicky kept staring at her, uncertain and then alarmed, because she had completely forgotten what she was supposed to feel. Indignation? Embarrassment? Anger? Should she report the woman to someone? Should she pretend she hadn't seen? It was as though her emotional responses had become tangled, frayed, messages leaping over the wrong synapses.

"Now listen," Amanda said, leaning toward Vicky, "I know I'm to empathy what Margaret Thatcher was to civilization, but I want to be useful to you here. You want me to come and stay with you tonight?"

"No," Vicky said. The woman by the door was getting

up, leaving. Vicky had let her get away with it. "I'm okay. Really. But thanks. I appreciate it."

"It'll be all right," Amanda said. "He doesn't sound like a monster. He probably *did* think he was just seducing you."

"I hope so." Vicky pressed her thumb into the small bowl of her spoon, felt her skin stick to the warming metal. How easy it would be to slide the spoon into her purse. Quickly she pushed it out of sight, under the rim of her plate. The impulse had been alarmingly reminiscent of her original Nasty Sub Habit. She had, she thought, enough other short circuits left in her personality without reactivating old ones or borrowing someone else's now.

"... if you just say no," Amanda was saying.

It took Vicky a moment to realize she wasn't talking about stealing the spoon. Concentrate. Something about saying no.

"There was this book," she said, sitting up straighter, "by Jane Austen, I think, and the hero is at a dance and says to the heroine how men have the advantage because they have the power of choice while women have only the power of refusal. And the woman says, 'Don't underestimate the power of refusal.'"

"And?" prompted Amanda when Vicky paused.

"I don't know. I suppose I must have had a point. Well, look, tell me something cheerful. What did *you* do Saturday night?"

"I went to a wake."

"Jesus Christ's, I hope."

"I wish. No, my great-uncle's. Everyone despised this man, but here they were, wailing and gnashing their gums and rending garments."

"Don't be cruel."

"I'm not being cruel. I just hate the hypocrisy. But

speaking of Jesus Christ—and note how nicely he segues from 'hypocrisy'—did you hear that Friday afternoon someone trashed his car?"

"Really?"

"Really. In the school parking lot. All four tires were slashed, a window was smashed, I forget what else. And there was a note on the windshield, kind of creepy. It said, 'Back off.'"

"Wow. Did they find out who did it?"

"Nope. They suspect some Grade 10 boys he'd had trouble with the day before, and one of the secretaries saw the proverbial suspicious man around the cars earlier, but there's no proof of anything. It could have been anyone."

"I'll bet it was a teacher. You'd think they'd be lining up to take the credit."

Amanda looked at her a little oddly. "I think you're enjoying this a bit too much."

"I am," Vicky said.

"Jesus Christ called the police to investigate. If they come knocking at your door you'll know why."

"Well, nothing is a coincidence. God, I sound like Leo."

"Who's Leo?"

"This nutty neighbour of my dad's. The one who got him his gun. Maybe Leo did it. Were there any bullet holes in the car?"

"Not from this particular incident," Amanda said. She was prodding gingerly at a red spot on her throat. "Shit. I've got a manitou growing on my neck."

Vicky began to laugh, too loudly. A few weeks ago they had watched a TV movie called *The Manitou*, mostly because they couldn't believe the description in Vicky's *Video Movie Guide*: "a woman wakes up one day with an ancient Indian growing on her neck." That was what the movie was about, though. It was supposed to be scary, but it was even more hilariously awful than they had expected.

"Doesn't look like anyone in *my* family," Vicky said, peering at Amanda's neck.

"I'm getting more zits now than I did when I was a teenager."

"God must think you're finally mature enough to handle them."

Amanda snorted. "If I were any more mature I'd be dead."

.

When Vicky got to the Matheson Pavilion she sat for some time in the car, looking at the entrance through the gauzy drizzle. For the first time since just after Conrad had been brought here she found herself not wanting to go in.

Damn Richard, she thought furiously, *damn* him. She remembered how when he had first kissed her she hadn't been able to tell Conrad, and how it nagged at her, a guilty secret. And now this. She tried to imagine telling him, like any other anecdote she had brought to him over the past year. *You know that neighbour I told you about, that Richard Menard with the peculiar kid, well, he came over last night, and—*

She couldn't tell him. She'd done nothing wrong; why should she feel ashamed? But there it was. Richard had come between them, as surely as if he were standing in the entryway, barring the door.

She made herself get out of the car, go inside. Nurse Nice looked up and smiled. She was wearing a new pink cardigan over her uniform.

"Well, hi," she said. "I missed you yesterday."

Vicky murmured pointlessly, "I know. I didn't come."

"Oh, hey, that's all right," Nurse Nice said, putting too much reassurance in her voice. "You come so much more often than we expect."

Vicky nodded, not meeting her gaze, and walked past her down the corridor. A television in Room 105 was shouting. To her right between Room 114 and Room 116 a woman was hunched on a small bench, fondling a pair of false teeth in her lap.

Room 121. Conrad was sitting in his wheelchair with his back to her, facing out the window. He was wearing his pajamas and robe—on Sundays if she didn't come to dress him nobody would.

"Hello." She put her hand lightly on his shoulder.

His head turned a little to the side, but not far enough to see her. He raised his shoulder an inch or two, pulled it forward, trying to shrug her off. Vicky lifted her hand away, feeling the rejection, even though his reaction was not unusual.

She turned his wheelchair to face her, and sat in the chair in front of him. His eyes moved slowly across the room, settled on the painting of the ocean. When he had first stared at it she had gone and stood in front of the picture, trying to force him into seeing her.

"So how are you today?"

Conrad lifted his right hand, scratched delicately at his nose with his forefinger. His nails needed to be cut. He settled his hand back into his lap, cupped in his left palm.

"You were watching the rain, were you?"

Someone was pushing a hospital cart past their doorway. One wheel squeaked with every revolution.

"Why don't you answer me, for god's sake?"

She got up, pushing her chair back so abruptly it would have fallen if it hadn't hit the bedstead, and walked over to the window. She pressed her forehead against it, watching her hot and ragged breath fogging the glass.

After a while she returned to her chair and sat down, took Conrad's hand. He let her hold it for a moment before pulling it away. She reached for it again. As she picked it up her fingers slid over his groin, and she could feel his genitals under his thin robe and pajama bottoms. She had had to touch him there often enough in the hospital, and always she had made her mind go dull and clinical, had finished whatever task she was doing as fast as possible. But now she left her hand there, pressed down slightly, began to stroke him through the cloth. After a moment she could feel his penis stirring.

She lifted her hand away, quickly. "I'm sorry," she whispered. "I'm sorry."

She got up again and began pacing the room. She could hear herself whimpering. Finally she lay face down on the bed and let herself cry.

.

When she was leaving, she noticed the woman she'd seen on the bench was still sitting there, her old face peaceful, smiling a little at something near the ceiling. One of her dentures had fallen to the floor. Vicky stopped, uncertainly, looking down at the row of teeth in their pink plastic gums. She would tell the nurse to come and pick them up. She began to walk away, then stopped, made herself go back, reach down and pick up the teeth, gingerly, between two fingers, touching only one of the molars. She set them carefully in the woman's lap.

The woman started, almost jarring both dentures from her lap, but her hands closed on them quickly. "Oh!" she exclaimed. "My goodness. I didn't even realize I'd dropped them. How clumsy of me. Thank you so much."

"It's all right," Vicky said, staring at the woman, her unexpected lucidity.

"I was daydreaming," the woman said. "One of the few indulgences left to me, I'm afraid."

"Yes," Vicky said. "I know."

At the nursing station, Nurse Nice looked up from a file she was writing in, smiled. Vicky shrugged on her coat, put her hand on the door. Then she turned back to the nurse and said, "Do you remember, a couple of days ago you asked me why I keep coming here?"

The nurse looked at her blankly. "I'm not sure I—"

"You said it was courage," Vicky said. "And I said it wasn't courage, it was something else but I didn't know what."

"Oh. Yes."

Vicky could tell the woman didn't remember, but she pressed on. "Well, I thought about it, and I decided that what it is is love. That's all. I come here because I love Conrad."

Nurse Nice gave her a warm smile. "He's lucky to have you, Vicky."

Lucky, Vicky thought, oh, yes, Conrad is so lucky.

•

By the time she turned into the alley behind her house the sun had broken through the clouds in the west, and she had to put her visor down. She was almost at the turn into her drive when she realized something was partially blocking the alley, and, squinting into the sun, she slammed on the brakes.

When she could finally see it in the glare she realized it was a hockey net, a small one, the size children used. If she kept as far to the left as possible she should manage to get around it. Annoyed, she inched forward, barely able to see, the laurel hedge scraping the side of her car. But she was able to squeeze past and pull into her driveway.

She got out and walked back out to the alley. The open end of the net was facing her like a huge mouth. Angrily, she took hold of the metal crossbar and pushed the net as far as she could against Birdy's fence. It could still be a danger, but surely somebody would retrieve it soon. She had never seen it here before; it must belong to some kids on another street. Or—of course—to Jason.

She turned quickly, knowing somehow that he would be standing there, just a few steps beyond her driveway. He was. Standing completely still, watching her. He was wearing a red tuque pulled down over his ears, an oversized hockey shirt with the number 99 on it, and brown corduroy pants with the hem on one cuff loose and worn ragged from being stepped on and scraped along the ground.

Her heart thudding, she walked towards him. She could see him shift his posture a little, could sense his tension.

"Hello, Jason," she said. Her voice sounded awkward, accenting the wrong syllables. "Is that your hockey net?" She gestured behind her.

"Yeah. So what?" His eyes blinked rapidly.

"You shouldn't leave it on the road like that. It's very dangerous. I almost hit it when I was coming in."

He shrugged. "I know."

"If you know, why did you leave it there?"

"Stay away from my dad."

"What?"

"Stay away from my dad."

"What do you mean?" she said, trying to sound calm.

"I know what you two did yesterday."

"You do?" she repeated stupidly. He *knew*? Could he

have seen, were her drapes open?

"Yeah."

"So what did we do?" she asked, taking a risk.

Jason reached over and snapped a twig off her forsythia bush, making her wait before he answered.

"You fucked," he said.

Vicky took a long breath. "No, we didn't. But, even if we had, it's none of your business."

"He's my dad. It's my business."

"You can't go around spying on him."

"I wasn't spying on him."

"So how do you know?" She was as good as admitting he was right.

Jason looked down at the twig he was poking into the palm of his left hand. "I just know," he said.

"Well, you're wrong."

"Just stay away from him."

What should she say now? She looked at the boy, dumbly, her hands clenching tighter in her pockets.

"Is this *your* thing, young man?"

The shout behind them made them both jump. Vicky whirled. Birdy, of course.

"I said, is this *yours*?" Birdy had grasped the hockey net by the crossbar and was dragging it towards them like some collared miscreant.

"Yeah, it's mine," Jason said. He sounded, Vicky was relieved to hear, a little afraid.

Birdy deposited the net with a thump in front of him. "Well, keep it out of my hedge, please."

Jason took hold of the net and, without a word, began dragging it behind him down the alley. It caught in a crack in the pavement, but he jerked it loose before it could fall over. When he reached his driveway he turned into it without looking back.

"Kids!" Birdy sighed, dusting her hands off in a gesture mostly rhetorical.

"Actually I was the one who dragged the net into your hedge," Vicky said.

"Ah," said Birdy. "It was you I should have yelled at."

"I nearly ran over it when I came home. He left it in the middle of the alley."

"In summer it was the skateboarders. Now we're going to get them playing hockey here?"

"It's just Jason. I don't think there are any other kids involved."

"He's an odd little bugger."

"That's putting it mildly."

"His old man isn't bad, though, is he?" Birdy looked up at Vicky, ingenuously.

"Don't *you* start." Vicky tried to keep her voice light. How much had Birdy heard of the exchange between her and the boy? Or had she been peeking through Vicky's windows, too?

"Well, you can't put your life on hold forever. If I were five years younger, the man wouldn't be safe in his bed." Birdy took a tissue from her pants pocket and blew her nose, a loud exclamatory snort.

"You're incorrigible."

"What's that? Some kinda cardboard?"

"You know what it means, you evil woman."

"Evil!" she hooted, giving Vicky a punch on the arm. "Evil!" She turned and stomped back down the alley, her big rubber boots whooshing with each step. She stopped at her driveway, shouted, "Want me to say a Black Mass for you or anything?"

Vicky laughed. "I can use anything you've got," she called back, heading down her own driveway.

If she had looked up then, looked carefully, she would

have gasped at what she saw. The rotten section of eaves-trough was gone, replaced with a length of brown plastic the same colour as the old eavestrough, the ends joined snugly to the wood. It would be a week before she would notice. She would stand there for a long time staring up at it, and she would say nothing about it, to anyone, ever.

When she got into the house she changed into more comfortable clothes, a T-shirt and over it a bulky-knit black sweater that came almost to her knees, tights, and leg warmers she had begun to pull down to her instep and use as socks. Then she went into the living room, turned on the stereo, CBC Radio with its talky Sunday programming, and lay down on the sofa, deliberately, as though she needed, like the cat, to physically reclaim the space after a territorial challenge.

She looked at the curtains on the main picture window facing north, remembered pulling them open this morning. They had been closed yesterday when Richard was here. But the curtains, left behind by the previous owners, were old and poorly fitted, and if they met securely in the mid-dle it often meant an inch gap at one of the sides. So it might have been possible, if Jason had been outside, espe-cially with something to stand on, for him to see into the room. But maybe he was simply guessing, trying to shock her. *You fucked.* She shuddered, hearing again his high child's voice. How much did he know, understand? Maybe it would have looked to him as though she and Richard *had* done it. Had fucked.

She got up and pulled shut the drapes, carefully.

She put on some creamed corn to heat for supper and cracked a couple of eggs into the frying pan. "This is your brain on drugs," she told the cat. He didn't seem to care.

After she'd eaten she turned on the TV, flipped aimless-ly around the channels. "This is also your brain on drugs," she told the cat, who didn't watch much television.

The doorbell. She jabbed the mute button, stared at the door.

She wasn't ready. She had known it would happen and still she had no idea what she should do. Get control of the situation, Amanda had said; make some rules and stick by them. But what were the rules? She remembered the feel of his hands, and she pulled back as though he were already in this room, touching her—

The bell went again, a loud bleat. Maybe it wasn't him, she pleaded with the air, and made herself tiptoe to the door and look through the peephole. Even in the dim light from the street she could make out Richard's face, distorted in the small bead of glass. Her heart was beating so loudly he must hear it through the thin door. Her whole house felt suddenly flimsy, a straw house, a huff and a puff and he could blow it over.

"Vicky? Please open the door."

She jumped back, pressed herself against the wall.

"Vicky, please."

She didn't move. She closed her eyes, thought, go away, go away, go away. He knocked at the door, four sharp cracks of sound.

"Vicky." She could imagine his voice audible on the whole block, the twitching back of curtains, the excited gossip of eyes on her front porch. "I just want to talk to you. I swear that's all. Please let me in."

She turned to the door, put the chain on. He must have heard it, because he said, "Vicky? I know you're there. I just want to talk to you."

Maybe he did just want to talk. If she opened the door and left the chain on, he could tell her what he had to say through the crack. At least he would lower his voice.

"Yes?" She snapped the door open abruptly to the

width of the chain.

"Vicky, thank god. Let me come in. I just want to talk to you."

"You can tell me what you want from there."

"No, I can't. I won't stay long."

"I don't want to see you."

"I know I was, I was ... pushy yesterday. I behaved like some adolescent, some idiot. I swear, I *swear*, I won't do anything you don't want."

She stood there a long time, staring at the chain, the crack, the slice of darkness that was Richard, outside.

And finally her hand, someone else's hand, reached up and pushed the chain slowly along the metal slide until it dropped out, swung like a pendulum in front of her eyes.

Why did she do it? (She was wondering that now, in the police station, her hand reaching up a little into the air as though she were reaching again for the chain.) It wasn't, surely, because she cared what the neighbours might think. Maybe it was cowardice, making her give in. Maybe it was the very danger that excited her, compelled her. Maybe it was simple itchy sexual desire shooting her brain full of endorphins, making it stupid, making it an accomplice.

When she'd freed the chain, the door had pulled almost completely shut. She stepped back, waited for Richard to press it inwards.

He pushed the door open, slowly. The cold air rushed in ahead of him; she felt her nipples tighten underneath her T-shirt. She kept her eyes pinned to the level of his right elbow. He was wearing a brown sweater and slacks with oversized pockets, and he smelled of the outside, of the crisp chilled air and, faintly, of pine needles, which could have come from outdoors or from a scent he was wearing.

He followed her into the living room, sat in the armchair he had chosen the first time he was here. Vicky sat on the sofa, facing him, the coffee table between them. She folded her hands into her lap, but one hand pulled itself free, began to fiddle with a loose thread on the seam of her sweater. Across the room the TV picture danced silently, people's mouths opening and closing. She considered turning the set off but decided against it, thinking he would find her doing so an encouragement.

"Well." Richard cleared his throat, leaned forward a little, rubbing his hands flatly together. They made a sound like leaves blowing against her front door. He smiled, nervously, Vicky thought, the sides of his mouth not quite synchronized. "Did you get called for work tomorrow?"

The question was so innocuous she almost couldn't answer. What had she expected? "Yes," she said stiffly. "There seems to be a demand for subs right now." She crossed her legs, pressing her calves together, latching the toes of one foot around the ankle of the other.

"That's good." He flicked his eyes to the cat, who sat watching him from the kitchen doorway. "Here, kitty, kitty." The cat, of course, ignored him.

"He's not very friendly," Vicky said.

"We had a cat. In our last place. But Jason isn't very good with pets."

"I saw Jason when I came home. He says he, he knows we ... made love." She had wanted to use the other word, Jason's word, but she couldn't bring herself to say it.

"What?" She could hear his sharp intake of breath.

"I think he might have been watching us. Through a crack in the curtains."

"Jesus."

Richard got up, walked to the other end of the room. He picked up a small box of paper clips sitting on the stereo speaker and tossed it lightly from hand to hand. Ching, ching, ching.

"Do you think he actually saw ... anything?" he asked. "He makes things up sometimes."

"It would have been a pretty good guess. I think he really saw us. There's always a little gap in the curtains—" she gestured at them "—so he could have been watching."

"Jesus." He tossed the box of clips harder. Ching, ching, ching. "I'm sorry. I'll talk to him. I'll explain." Behind him the images leapt soundlessly on the TV.

"He said I should stay away from you."

Richard set the box of clips back on the speaker and sat down in the armchair.

"He's probably right." He looked at the floor. After a moment he cleared his throat and said, "I'm sorry about yesterday, Vicky. I told myself that you wanted it as much as I did, but you kept telling me you weren't interested, and I didn't listen. When I got home I felt like such a shit. I just want to say I'm sorry. I had no right to pressure you like that. I'm just ... really sorry."

His voice had been full of such self-recrimination that her own anger faltered. She had to stop herself from saying, oh, that's okay, or, it wasn't that bad, or, it was my fault too; and when she did say something, finally, it was one of those things after all, as though she couldn't help it, as though it were a conversational equation she had to complete.

"It wasn't all your fault. I was so ... inconsistent."

"And I took advantage of that."

Took advantage of. It made her seem like a simpleton. "Well, I'm glad you understand. That, you know, it would have been a mistake."

He nodded, rubbed at a little swirl of cat hair his pants had picked up from the chair. "Probably neither of us is ready for anything like this. Christine and I were together for twelve years. She was the one who wanted to end it. Maybe I'm still too, too raw or something. Maybe I'm like

Jason, acting out."

"Maybe," she said, uncertain how else to reply.

He had rubbed the cat hair into a small ball, and he set it on the arm of the chair. "I feel like some goddamned predator: you're there, you're attractive, you're nice, you're vulnerable. I know you still love your husband—"

Vicky winced. *Your husband.* "I *do*," she said. "It's not like divorce, or even death, it's ..." She couldn't continue.

He got up, came over and sat beside her. Like yesterday, she thought dully. She felt his arm go around her, but it was light, barely touching her.

They sat that way for a long time, not moving, not speaking. Outside, a car door slammed, freeing a short burst of loud, laughing voices which were cut off by another door slamming: a parenthetical interjection in the silence between them.

"It's just all such a pile of shit sometimes," Richard said.

There was a hoarseness to his voice that made her turn to face him.

"You're crying," she said. She stared at the dampness on his cheeks.

He turned a little away from her, shrugging. She saw his Adam's apple move as he swallowed.

"I should go." He stood up.

Vicky got up, too, and they stood there, awkwardly, avoiding each other's eyes. Richard leaned over and picked up the little ball of cat hair and started rolling it again between his fingers. Then he turned and walked to the door. Vicky followed him, not knowing what to say. He put his hand on the doorknob, turned it back and forth several times without opening the door. She could hear the metallic grate of the latch moving in and out of the receptacle on the jamb. Finally he opened the door, then reached for her hand, turned it palm up, and put the cat hair into it.

"In case you're saving it," he said. "For a cushion or something."

When he was gone Vicky leaned her back against the door, let herself slide slowly to the floor. She pulled her knees up to her chest, pressed her face into them. Why did he have to behave so damned well, why hadn't he made it easier for her?

I want him, she thought, pressing her face down harder. Want: the way it began not with the verb but with the noun, meaning a lack, an absence. Want: the way it became need, became desire.

Part II

LATER

RICHARD

$\mathcal{V}$ICKY AND AMANDA sat watching the teachers file list-
lessly out of the gym after the AGM had failed to get a
quorum. The walls were flecked with bits of pink crepe
paper from where streamers had hung for a dance on the
weekend.

"I mean," Amanda was saying, "if all the subs showed
up and voted, we could make a real difference as to whose
interests the negotiating team takes to the table. But do
they come? Noooo."

"I think they just feel the union isn't set up to represent
them."

"And of course they're right," Amanda sighed. "We
should join the Teamsters. Really."

The gym was deserted now except for them. A tall man
in an immaculate, grey suit came in and stopped short
when he saw the empty room. He glanced at his clipboard
and then at Vicky and Amanda and said accusingly,
"Where's Mr. Timms?"

"Two men in white suits dragged him kicking and
screaming out of here," Amanda said.

The man didn't seem surprised. "I see," he said coldly,
and strode away.

"Well, I suppose we should go home." Amanda
yawned, rubbed her right shoulder. "Have you run into
that neighbour of yours yet? I don't know how you've managed to avoid him for two months."

Vicky reached down to pick up her books, set them

carefully on her lap. She'd known she would have to tell Amanda about Richard eventually, but it was hard enough to explain things to herself, let alone to someone else. She'd practised what she would say on the cat: *Amanda, you'll never believe what's happened—* The cat had heard her out but was skeptical.

She lifted the cover of the top book, let it fall shut. "I'm having an affair with him, Amanda."

"What?" Amanda's arm stopped halfway through its plunge into her coat sleeve. "The bodice-ripper? You're having an affair with the bodice-ripper?"

"I know. It's crazy."

Amanda pulled her arm slowly out of her coat sleeve. "Jesus, Vicky."

"I should have told you before. I was just ... embarrassed."

"As well you should be!"

"I know we got off to a bad start, but it's different now. He's actually very considerate. He lets me choose."

"If he *lets* you choose, is that really choice?"

"You know what I mean. It's mutual. He's—" she looked down at the cover of her book, a picture of trees, a forest "—a great lover."

Amanda looked at her for a long time without answering. Then she said, "I always suspected your brain was not your favourite bit of anatomy."

Vicky began to laugh. Oh, it was all true. She was having an affair with the bodice-ripper. Her brain was not her favourite bit of anatomy.

She couldn't even quite remember how it had started, who had made the first move that day he'd come over to bring her a piece of wrongly addressed mail, but suddenly there they were, breathless and tangled in each other, and since then she had been seeing Richard nearly every day.

She would drive home from school oblivious of her surroundings, of the highway and traffic, of the buildings sliding by, of everything except her own anticipation. Her skin would feel tingly, electric. She would turn into the alley behind her house and feel her heart beat faster because she knew he would be there, coming over sometimes to meet her as she got out of the car, and they would go inside, so eager they began to undress each other even before they got through the kitchen.

"I know you think I'm making a mistake," she said to Amanda, "but Richard is really very nice. And physically it's so, well, exciting."

"Exciting," Amanda said. "I see. As in lust. As in those close-up movie shots of skin and writhing and moaning. All that stuff before the trouble starts."

"Let me enjoy this, will you?"

"All right," Amanda said, shrugging. She shoved her arms back into her coat sleeves and pulled her coat on.

"Don't be pissed off with me, Amanda."

"Look, it's not like I think you're his love slave or something, but I do think you might just be getting in over your head. You're, well, needy now, and pardon me if I'm suspicious of this sudden passion."

"Needy," Vicky said coldly.

"Oh, we all are—you know what I mean."

"I'm not an infant, Amanda. I haven't entirely abandoned all common sense. I'm having an affair. So what?"

"Okay, okay," Amanda sighed, slumped in her chair. On the gym wall, a piece of pink crepe paper came loose and drifted slowly across the room.

"Oh, maybe I'm just envious," Amanda said finally. "The last man I slept with had the sex drive of a dishrag. God, why do we bother? We should just stick to masturbation. We'd spend less on clothes and makeup. Speaking of masturbation, did you know Dorothy Parker had a parrot she called Onan because he kept spilling his seed?"

"That's useful to know. In case I get a clumsy parrot."

"I don't suppose you need any more pets. Not when you've got *Rich*ard. When am I going to get to meet this priapic wonder, by the way? Sometime before the last of your brain cells fall into your crotch, I hope."

"I'm saving a few," Vicky said. She knew she wasn't answering Amanda's question.

"Well, remember to send me a Christmas card."

"Oh, come on, Amanda. It's not going to be like that."

"Yeah, yeah." Amanda stood up, slung her purse hard across her shoulder, like a missile she was trying to fire.

"It's not going to *be* like that."

They walked out together to the parking lot. They reached Vicky's car first. As Vicky unlocked the door, Amanda, pulling on her gloves, said, "What about Conrad?"

"I'm going to see him now." Vicky turned and got in the car, pulled the door closed, abruptly, and drove off.

Conrad. Trust Amanda to slide his name in like that, a cold twist of the heart. Vicky had been trying determinedly to keep Conrad in some separate place in her mind, untouched by what she was doing with Richard. Conrad was her husband; she loved him, was committed to him. That hadn't changed, wouldn't have to change. Richard gave her pleasure. And if sex were all, or even the most important thing, they had between them, what was wrong with that? It made things easier, really.

Still, later that night, after they had made love, she felt guilty, watching him get dressed in silence, thinking that they didn't talk enough to each other, that they talked less now than they had before they'd begun sleeping together; and she said, "Stay and have a drink before you go home."

He paused from buttoning his shirt, looked at her. "All right," he said. "If you want."

And then she was annoyed at herself because it was late, ten o'clock, and she had to work the next day. But she pulled on her robe, went to the kitchen, poured him a glass of wine and herself a glass of milk, and they sat down at the kitchen table. He had a bit of fluff from her pillow caught in his hair, and for some reason she felt shy about reaching over and brushing it off.

"So," she said, "what should we talk about?"

"I don't know. What do you want to talk about?"

"I asked you first."

"The weather, then," he said. "How about that cold front?"

"Oh, come on. Tell me something about yourself."

"What do you want to know?" He took a swallow of wine.

"If you ever broke a bone. The name of your best friend in high school. Your favourite vegetable. How many wisdom teeth you have."

"Yes. Walter. Corn. Two."

"See?" she said. "You're good at this."

He laughed, stretched his arms over his head, yawned. She could see the swirls of blond hair on his chest where his shirt was unbuttoned, and she looked away. Sometimes she thought she could give herself orgasm just by looking at him.

"Okay, try these, then," she said. "Your parents. Your work. Your ex-wife." Oh, she was reckless.

He lowered his arms slowly. She could feel him withdrawing. "Dead. Dying. Painful."

Painful. It meant, *Don't pry.*

"Now let me give you some," Richard said before she could think of how to answer. "The worst thing you ever did. The best thing you ever did. Why your kitchen walls are the colour of stale processed cheese."

She laughed. "No fair. I can't give one-word answers to any of those."

"Sure you can. I could."

"Bet you can't," she said.

"Jason. Jason. Jason."

It took her a moment to realize he was answering her. "The best and worst things are both Jason?" She wouldn't even bother pursuing the kitchen wall connection.

"Of course. Speaking of whom, I should go, see if he's in bed yet. Not that he will be." He stood up.

"Well—I'm glad you could stay."

He smiled, enigmatically, put the back of his hand for a moment on her cheek. "You shouldn't ask me things. I just might tell you."

After he'd gone she sat for some time toying with her milk glass, thinking about what he'd told her. His responses had been like Conrad's, she realized suddenly. Single words she was trying to link into something meaningful.

.

After that night Richard seemed to want to spend more time with her. He would drop over oftener in the evenings when, he said, he and Jason needed a break from each other, and he came for supper several times when Jason was at his mother's. He always brought at least his share of food and wicked desserts, which they would eat lying on the living room floor, watching TV and making jokes about the programs, having casual arguments about politics, the environment, food, travel, Alberta, never anything too contentious. When their conversations got more personal she sensed a carefulness in what he told her, and she wondered what things he was leaving out. Of course, she was being careful, too, leaving things out. Leaving Conrad out.

There were not many times when the companionable moments between them did not turn into lovemaking. And when they didn't, Vicky could feel a fear rising in herself that their involvement might be turning into something else. She wondered if, in some irrational way, she wanted him to hold emotionally back from her at the same time as she resented his doing so.

She wished she could talk it all over with Amanda. But Amanda would just tell her she was expecting Richard to be the Gothic uncommunicative type whose appeal was his broody mystery. Or she would say that Richard was another man manqué Vicky needed to nurture.

And she would deserve it. In spite of her promise, she was spending less time with Amanda. She was turning into just the kind of woman Amanda had accused her of being, one who neglected her women friends when a man came along. Well, she told herself vaguely, I am only ... sidetracked now; I'll make it up to her later, when this is over— a part of her mind telling herself her affair with Richard would not last, that she did not want it to last. But another part of her ached and desired and cared about little else. She seemed unable to make her thoughts and feelings synchronous, and when they did come close together they seemed only to abrade.

Richard never, to her guilty relief, brought Jason over to her house, and she hadn't talked to him since their last encounter in the alley. She would see him, briefly, in his back yard, but did not see him on her property until a Saturday in early February, a day she would want, for other reasons, to forget.

She was doing her breakfast dishes and looking out the kitchen window, which overlooked her driveway, when she thought she saw him in the driver's seat of her car. Astonished, she dropped the plate she was washing back into the water, and, not bothering to dry her hands, ran to the back door. By the time she got down her steps and around the corner he was gone. She approached the car warily, as though she expected it to detonate. The driver's door was unlocked. Could she have left it that way? She opened it, carefully.

"Jason?" Her voice was trembly.

He wasn't in the car, not that she really expected him to be. She slid slowly into the driver's seat, looked at the dash, the windshield. Nothing seemed to have been touched. Except for the passenger seat.

It was nothing horrible, but its very ordinariness frightened her. On the seat lay a neatly-bound bundle of twigs, almost the thickness of her arm. She picked it up, her heart racing, turned it over. There was nothing else attached; it was a simple bundle of twigs gathered, probably, from her front yard but possibly from any of the trees in the neighbourhood and tied together clumsily with green string. There was no message, nothing aside from the thing itself, and what kind of a message was that? What did it mean?

She got out of the car, said his name again, but of course there was no answer.

She kept a watch out for the boy that afternoon, knowing she should try and talk to him, but when she did see him, playing with a skateboard in the alley, he ran into his house when she opened her back door.

She should have told Richard about the incident that night, but she didn't, for whose sake she wasn't sure. She found herself, instead, asking him about his art, deflecting the evasions that only increased her curiosity and asking to see his paintings.

Finally, he got up, abruptly, from where he had been

sitting cross-legged on the floor, and said, "All right. Let's go, then."

"Right now?"

"Why not?"

"Well, I mean, will Jason mind? My barging in all of a sudden?"

"He won't care. He's just watching TV. Come on."

So she could hardly refuse. Why had she been so insistent?

"I haven't done anything for a long while," he said for the third time as she followed him nervously up the back stairs into his house. "You'll be disappointed."

She hadn't been in Richard's house since the night she had helped him move the stove. The place was untidy and needed a good vacuuming, but it no longer looked chaotic. The stove was in its proper place now, and the dishes, except for a pile in the sink, put away in the cupboards. In the living room she noticed the furniture was not old but well used. One armchair had a long slash near the bottom from which stuffing was leaking; it looked as though it had once been fixed with tape. The hardwood floor was covered with a worn blue-and-white carpet, which was about a foot too long and curved up onto the wall on either end. Along the west wall an arrangement of shelving extended to the ceiling, and on it sat pieces of stereo equipment and rows of books, CDs, video cassettes, and small ornaments, all of them blue.

Vicky looked around for Jason. He was nowhere in sight, although the TV was on, a cartoon show.

"*The Simpsons.*" Richard nodded at the set. "I wish someone could convince Jason that Bart was not meant to be a role model." He started down the hallway. "The paintings are in my bedroom," he said over his shoulder. "It's the only place in the house with enough space. I don't know what I'll do if the gallery in Seattle returns everything it has."

He led her past two closed doors, one of which, she assumed, was to Jason's bedroom, but she heard no sound from behind either of them. Richard's bedroom was at the end of the hall and, she was surprised to see, it was the tidiest room in the house, the bed neatly made; the clothes all hanging, in careful groupings of slacks and long-sleeved and short-sleeved shirts; several stacks of folded sweaters on the shelves; a dresser on top of which were two pairs of cuff links, his pajama bottoms, and two books, whose titles she could not make out.

Richard opened a door beside the closet, which led into a larger, walk-in closet. As soon as the door opened, she could smell, although faintly, paint.

"Don't be disappointed," he said, turning on the light. "I'm no Rembrandt."

"And I'm no art critic."

She walked into the closet. On one wall was a small corkboard, covered with notices and brochures—an exhibit at a Seattle gallery, a postcard of a painting by van Gogh, a newspaper clipping about Emily Carr College—but what interested Vicky most were the typed quotations from famous artists that took up most of the space. There were about a dozen of them, tacked onto the board at various angles, making it look like a collage. "Give me a museum and I'll fill it," said Picasso. "Life being what it is, one dreams of revenge," said Gauguin. "A portrait is a painting with something wrong with the mouth." Sargent. "Orange is the colour of insanity." Van Gogh. "The world is divided into two classes—invalids and nurses." Whistler. That one made her look away, uncomfortable.

"Pretty acerb," she said.

"Oh, those," Richard said. "They're Christine's, actually. I should take them down, I suppose. She was an art student, too. It's how we met."

Vicky nodded. Was that the tweak of jealousy she felt, for the woman who had been able to share this with him?

Behind her Richard shifted his weight, began drumming his fingers on the doorknob, so she turned quickly to the canvases. There were about two dozen of them, stacked in three rows. She looked at the first row, pulling each painting forward and looking at the next, and the next, until she had them all leaning against her legs. Then she put them back, one by one, looking at them again in reverse order, trying to think of what to say.

She had expected, perhaps, that they would reveal to her something about him, or that they would be on subjects or in styles she could talk about, even with her limited knowledge of art, but she was at a loss with these. The one she was looking at now, for instance: what could she say about it?

It looked as though it had been designed using a set square, daubs of green paint close together and running in a rigid right angle across the upper left corner, then the pattern repeated, but with the right angles in different sizes and slants, in about a dozen places on the canvas. The others were similarly abstract, right-angled shapes that may or may not have been meant to suggest something else. In one that used about thirty of the right-angle shapes she thought she discerned, if she made her eyes go a little out of focus, a running figure.

She could hear Richard fidgeting behind her, playing with the chain attached to the light switch. "These are so minimalist," he said. "They're old. The ones in Seattle are better."

"I know so little about art," Vicky said, leaning the front painting carefully back against the others. "The modern styles and everything."

"Well, you wanted to see them," Richard said, jerking the light off, so that they stood in semi-darkness.

"Wait. Let me see the rest."

He hesitated, then turned the light back on. She was determined to be more enthusiastic about the other two rows.

"She doesn't like them. She thinks they're dumb."

They both turned quickly, startled, jostling each other. Jason was standing in the doorway, silhouetted in the light from the bedroom. With one foot he kicked at the corner of one of the canvases.

"Stop that!" Richard clamped his hand on the boy's shoulders and yanked him away from the paintings.

The boy's head jerked back to barely an inch from the wall. Richard's fingers were pressed so deeply into the hollows below the boy's clavicle Vicky could see the pressure on his knuckles, could imagine the bruises building underneath Jason's skin. Abruptly Richard released him, then pushed him, hard, away through the doorway. Jason stumbled back across the bedroom, fell against the foot of the bed.

"Oh, don't," Vicky cried.

Jason picked himself up, stood pressed against the bed, looking at them, his right arm held across his chest, his hand clenched on his left shoulder where Richard's fingers had grabbed him. His face was contorted, his lips pulled up and his eyes squeezed almost closed, but whether it was an expression of pain or fear or anger Vicky couldn't tell. He began to say something, but it was only a sound, not even a word, and then he turned and ran out of the room, slamming the bedroom door behind him. It didn't latch and bounced open again.

Richard walked out of the closet, over to the door,

catching it before it banged on the wall. Vicky followed him, numbly, stood looking at his back.

She should go to the boy, she thought, talk to him, see if he was all right. But she didn't. (If she had gone, would it have made any difference, she wondered, sitting in the police station with a headache pressing at her temples.)

Richard stood in the doorway for a long time. Finally he closed the door, turned, not looking at her, and sat on the bed, put his face into his hands.

"Oh, Jesus."

"It's okay." Her words sounded scratchy, barely recognizable. She sat down beside him, not close enough to touch.

"It's not okay. Didn't you see what I did?" He dropped his hands, let them dangle between his knees as though the tendons had been severed.

Vicky waited for him to continue, and when he didn't she said, "Why don't you go tell him you're sorry?"

"He doesn't care what I have to say."

"Of course he does. Imagine how he feels right now."

"He just ... seems to know what to do to make me crazy."

"He's only a child."

Richard got up, so abruptly Vicky had to steady herself from the sudden movement of the bed. "Don't you think I know that? Of course he's a child. That makes this child *abuse*, right?"

Vicky stared down at her own hands, pressed tightly into each other in her lap. *Child abuse.* It was what Jesus Christ had accused her of, when she had struck her student. Who was Jesus Christ to judge her? Who was she to judge Richard?

"You overreacted, you lost your temper, but he was provoking you. You had to stop him from kicking the paintings—"

"For Christ's sake don't say that." He strode to the door, stood facing it. "It's what she would do. Make excuses for him." His voice was low, shaking.

Vicky stood up. Her mouth was dry. She had to lick her lips twice before she could speak.

"Make excuses for whom?" But she had already guessed.

"My loving father." His knuckles were white on the doorknob. "I almost told you about it last week, when you asked if I'd ever had any broken bones. Oh, yeah, I had broken bones. One in my face. My right arm. Probably one in my foot.

"Oh, Richard."

"My mother would protect him. 'He fell,' she told the doctor. 'You know boys,' she'd say, 'so clumsy, always getting into things.' He never hit *her*. He never hit my sister. God knows why he chose me, why I was the lucky one."

"What ... how did it stop?"

"He died. When I was fifteen. He was drunk and rolled the car. I never had the satisfaction of once, just once, beating the shit out of him. His life insurance paid my way through art school, though. I suppose that was some satisfaction. He'd never have let me go."

Vicky put her hand on his upper arm, lightly, hesitantly. His biceps felt like a fist. "I'm sorry," she said. "I'm so sorry."

"Let me show you something." He turned from the door and went back into the closet. Vicky could hear him sliding one canvas over another, the shuffle of paper.

When he came out he was holding four canvases and about a dozen pencil drawings that may have been torn from a large sketch pad. He tossed them onto the bed.

They were completely different from the other work she'd seen, different and, she was sure, better. They were all of the same subject, a pair of hands, thick-fingered, callused, done in varying degrees of abstraction. The most striking was a canvas in which the detail was as exact as a photograph, the fingers interlaced awkwardly and resting on a single, not-quite horizontal line. In this, as in all the pieces, the body was only sketchily represented, suggested more than drawn, and the hands were disproportionately large.

"You like them, don't you?" Richard said, watching her. "Everyone does. The gallery in Seattle has a bunch more of them. They're beautiful, the curator said. They're my father's hands. The ones he used to beat me half to death."

He began gathering up the canvases and sketches, carelessly, tossing them on top of one another.

"Well, now you know," he said. "Now you know what I'm up against with Jason. I'm up against myself. Myself turning into my father."

"But ... you're aware of the danger. You aren't telling yourself it's okay. You don't do it habitually. I mean, I assume you don't. Jason doesn't seem to be afraid of you."

Richard sat down on the bed. The canvases slid towards him, rested against his thigh. "Maybe we're afraid of each other." He laughed, unamused. "I'm going to talk to the lawyer. I have to make Christine take him more of the time. Maybe even full-time."

Vicky nodded, looking at the canvases on the bed.

CHILDREN

$\mathcal{R}$ ICHARD HAD NEVER explained precisely what his custody arrangements were with his ex-wife, but it was apparent now that Jason was spending more time with her, even though he was still living with Richard and continuing at the local elementary. Several times Vicky saw a rusty red Toyota pull up in front of the house after school, driven by a woman who would wait in the car until Jason came out of the house and got in. Vicky peered at her through the window, but she was only a dark shape behind the steering wheel.

What Vicky hadn't expected was that Richard must have made some arrangement to be seeing more of Lisa. She was dismayed when he asked to bring her for supper one evening, but she felt she had to agree. The girl, however, was so polite and well mannered that Vicky actually found herself enjoying her company.

"You like Lisa, don't you?" he asked her, when the girl went outside to chase the cat in the back yard.

"Of course." She almost had to laugh. He was being so obvious. He wanted her to fall in love with the child, knowing how easy that would be. And she had told him, only a few days ago, just the right story about herself, almost as though she had wanted to leave herself vulnerable.

Conrad's childhood had been so full of pain and loss, most of his family having died in the war, that he did not want children; and besides, he said, people should stop thinking in terms of what they would leave behind—monuments, possessions, children—and aim at leaving nothing, no mark on the burdened world. Vicky agreed. But the older she got the more nature's ironic reproductive imperative pulled and whispered at her. She had almost worked up the nerve to raise the subject again, but then they'd had that argument with Ernest and Helen, with whom they never argued, one evening when they'd all had too much to drink.

Ernest, shooing off his three pretty and amiable daughters into the kitchen to do the dishes, said they were missing a lot, not having children; and Conrad said the world hardly needed more children; and Ernest, sensing some personal accusation, said Conrad was just justifying his own selfishness; and Conrad said he and Vicky were the unselfish ones, that every child born into this society would produce over fifty tons of garbage and be the equivalent of a hundred in the Third World in terms of its consumption and pollution; and, oh, great, Ernest said, you call my kids pollution. And who knows what they would have said next, except that one of the children came into the room then, and Ernest picked her up and set her, in what seemed to Vicky like defiance, on his lap. It annoyed her, but it was also what she remembered as they drove home, the child in her father's lap. When they were going to bed she began to cry.

"What's wrong?" Conrad asked, helplessly, putting his arms around her.

But she couldn't tell him, couldn't betray him like that, couldn't explain even to herself her terrible ambivalence. She sat on the edge of the bed and cried, for her lost children, for what was denied the two of them.

When she had told Richard about the episode, at least she didn't tell him about the end of it, her crying; she had even tried to make it a little comic. But she knew he understood more than she wanted him to, knew he could use her desires against her, could say, just as he had now, ingenuously, "You like Lisa, don't you?"

"Of course," she said.

"She likes you, too. You're a good influence on her."

Vicky laughed. "I don't think she needs any more good influences."

"She's the way she is in spite of her parents, not because of them, believe me."

"Some recessive gene, then? Some saint in your family tree?" Stupid thing to say: had she forgotten what he'd told her about his father?

But if the comment had bothered him, Richard gave no sign of it. "Must be," he said. "Couldn't be from Christine's side."

"It's amazing how different Lisa is from Jason. It's as though she's decided to be the exact opposite of him."

"Maybe she has."

"I missed out on all that sibling rivalry stuff, being an only child."

"You didn't miss much," Richard said. "My sister was older and the favourite, and I resented her enormously. We fought all the time. Even now I don't like to see her. We haven't talked in years."

"That's a shame. I always thought it would be so great to have more family around. I suppose that's why I let my father back into my life."

"There are things you can forgive and things you can't."

"Of course," she said, a little too quickly. "Well, it'll be interesting to see how Jason and Lisa develop. Maybe they'll become more alike, now that they aren't together. They won't have each other to react against."

"Yes, Sigmund."

Vicky laughed, but Richard's words had a sting to

them. Then he began talking about having his kitchen painted, Jason having drawn on it with permanent felt marker, and what colour would she recommend?

The next weekend when Richard brought Lisa over again for supper Vicky found herself watching the girl, curiously, observing her helpfulness and deference, wondering if she really might be modelling herself on the reverse of her brother. Or was Jason modelling himself on the reverse of his sister? What peculiar children they were. Certainly Jason seemed to be the problem child, but Vicky wondered if it might be healthier for the girl to show some of her brother's rebellion. Vicky had seen too many girls, by the time they reached high school, stifle their personalities in order to please.

When they were finished eating, Richard leaned back, sighed, reached for another grape cluster, and said, "Great meal. Thanks."

"You did as much work on it as I did."

"Still, it's your place. We always seem to be using your place."

"It's easier," Vicky said, hoping he wouldn't disagree, because she preferred it like this, didn't want to think of them meeting in his house, where her experiences had been far from pleasant.

"Easier for us, anyway, eh, Lisa? We can live like piggies and Vicky will never know."

Lisa giggled. "Like the three little piggies." She reached up and refastened one of the gaudy, purple barrettes she was wearing again in her thick hair.

She helped Vicky clear the dishes while Richard went to the bathroom. As Lisa brought the last plate to the sink, Vicky said, trying to sound casual, "How's Jason doing?"

Lisa set the plate carefully on the counter. "Okay."

"Does he like being with his mother?"

"I don't know."

"Of course Jason likes being with his mother, Lisa," Richard said. He was standing in the doorway.

Guiltily, feeling she had been the one corrected, Vicky reached down to scrape the potato peelings into the garbage can.

"Shouldn't those go into the compost?" Lisa asked.

"So they should," Vicky said. "Thank you." She began picking the parings from the garbage and dropping them into the bucket she used for compost.

"A few potato peelings going into Garbage A instead of Garbage B isn't going to make much difference in the long run," Richard said.

"Sure it will," Vicky said. "Besides, it's a question of attitude—"

"It's *only* a question of attitude. People compost their potato peelings and recycle their newspapers and think smugly they've saved the planet."

Vicky picked the last paring from the garbage can and felt annoyed enough at Richard to want to toss it at him. She was trying to think of how best to answer when he went on, "Look, terrestrial life originated, what, about three and a half billion years ago, right?"

"Yes—"

"And in another billion years the earth will be incinerated when the sun bloats up into a red giant. So life here has already used up three-quarters of its time. No matter how we treat the planet it's destined for the scrap heap, anyway."

Maybe she *should* have thrown the peeling at him. "That's awfully cynical. Besides, we're programmed to care about the next generation." She glanced pointedly at Lisa.

"Are we?" Richard smiled down at Lisa. "Well, *that's* sure a relief, isn't it, kid?"

Lisa regarded him thoughtfully. "You're just being

provocative, aren't you?"

Vicky looked at her, amazed. "That's an impressive word for you to use, Lisa."

"I expect it's what her mother says about me," Richard said.

Lisa giggled. "Pro-voc-a-tive, pro-voc-a-tive, Daddy is pro-voc-a-tive!"

"You two."

They looked at Vicky with the same expression, one that smiled but that held something else, too, something private, a knowledge that excluded her. But there seemed little point in continuing to be annoyed at Richard, so she made herself shake her head and laugh.

Richard had to take Lisa back to Burnaby that night, but he returned a few hours later with a video he'd rented, a violent film about Arab terrorists and American heroics called *Executive Decision*. At least he admitted afterwards that, yes, it was a bit supermanly.

"Did you notice," Vicky said, "how halfway through Kurt Russell loses his glasses, which in true Clark Kent fashion he didn't seem to need and after which he's no longer the mild-mannered professor but as macho as the soldiers? The glasses are just a prop, tagging him as a weak intellectual, and without them he becomes more confident, more aggressive. For women in film it's the opposite— when they take off their glasses they become weaker, less assertive, more passive."

She was aware she must have sounded lecturing, and she wondered if he would say something argumentative, if he was still in his pro-voc-a-tive mood, but he only said, "Mmm. That's interesting."

"It was just a footnote in my thesis."

"Are you sorry you gave it up? The PhD, the academic world?"

"Sometimes. I'll do it in my next life. What will you do in your next life? Who are you going to be?"

Richard pushed the eject button on the VCR. "My next life." He hefted the tape in his hand. "I think I'll be a woman."

"A woman."

"Sure. All that macho stuff to impress you, who needs it? Even if it does give us perfect eyesight."

"Well, you're just going to love menstruation."

.

Richard began wanting to do things with her more often, ordinary things like going to the drugstore or walking down to the garage to pick up his car. Although a part of her was pleased, she found herself pulling back, afraid it was too much. She would say she was too busy, that she had papers to mark, but then she would find herself sneaking looks over at his house, waiting for his lights to go on, his car to come back, his footsteps on her back stairs. Just thinking about him made her breathing trembly, made the insides of her thighs warm and tighten, and she would throw on her coat and go out and walk around the block, counting her steps, as though he were something she could walk off, like a leg cramp, a headache, a movie with a disturbing ending.

One Saturday afternoon he talked her into taking him along to see her father.

"I'm bringing a friend," she told her father on the phone. "Now please be nice to him, okay?"

"A him, huh? A boyfriend?"

"Just a friend. Promise you'll be nice to him, or I won't come." How could she have let Richard convince her to do this?

"When am I ever not nice, for Christ's sake?"

But, to her surprise, her father did not behave badly. He wanted Vicky to move his swag lamp from the corner to hang beside his armchair; and when Richard, not waiting for Vicky to ask, got up on his chair, unscrewed the hook and moved it and the lamp to where her father wanted, he said, "That's great. Thanks a lot. That's much better."

Vicky went into the kitchen, unpacked the groceries she had brought. It was so easy for him to say thank you to a stranger, she thought. She could hear them talking in the living room, something about hockey.

On the way home Richard said, "I think your father must be sorry for walking out on you all those years ago. He seems like a decent enough guy."

"Yeah—*seems*." Vicky shifted into second gear with twice the force necessary. "When it's just him and me he's ..." She tried to find the right word.

"He's a vicious bastard," Richard said. "He hates you and resents you and blames you for everything that's wrong with his life. He used to beat the shit out of you when you were a kid."

Vicky's foot eased off the accelerator, and she looked over at Richard, who was gazing out the window as though he had simply commented on the weather. "Of course it's not anything like what you had to put up with," Vicky said, carefully. "He never hit me. I mean, if he was abusive it was in more of an emotional way."

"In an em-ot-ional way," Richard said, drawing the word out like a foreigner saying it for the first time, like Lisa saying pro-voc-a-tive.

"Yes," Vicky said, glancing at him again, his smooth profile telling her nothing. "Maybe he just wanted everyone around him to be as unhappy as he was. Living with him wasn't easy. And then the way he left us. It was horrible."

"Maybe he left because he was afraid of what he might do. Maybe he was saving you from something worse. God knows I wish that my father had left, that he'd done one decent thing in his goddamned ugly life."

"Still," Vicky said stubbornly, "abandonment is abuse, too. There are other ways of being cruel, besides just physical. Besides just violence."

"Easy for you to say," Richard said, his voice tight and angry. "You have no fucking idea."

Vicky winced, didn't answer.

When she had reached her driveway and parked the car, they turned to each other, but they didn't speak. She imagined her own face looking like his in the shadowy light: strange, gaunt, features redrawn by the pain of old betrayals.

"I better go in," she said quietly. She opened the car door.

The dome light made them blink. Richard gave her a smile, but it clung to his lips with obvious reluctance.

"What a pair," he said. "My father was meaner than your father."

She laughed, but uncomfortably. She had heard nothing in his voice that was light, that was amused.

She knew he expected her to invite him in, and perhaps that was why she didn't. As she walked across the lawn to her back door she knew he was still standing by the car, watching her, but she didn't turn around.

She had just hung up her coat when the phone rang. It was her father.

"So what's the story on this Richard?"

Vicky sighed, sat down, kicked off her shoes and curled her toes into the fur of the cat sleeping on the floor. "No story. I told you. He's just my neighbour."

"Don't give me that. If he was just your neighbour you

wouldn't have brought him over here."

"He wanted to come. I didn't ask him to."

"So why did he want to come?"

"For Pete's sake—I don't know. He just did." The cat began jerking his tail crankily from side to side and Vicky moved her feet away from him.

"Well, it's a good thing. You should be getting over Conrad by now."

"Goodbye," she said grimly, and hung up.

The old bastard.

·

She had still been going to see Conrad, but not as often, and not staying as long, and she felt such pain and guilt sometimes that she simply paced his room, not speaking. Occasionally she would take him for a ride in his wheelchair up and down the corridor, but she felt like an animal patrolling the limits of its cage. Conrad gave no indication of whether the change of scenery made any difference to him, although once when they met the old man who had made the lewd comments to her Conrad looked at the man as though he might recognize him. But the next day when they passed him Conrad ignored him, even though the man said something to them that sounded like, "The horses are out," and tried to stick his cane into the spokes of Conrad's chair.

When the small lounge at the end of the hall was unoccupied they would stop there, but it was a bleak place, smelling of disinfectant and urine, the magazines and decks of cards on the table thumbed and dirty. A few times it was warm enough for her to take Conrad outside, up and down the walk, through the parking lot. She looked forward to the summer, when they could do this more often.

A few days after Richard had come with her to see her father, he asked her to take him sometime to see Conrad. She was aghast.

"Why won't you?" he said. "I just want to share that with you."

"I'd feel too uncomfortable."

"Why should you?"

"I'd feel guilty. It's bad enough as it is."

"If you bring me maybe you'd stop feeling so guilty."

"Richard, please don't ask this of me—"

"Why should this make you feel so threatened?"

"I don't feel threatened. I'm not ready, that's all. Later, maybe."

"I just want to see him. Just once. What's wrong with that?"

"He's my husband. You're my lover."

"It's not like it's some social occasion, Vicky. It's not like we're going to sit around and chat."

"I just don't want to, all right?"

"Look, I respect your loyalty to him—"

"If you respect it, you wouldn't ask to come."

"I care about you. I want to share some of the more painful parts of your life as well as the good parts."

"I can't share this with you. How would you feel if I invited myself along when you see Christine?" Maybe that wasn't fair, but she was alarmed at where the conversation was going.

"That's different," he said tersely. He got up and went into the kitchen. She could hear him opening the fridge, the grate of a pop-can tab being pulled.

"Why is it different?" she asked doggedly, when he came back into the living room.

"We're divorced. It's over. It's boring."

"It's not boring to me. She was an important part of

your life."

"Right. *Was.* I've told you as much about her as you need to know."

"I see," she said, stung. "As much as I *need* to know. You expect me to tell you everything about Conrad, even take you to see him, but your ex-wife is none of my business."

He swung around, so quickly that a small streak of Coke leapt like spittle from the can, dotted his jeans.

"She walked out on me, Vicky. On me and Jason both. One day I think we're doing okay, more or less, and the next day she's gay and going to live with some woman. Pardon me if I don't enjoy talking about it."

"Oh. I'm sorry." His ex-wife was *gay?*

"The thing is, I wonder if she actually *is* gay. She just started making all these gay friends, and they got her thinking she wasn't fully evolved or something if she was still living with a man."

"But surely she—"

"I tried to understand. I tried to get along with them, but all they could talk about was how men had oppressed women, there wasn't a conversation we could have that didn't turn into an argument. I was sympathetic, I swear I was. I know men have done rotten things to women over the years, but it was like I was personally the enemy." He brushed his hand, hard, several times along the back of the armchair. "Well, men can be victims, too."

He went into the kitchen. She heard him running the water in the sink, for so long she thought he must want her to go in to him. She sat there miserably, not knowing what to do.

He came back, stood in the doorway drying his hands on her kitchen towel. "I'm sorry," he said quietly. "It's just that I still get upset thinking about it. Maybe she really was gay all along. Maybe we didn't need all those fights, those political arguments. Maybe she just needed them to make it easier to leave."

"It's complicated," Vicky said cautiously. "Gay, feminist, feminine."

Richard dropped the towel onto the table and came over to her, put his hand on her shoulder, began kneading it lightly. It sent prickles of pleasure along her spine.

"Well," he murmured, "I know which one you are. You are definitely feminine."

"Am I?"

She should have said, it's not that simple, or, they're not mutually exclusive; but he knew that already, didn't he? And how could she object to being called feminine? He hadn't meant it as an insult. She should be relieved the conversation had gone where it had, that at least they were no longer arguing about Conrad.

But when he slid his hands under her sweater, began touching her in the places he knew she liked, she felt she had compromised somehow, lied about something; she felt like the movie women in her thesis when the hero removed their glasses and told them they were beautiful after all; and why, after that, would they ever again want to be more than just beautiful?

AMANDA

*W*HAT SHE WOULD BE forever grateful to Amanda for was the tutoring students. Amanda had recommended her to two of her own several weeks ago, and now Vicky had four regulars. For the first time her financial survival wasn't depending completely on substituting.

The tutoring was time-consuming but not difficult, the students slow but motivated. One of them, a depressed and overweight girl in Grade 10, was, Vicky discovered, basically illiterate. When Vicky told the girl's mother she needed more help than Vicky could give, the woman began to cry, pleaded with her to do what she could, so Vicky took the girl back, although she had no idea how to teach someone to read. But she began to enjoy the challenge. The girl was so used to failure that the biggest hurdle was just getting her to try. When, after two weeks, she sounded out, syllable by painful syllable, the word "exploration," they were both delighted.

She would talk to Richard, excitedly, about her success with the student, and he would nod and say vaguely, "Yes, isn't that good," but she knew he was resenting the amount of time she was putting into this new work.

"It's just too much," he said one Saturday night as they sat on the sofa waiting for Amanda, Vicky having at last given in to Amanda's ultimatum that if she didn't get to meet Richard soon she would go to his house naked and say Vicky had sent her. Richard was looking particularly handsome, in grey slacks and a blue blazer. Vicky, wearing an oversized flowered blouse and her black tights with the small hole beginning a run at the back of her knee, felt frumpy next to him.

"You put in a full day at school," Richard went on, "and then you have kids over in the evening and weekends, too."

"I need the money," she said.

"But I hardly get to see you any more."

"We see each other almost every day."

"It's so rushed."

Vicky pulled away his hand from where he had lodged it inside the waistband of her tights. "I don't complain about your work," she said. "You have to work some evenings, some weekends. You have the time with your kids."

"I just want us to be important in each other's lives, that's all," he said.

"We are," she said. "Aren't we?"

"Maybe we should live together."

"*Live* together?"

"Well, why not? We could rent out one of the houses. It would save us both a lot of money."

"I guess it would," she said carefully. She pulled her left leg up, hugged it to her chest. "It would make sense in some ways. But—live together. I mean, Richard, we've only known each other for, what, four, five months."

"I know, but, well, why not? We could try it for a month, maybe, before we commit to a renter."

Vicky drew in a breath, let it out slowly. "I don't know." But she did know—why was she afraid to tell him? "I'm flattered you'd ask."

"I'm not trying to flatter you. If you don't want to do it just say so." His eyes went squinty, the way Jason's would, pulling in a fine pattern of lines at the corners.

"There's the children to consider," Vicky said. Of course: why hadn't she mentioned them right away? "You know Jason doesn't like me. He'd make it miserable for all of us."

"I know Jason's a problem, but I'll talk to Christine again. I'll just insist that she take him, that he go live with her. I'll pay her however damned much she wants."

"It would be so disruptive for him, a new school again—"

"It's Christine he wants to be with. He'll have no trouble adjusting."

"And Lisa."

He shrugged. "Christine's never minded keeping Lisa. Besides, you're so good with her. She likes you, she keeps telling me she likes you."

"Still—" Vicky dropped her left leg, pulled her right one up to her chest. "It's nice the way it is, isn't it? We live so close to each other; it's easy to be together when we want, and it gives you private times, to do your painting, to be with the kids—"

"Don't tell me *my* reasons for not wanting it, Vicky."

"I'm sorry, I just ..." She gestured helplessly at the air. "I'm just not ready."

"It's because of Conrad, isn't it? He still comes first."

"That's not fair." She looked away from him, knowing he could read the truth on her face. Of course it was Conrad. He was her husband. She loved him. She could never let him go, and Richard would expect her to, already expected her to.

"You're the one not being fair," Richard said, his voice tight. "Not to me, not to yourself. Your husband is gone, Vicky. He's never going to come home. He's a vegetable. When are you going to face up to that?"

"Stop it," she whispered.

She twisted herself away from him, got up, walked across the room. She found herself in front of the stereo, and she shoved a tape into the cassette player, her mind barely registering what her hands were doing. The adagio of a string quartet filled the room, like parody.

"I didn't mean to just ... say it like that, to use that word. But it's true, you know it is."

And then Amanda was at the door.

Vicky would tell herself later (yes, she was telling herself this now, sitting on the hard bench in the police station listening to the brittle hum of the light above her, waiting for someone to come for her) that perhaps if Amanda hadn't arrived just then they would have argued it all out, somehow, that she could have changed what would happen. Later—when she was looking for excuses, reasons to blame herself, reasons not to blame herself.

Amanda had come from a birthday party. She was carrying a black, helium-filled balloon on which was written, "Fart if you like being forty." She let go of the string, and the balloon rose to the ceiling, where it hovered like a severed head.

"A present," she said, gesturing vaguely at the spot the balloon had been before she released it. She was wearing a tight, low-cut black dress, an overdose of makeup and perfume, and earrings with silver arcs like small sickles swinging against her neck.

"You look nice," Vicky said halfheartedly, finding it hard to breathe through the perfume mixing toxically with the alcohol on Amanda's breath.

"To quote Dolly Parton," Amanda said, her eyes already fixing on Richard in the living room, "you'd be surprised how much it costs to look this cheap." She walked up to Richard, held out her hand. "And you're Richard. Vicky's told me so much about you."

Richard flicked a look at Vicky, took Amanda's hand. "Pleased to meet you," he said.

Amanda dropped herself into the chair opposite him. Her earrings swung dangerously. "You *are* a sight for sore eyes," she said.

"You're drunk," Vicky said coldly, standing in the doorway. She had an urge to open the door again and ask her to leave. Amanda had said once that she had been going for interesting but had overshot it all the way to weird. Vicky felt like reminding her of that now.

"I'm not drunk. Really. Cross my heart. Or the organ of your choice." She spread her arms dramatically.

"Yeah, sure," Vicky said.

"Okay, okay, maybe a little. But I had to get drunk. It was either that or admit I was in a roomful of people so stupendously boring I was the most exciting one there. You ever notice how after a few drinks people get more interesting? A terrific guy talked to me for two hours about his sailboat. Sober, I'd have thought he was a jerk. You miss out on a lot, being sober." She sighed.

Richard laughed, throwing Vicky an ambiguous glance. Maybe it was a challenge—he would prove to her what a gentleman he could be; he would charm even her drunken friend. "Vicky tells me you're a languages teacher," he said. "How many languages do you speak?"

"I can say, 'I am innocent,' in all of them." Amanda giggled. "That wasn't original. That was Ilie Nastase, the tennis guy."

"She can speak French, Spanish, English, and Chinese," Vicky said, too primly.

"Yeah, I can go senile in four languages."

Richard laughed again, leaned back, spread his arms out along the back of the sofa.

"Offer me a drink, will you, Vicky?" Amanda looked

down at where one breast was leaning precariously out of her dress, and she pulled at the bodice to tuck it back in. "What kind of a hostess are you?"

"A sober one."

Vicky went to the kitchen and poured a cup of coffee from the thermos and set it in the microwave. Amanda wouldn't like it, but Vicky didn't care. She heard them in the living room, laughing, Richard asking her questions, being charming. The microwave beeped. She added sugar and cream to the coffee and brought it into the other room. Amanda was telling Richard, "Well, you know what they say: whether life is worth living depends on the liver." She cackled. Vicky set the cup in front of her.

"Coffee!" Amanda made a retching sound. "Jesus, Vicky, it looks like coagulating urine. Couldn't you do better than this?"

"Sorry. The bar is closed."

Amanda sighed, took the coffee. "You used to have such a polite demeanour, Vicky. But the longer I know you de meaner you get."

Vicky allowed her a smile for that one. "I think I should take you home. You shouldn't drive."

"Yes, *sir*." Amanda saluted her, then took a large mouthful of coffee, held it in her mouth for so long before swallowing that Vicky thought her throat must have seized up.

Richard stood up. "I should go, too," he said.

"Don't leave on my account," Amanda protested.

But Richard was already at the door, opening it. Vicky went over and held it for him. The string from Amanda's balloon dangled down between them.

"Well. Don't stay up too late," he said.

Vicky didn't answer, didn't look at him. *Vegetable,* she heard his voice saying. She would never forgive him for that, never.

"Are you two talking about me?" Amanda shouted from the living room.

"No," Vicky said. "You're not really here."

Richard leaned around the corner into the living room and said, "Goodnight. It was a pleasure to meet you, Amanda."

"Likewise, I'm sure," Amanda said, struggling up from her chair, her right breast tipping again almost out of the top of her dress. By the time she was on her feet Richard had gone. "Well, *he* left awfully fast. Was it something I said? *My* men at least wait until they get paid."

Vicky dropped onto the sofa, feeling suddenly so exhausted she could hardly stop herself from sliding down into sleep.

"I'm starving," Amanda said, wandering into the kitchen. "What you got to eat around here?" Vicky could hear her opening cupboard doors, humming. "Food, glorious food. Who needs sex when you can have food?"

She reappeared in the living room carrying a box of cereal. She poured out a handful, shoved it into her mouth. "God, what is this stuff?" she demanded. "It's got pieces of gravel in it." She squinted at the box. "*Post Grape Crunch.* That must be post as in 'past.' Post-grape."

"I'm not forcing you to eat it."

"Cranky, cranky." Amanda set the box on the coffee table.

"I'm sorry. Richard and I had an argument before you came. It has nothing to do with you."

"An argument, eh? Tell me all."

"I'm too tired. You're too drunk."

"Don't give me excuses. Give me dirt." Amanda took another sip of coffee, made a face, sat down.

"He said we should move in together."

"Isn't that rushing things just a tad?"

"Of course it is. Everything that's happened with him has felt rushed. It's my fault, too, I suppose, but sometimes I think he's like a man under a death sentence or something, and he has to put us on fast-forward."

"So in a couple of days he'll be asking you to marry him."

"I wouldn't be surprised."

"Doesn't sound too bad to me."

"Amanda." Vicky sat up straighter. "I count on you for some common sense. Bizarre as that seems at the moment."

"Okay, okay. But I liked him. I didn't expect to, you know. The bodice-ripper and all that."

"Wasn't it you who just said that after a few drinks you find jerks interesting?"

Amanda scratched at her nose, looked thoughtfully at whatever she had scraped off under her fingernail. "It's as though you didn't want me to like him, Vicky."

Vicky was silent for a few moments, staring dully across the room at the light on the cassette player, which had long since finished playing. "Maybe I didn't," she said.

•

The next day was Sunday, and Vicky made an effort to do some laundry and catch up on her bills and correspondence. Amanda's black balloon seemed to follow her around the house. It was slowly losing its helium, and its string began dragging on the floor. She tied it to the leg of her desk, where the cat kept a nervous eye on it.

She kept glancing at the door, expecting to hear Richard there, not knowing what she would do if he did come. Amanda called, full of apologies for her drunken lushness, as she called it, assuring Vicky the mighty god

Hangover was making her suffer. They didn't talk about Richard.

In the afternoon, rummaging in a kitchen drawer for scissors, she found the instruction booklet for programming the thermostat timer. The directions didn't seem hard to follow, she thought. But her finger hesitated over the buttons. She wouldn't just be setting her own program; she would be erasing Conrad's. But she made herself continue— it was just a thermostat, nothing to get sentimental about. There. Why hadn't she done it long ago?

At the hospital she stayed longer than she had for weeks. She fed Conrad supper, went out to get something of her own to eat, came back again. On impulse she began to read aloud to him from a magazine she had picked up at the nursing station, an article on new Canadian films, and he sat as though he were listening attentively.

Halfway through he said suddenly, croakily, "Stones."

"Yes, stones," Vicky said. She went back to reading. She had almost finished when she glanced up and saw he had fallen asleep. His eyes were moving under his lids, and she watched him curiously. Since his accident she hadn't noticed him dreaming. Although surely he must have had dreams; they were necessary, she supposed, even to damaged brains. Dream of me, she thought, willing herself into whatever broken pictures his mind was seeing.

It was almost ten o'clock by the time she got home. She was just getting ready for bed when she heard the doorbell. She looked at herself in the bathroom mirror, her hand on the toothbrush pushing out her right cheek. There was a part of her that might have said, *Don't answer*, but the rest of her was already responding, eager. She rinsed out her mouth, let the toothbrush drop onto the counter and went to the door. The bottom of her robe caught on the hall table and pulled open the belt loop.

They were like people who had forgotten language, wordless. They made love wildly, knocking down the bedside lamp, nothing mattering except their physical need for each other, for that unmindful hemorrhage of blood and desire.

SEARS

*I*T WAS THE NEXT DAY. Her father was on the phone. "Is that too much to ask? How would you like to be stuck in this apartment for weeks, nobody to take you out anywhere—"

"You can book the transit van any time you want, Dad. You've done it before." Vicky hunched her shoulder irritably higher to hold the receiver and continued cutting her nails.

"Yeah, sure, and I get there and then what? You ever tried getting around a mall on your own in a wheelchair?"

"I haven't time to take you. I've got the extra tutoring now."

"Who? Your new boyfriend?"

"He's not my boyfriend." The scissors slipped, and she cut closer to the quick than she had intended.

"Is it too much to ask? That you take your father out to a shopping centre so he can buy a new sweater? Just once. Is that too much to ask?"

So she agreed to take him, the next day after school. Leo managed to get himself invited along, which annoyed her, but at least he helped her get the wheelchair into the trunk, while her father stood by the car door watching them and not nearly as helpless as he pretended to be.

"So how's school been?" Leo asked, easing the trunk lid closed. He was wearing his Arctic-strength parka but with the hood down, maybe so as not to disturb his comb-over, which had been done with such care that Vicky had felt some need, which she suppressed, to tell him how nice he looked.

"Oh, okay, I guess," she said vaguely.

"That's good, that's good." Leo rubbed his hands together. "Okay is good. Okay is better. And the husband? He still the same?"

"Yes. Still the same." She went over to the driver's side, opened the door.

"'The husband,'" her father muttered. "Not much of a husband anymore. Just takes up your time for nothing."

"*You* take up my time for nothing," Vicky snapped. "Now get in the car before I get Leo's gun and shoot you."

Leo scuttled quickly to the back door and got in, as though he were the one she had threatened.

"See how she talks to me, Leo," her father whined. "I tell her the truth and she talks to me like that."

"Get in the damned car."

"See how she talks to me." He got in, sighing, fumbling with the seat belt until Vicky reached over and jerked the clip into the slot. "Be glad you don't have a daughter, Leo."

"Oh, Vicky's okay. One like that's okay."

Vicky laughed. "Thank you, Leo."

"That's a new light, isn't it?" her father said as she pulled up to a light that had been there for ten years. "It's nice to get out and see the changes. Stuck in that apartment. It's like a goddamned jail. They throw food at you and let you rot. Nobody gives a shit."

"That's right," Vicky said. "Life is hard."

In the shopping centre Leo went off to do some chores of his own, and Vicky took her father to several men's clothing stores where the sweaters were, apparently, all too expensive.

"I don't have money to waste," he said. "Not like some people."

"Well, where do you want to go now?" she asked, exasperated. "Sears?"

"Yeah."

The mall was crowded, and they got stuck behind a young couple tugging a toddler along between them. The soles of the child's shoes had a whistle built into them, and every step he took produced a shrill squeal.

"What the hell is wrong with that kid's shoes?" her father asked loudly.

The child's father turned, his face assembling a belligerent expression, which changed to uncertainty as he saw Vicky's father glaring at him from a wheelchair. The man picked up the child, said something in a low voice to the woman, and they edged away. Vicky was glad her father couldn't see her smiling.

She wheeled him at last into Sears, but they were in the wrong section, the wrong floor, even; so, her father saying something she was trying not to hear about how women never knew where they were going, they went looking for the elevator.

They were going through the appliances section when her father suddenly said, "Isn't that your boyfriend there?"

"What?" Vicky stopped abruptly, and her father had to grab the arms of the chair to keep himself from sliding forward.

"Jesus. Be careful. You want to dump me onto the floor?"

"Did you see Richard?" She was looking around, couldn't see him.

He had called her that morning and asked if he could come over later, and she had agreed, reluctantly, knowing he might want to resume their argument about moving in together. *Vegetable.* She'd winced, remembering both her anger and how easily she had let it go, let her physical desire forgive them both.

"I thought you said he wasn't your boyfriend."

"Oh, for Pete's sake. Stop playing games." She pushed the wheelchair forward again.

"Well, I thought I saw him. Over there." Her father gestured to his left. "Waiting on someone."

"Waiting on someone?"

"That's what I said. He was wearing a name tag and showing that woman in the red coat one of those little ovens."

"Microwaves," Vicky said absently, her eyes skimming the room. She saw the woman in the red coat, but there was no one with her. Well, it was ridiculous; her father was mistaken.

And then she saw him. She stopped moving, ignoring her father's indignant exclamation. Richard was coming out of the storeroom carrying a large box. He brought it to the woman in the red coat, opened it, checked inside and took out some papers, and then they talked and pointed at another microwave on the shelf.

Vicky watched them, transfixed.

"That's him, isn't it?" her father said. "Didn't you say he was a teacher?"

"Yes," Vicky said. Her lips felt numb. "Art teacher. I guess he must work part-time here."

"I always said there's no money in teaching."

Vicky couldn't take her eyes from Richard: the slight, attentive smile, one hand now holding out the papers to the woman, the other hand set lightly on the boxed microwave, his grey suit and tie, the name tag pinned on his lapel—what did it say, she was suddenly desperate to see what it said.

"Are we going to sit here all day?" Her father's voice made her start. "You see enough of him, you don't have to stand here gawking at him."

"I just didn't know he worked here," Vicky said, making herself move, pull her eyes away.

"Some boyfriend. Well, at least he has a real job."

"Yes," Vicky said, pushing the wheelchair through the tunnel of refrigerators. She found it hard to remember why they were here, what store, what city, who she was with, where they were going.

·

She told herself she would have to bring it up that night. She paced the floor, waiting for him, trying out tactful, non-judgemental questions on the cat.

There was no way to ask that didn't sound wrong, accusatory. Unless he had an identical twin, what answer could he make except, *Yes, it was me*. Obviously he hadn't told her because he didn't want her to know, because he felt embarrassed. His teaching position must not pay as well as she thought; perhaps he was hired on temporary contracts, not unlike hers. She had taken on a part-time job, too, after all; there was no disgrace to it. So why didn't he tell her about his? Did he trust her so little? Or maybe he had expenses she knew nothing about—the ex-wife, a drug habit, gambling, a blackmailer. She shuddered. The more she thought about it the more she liked the identical twin explanation.

When he called and said that the high-school student who usually babysat Lisa had cancelled and that he hoped he could bring Lisa along, Vicky was actually relieved, because she wouldn't be able to raise the subject with Lisa there. They helped Vicky make supper, and she found herself sneaking nervous looks at both of them.

"Is anything wrong?" Richard asked finally, turning on

the burner under the broccoli. "You seem kind of distract-ed."

"No, no," she said, looking with concentration at the chicken breasts from which she was peeling the skin, which reminded her alarmingly of the skin of testicles.

She put the chicken in the microwave. Had Conrad bought the microwave at Sears? Maybe he had; maybe he'd bought it from Richard. She began cutting up the toma-toes. Slice, slice, went her knife; all those fingers to avoid.

Over supper she made herself smile, pass the dishes of food, eat. She told herself that Richard had omitted telling her something about himself, that was all. It wasn't as though she had seen him doing something shameful, ille-gal, illicit. Maybe she should even be pleased that he would care enough about her opinion to hide the fact he needed extra work. So he wanted her not to know—couldn't she do that for him?

"Have another piece of chicken," she said to Lisa.

"No, thank you," said the girl, poking at the tomatoes on her plate.

"Eat what you have, then, come on," Richard said.

"Yes, Daddy." She put a piece of potato in her mouth, chewed, swallowed, reached for another. Her compliance could be unnerving.

"You should write a book on how to raise obedient chil-dren," Vicky said, thinking too late of Jason.

But Richard only smiled, said, "Oh, Lisa can be naughty, too. But I make her pack up her company man-ners when we go out." He poked his finger lightly into the girl's cheek, wiggled it.

Lisa squirmed, giggled. "Stop that," she said.

After he left to take Lisa home, Vicky cleaned up the dishes, waiting, dreading his return. She *had* to ask him. She couldn't stand not knowing. She poured him a large glass of white wine and herself a ginger ale and stood by the door, listening for his steps.

"This looks nice," Richard said, taking the glass. "Shall we make a toast?" He sat on the sofa, laid his arm along its back.

"I want to ask you about something."

"Oh, oh." He took his arm down, leaned forward a little.

Vicky sat down facing him, immediately got up again. "This afternoon—" she licked her lips "—I was shopping with my dad. In Sears."

Richard's face went pale. He set the wine glass on the coffee table, bumping the base, as though he had lost his depth perception, as though he might be trying to set it down into water.

"Why didn't you *tell* me you worked there? It's no disgrace, for god's sake. What was the point of keeping it secret? Most of us have to scrounge part-time jobs to survive."

"It's not a part-time job. It's my regular job. I've been selling appliances at Sears for fifteen years."

"Oh." Vicky sat down. Her legs felt weak. "Why didn't you tell me?"

"Because you'd have reacted just as you did now. Oh, a *sales*man. But an *art* teacher, well, that's different."

"That's not fair! I'm 'reacting' because you didn't tell me about it, not because it's inferior work."

"Inferior work." Richard snatched up the wine glass, took a deep swallow. A little wine dribbled from the corner of his mouth and he wiped it away with the back of his hand, making the gesture deliberately coarse, ugly.

"I don't mean it *is* inferior. I mean ... You know what I mean. You're trying to make this my fault."

He took a deep breath, held it, his eyes roaming the room as though looking for a safe place to exhale. "Okay, look," he said. "I told Birdie the truth, but I suppose all she remembered was that I teach this course—a continuing ed. course, not even an academic one—at the college, so that's what she told you and it was just so easy to let it slide by when you mentioned it and suddenly it was too late to correct you. I told myself it wasn't really a lie, just an ... omission."

"A big omission." But if he did actually teach a course he hadn't outright *lied*, had he? "You could have trusted me."

"I know."

They were silent for a while. Richard took another swallow of wine. Vicky watched the way he tilted his head, the way his throat moved, its sudden vulnerability.

"What I hate most about the job," Richard said abruptly, "and maybe that's why I couldn't stand to talk about it, is that it's what my father did. All his life he worked for Sears. It's why I got the job in the first place. And here I still am. Doing the same work he did. Hitting my son the same way he did—"

"Oh, Richard, you don't, you aren't the same as your father."

He leaned his head against the back of the sofa so that he was staring up at the ceiling. His face seemed pallid, over-illuminated by the swag lamp above him.

"I omitted telling you some things about him, too. Some of the things he did to me."

She wanted to cover her ears, to stop him. Because she knew what he would have to say.

"My earliest memories were of him ... touching me. By the time I was ten it was more than that, a lot more than that."

He began to cry. He stared up at Vicky's ceiling, his features twisted, tears filling his eyes, his breath shaky, all of it more terrible because he made no effort to turn away, to cover his face, to stop her from seeing.

She came over and sat down beside him, took his hand, folded his fingers around hers, tightly. They sat that way for a long time. At last Richard got up and went into the bathroom. Vicky remained on the sofa, put her head back, the way Richard had done, and stared at the beige circle of light on the ceiling made by the floor lamp across the room, at the way the light diffused into near-darkness by the time it reached the far wall.

She wanted to cry, too, but she couldn't. There was one more thing she had to ask, one more thing he had to tell her.

He came out of the bathroom, sat in the chair opposite her. His face was reddened, unevenly, like a fading rash.

"So now you know," he said.

She watched his fingers, pulling at the loose fibres of the tissue in his hands. "I have to ask you, I know you'll be upset but I have to ask you—"

"If I ever did it to my own kids?"

"I'm sure—"

"But it's what you were going to ask, wasn't it? It's what the research tells us, right? That the cycle repeats. That most sexual abusers were sexually abused." He threw the tissue onto the coffee table, rubbed his palms up and down on his thighs as though trying to rid himself of the feel. "Well, maybe you *should* ask. Everybody should ask. Maybe if someone had asked about me it would have stopped it."

"Maybe it would have."

"To answer your question." He straightened, looked at her. The redness had left his face, and it was pale again. "I haven't. I haven't. But I've thought about it. With Jason. Only with Jason. When he was little I was diapering him and I felt, oh Jesus, I felt like touching him, touching him there—" He closed his eyes.

"But you didn't."

"I wanted to."

They were silent for a moment, their eyes flicking over each other, never quite meeting.

"So," Richard said. "Are you repulsed? This man you've been sleeping with, well, it's so sordid, isn't it?"

"It's *not*. It's ... courageous of you to admit to things that have humiliated you. And to admit to inappropriate feelings. Only then can you do something about them."

"Yes, Doctor."

She smiled uncomfortably. "But it's true, isn't it?"

"I suppose so." The refrigerator cut in, a sudden shudder of noise. After a moment he said, "There was a bright side to all this. I told Christine, and she never made me diaper Jason again."

They began to laugh, giddily, out of proportion, the tension in them suddenly released, frightening the dozing cat, who sprang to his feet, the hair on his back and tail bristling, spiny as a porcupine. The phone rang. They kept laughing.

"The machine will get it," Vicky said.

It was a child's voice. "This is Lisa. Daddy, are you there? There's something wrong with the toilet. It runs over when I—"

Richard snatched up the phone. "I'm here. It's okay, don't worry. I'll be right over. Don't flush it again."

He hung up, made a shrugging motion with his hands. "Sorry. I have to go. Another emergency. And I've got to get Lisa back to Burnaby tonight and pick up Jason. He was probably the one who plugged up the damned toilet." He ran his hand through his hair, looked towards the door.

Vicky stood up, faced him. "I'm glad you could ... tell me about everything."

Richard picked up the tissue, fixed his eyes on it. "I hope it won't, you know, change things between us."

After he'd gone, Vicky put a tape in the cassette player (Vivaldi, Mozart, something stringy, she didn't care, whatever her fingers had touched first), turned out the lights and lay down on her back on the living-room floor. The cat curled up on her chest.

She lay there for a long time, well after the violin concerto had ended. She supposed she might be lying there without the lights on so that Richard would think she'd gone to bed. *I hope it won't change things between us.* Would it? Had it?

She closed her eyes, made the darkness darker. She remembered reading about automated Japanese factories where work went on all night, but no lights were ever turned on, because everything was done by robots, who didn't need light. She thought about all those blind inhuman hands, and she shivered, got up and turned on the lamp.

.

She didn't hear from Richard the next day. She could have called him, of course, but she didn't.

As she was pulling out of the alley on her way to work the following morning, she saw Jason standing at the side of the road in front of his house, obviously waiting to be picked up for school. Not giving herself time to think about it, she turned down the street towards him. He saw her coming but didn't step back off the road or smile to acknowledge her, only tightened his grip on the backpack he was holding against his chest. He was wearing jeans and a blue T-shirt with a cartoon logo she could only partly see under his open nylon windbreaker. His hair was cropped even shorter than she remembered it; she supposed that was the style now, but it reminded her of the skinheads she had met in Germany.

She rolled down her window. "Hi! Are you waiting for a ride to school?"

"Yeah."

"Well, good. It's a long way to walk, isn't it?"

"Yeah."

"Do you usually walk?"

He shrugged. "Yeah."

"At least the weather's nice now. Spring. You can smell it in the air." She inhaled deeply, as though she expected him to imitate her.

"It snowed in Spokane. I saw it on TV."

Finally. "Really? In Spokane? You have relatives there, don't you? It's where your dad's from."

"Yeah." His face closed again, squinty, scowling, and he looked away down the street, obviously wishing his ride into sight.

"Jason, look—if you ever want to talk to someone, about anything, you can talk to me. Okay? It'll be private. Just between us. About anything at all."

He swung his eyes towards her, then immediately back to the road. "I can talk to my mom." He was running the zipper of his jacket up and down, up and down.

"Of course, well, that's good—"

"There's Mrs. Novak."

He walked away, towards the blue minivan that had just turned the corner. Vicky could see a dark-haired woman driving, two children's heads. The van pulled in behind Vicky, the woman's expression unsmiling, wary. Vicky could imagine what she was thinking: a strange car idling beside a young boy, the boy obviously glad to get away, jumping eagerly now into the back seat of the minivan— It would be funny, Vicky thought, pulling away, if it weren't ... Weren't what?

Why had she decided to stop and talk to Jason? Could she still have doubts that Richard had told her the complete truth? *It wasn't really a lie, just an ... omission.* But that was just about working at Sears, she told herself angrily, nothing important. He must have told her the truth about his father, about Jason. It wasn't possible to disbelieve the pain she had seen in him, his struggle not to become his father. She would be victimizing him again if she didn't believe him. Jason had problems, certainly, but were they signs of sexual abuse? And if Richard had problems, they didn't, they couldn't, oh surely they couldn't, include abusing his children.

After school she had three hours of tutoring, at the student's home in South Surrey; it seemed a tad greedy, she'd told Amanda, to charge more if she went to the student's house, especially if the house was a quasi-Versailles like this one and the parents coaxed food and drink upon her; but Amanda insisted they keep ruthlessly to the rate schedule they'd worked out.

"The more they pay you the more you're worth," Amanda said. "Simple."

"They must be," Vicky sighed.

On her way home she stopped to see Conrad. She made herself stay to feed him supper, perhaps precisely because she was so eager to get home, to phone Richard, to say, come over, I want to see you, nothing's changed, come over.

As she was leaving, she had the sudden impulse to stop at the nurses' station and ask to use the phone to call him. She almost ran from the lobby, whether in flight from her own urgent desires or in pursuit of them she wasn't sure. In the car she turned the radio up, loud, the carpe diem of rock 'n' roll.

CONRAD

T WAS several days later.
She would remember it exactly.
The nurse had just brought Conrad back from physio, and Vicky had begun reading to him, from her old Norton anthology, Wordsworth's "Intimations Ode," parts of which she had long ago learned by heart. By heart, she'd thought, listening to her voice. Not "by head," but "by heart."

> A single field which I have looked upon,
> Both of them speak of something that is gone:
>> The Pansy at my feet
>> Doth the same tale repeat:
> Whither is fled the visionary gleam?
> Where is it now—

She would remember it exactly. She had just said the word "now," her eyes already on the next line.
"Vicky," Conrad said.
She stared at him, the book sliding closed on her lap.
"Yes," she whispered. "Yes. Vicky. That's my name."
"Vicky," he said again. His hand lifted, dropped back.
His eyes: there was a difference in his eyes. They seemed to be trying to focus on her. Hardly daring to breathe, Vicky got up, the book thudding to the floor, and went over to him, crouched at his feet. She took his hand, squeezed it.
He pulled away, but said again, in his rough, unused

voice, "Vicky."

"Yes," she said, "I'm Vicky."

Not taking her eyes from him, she stumbled over to the bed, pushed the call button, urgent jabs. It seemed hours before someone came. Nurse Ratched. Her uniform looked too large for her, as though she had shrunk since she had put it on this morning.

"He said my name," Vicky exclaimed as soon as she came in. "He said my name!" She went back to Conrad, looked into his eyes, willing him to see her. He was blinking rapidly, looking somewhere across the room.

"He does say words sometimes," Nurse Ratched said, her hand still on the door.

"This was different! He said 'Vicky,' said it twice, and he's never done that before, and in his eyes, you can see, something's happening. He's trying to remember!"

The nurse came over to Conrad. "What's this?" she said. "You're going to talk to us?"

He blinked several times, quickly, turned his head a little to one side.

"Conrad?" The nurse leaned over, looked more closely at him. "Say something to us."

He lifted his hand, waved it vaguely in the air.

Nurse Ratched sighed. "I'm afraid I don't see any difference, Vicky."

"But there *was*! He said 'Vicky' and then his eyes, they seemed suddenly more animated. As if he were trying to, to put it all together!"

"Maybe you're right," she said. Vicky could tell she didn't believe it.

"Well, tell the doctor. Please. It's important. He should see him as soon as possible."

Nurse Ratched gave her a little smile. "All right."

When she was gone Vicky pulled her chair close to

Conrad, their knees almost touching, and searched his face for any sign of understanding, recognition. Her hands fluttered at him, lighting in quick, almost furtive, touches on his arm, his leg, his cheek.

"Say something," she said, half laughing, half crying. "Say my name again. Please. Look at me. Say 'Vicky.' Say anything."

But he didn't. Still, Vicky was sure there was a change in his face, a frowning concentration, eye movement that seemed more purposeful, intelligence straining to reclaim consciousness. Several times his lips began to pull and twist, as though words were struggling to form, and twice more she thought his gaze rested on her, the way it would if he were well, if he were normal, if he were coming back.

She began reading aloud the Wordsworth poem again, slowly, glancing up at the end of every line, encouraging interruption. She had to stop when she got to "Where is it now," her throat locked tight, willing him so fervently to repeat her name she felt she could wait forever, if only he would say it.

(Remembering that moment now was almost too much to bear, and Vicky leaned forward on the hard bench in the police station and pressed her head into her folded arms; and Amanda, misunderstanding, put her hand on Vicky's shoulder and said, "Don't worry. Don't worry.")

Finally, late, Nurse Ratched came by and told her, not unkindly, that she really had to go home now.

"I'll be back tomorrow," she said to Conrad. "I promise."

On the way home she was still so excited she could hardly drive. She could feel the smile on her face, cocked the rear-view mirror to look at herself, smiling, laughing out loud. She told herself she was overreacting, that all he had done was say her name, and he had said words before.

But the look on his face, in his eyes—she couldn't dismiss that; there *was* a difference.

When she got home and out of the car she stood for several moments feeling the warm westerly wind blowing at her, not caring about the specks of rain it tossed in her face. The air smelled fresh, full of spring, new grass and the stirring of sap, the promises of March. She could see the stars of the Big Dipper visible even through the cloudy glow of city. The cat came over and rubbed himself, first on the car tires, then on her leg, welcoming them all home.

"Vicky."

She jumped, took a step back and nearly trod on the cat, who leaped straight up and then galloped away down the driveway.

"You scared me half to death!" she exclaimed, peering at Richard across the hood of her car.

"I was worried about you. It's so late."

"I was at the hospital." And she should have thought about what she was doing, but her excitement was too great, and she showered her eager story onto him. "So I'm sure there's been a change, it's so incredible, after all this time—"

She stopped. Richard said nothing. He was a black shape on the other side of the car, faceless.

"I'm still a bit in shock about it. You know," she said lamely, thinking for the first time about Richard, about how he would feel. "Well ..." She stood there helplessly. "Do you want to come in for a while?" she said at last.

"So you can tell me more about Conrad?"

"Richard, I'm sorry. It was insensitive of me."

"Insensitive. I suppose that's a good word for it."

"It's not like he's coming home, cured, tomorrow. There was a slight improvement, that's all."

It sickened her, hearing herself say that, the pleading

tone, minimizing the change, as though that were the good news. She turned away, looking across the lawn at the empty branches of the cherry tree.

Richard came around the car and stood beside her, put his hand on her arm. "Look, I know you—"

She pulled away from him. "I'm going in," she said. "Goodnight." She began to walk toward the house.

"Jesus," she heard his voice. "You can be such a bitch."

She winced, her step faltering, but she made herself keep walking. She felt his eyes on her back like a hand, pushing.

When she got inside she ran a bath and lay in it until the water was barely tepid. She closed her eyes, trying to think, to work it all through, but her head felt swollen with confusion and excitement, and finally, chilled, she got up and took a sleeping pill and went to bed.

It was well after midnight when the doorbell sounded, over and over, and she dragged herself up at last from her drugged sleep and went to answer it, stumbling, barely awake.

"Vicky," he said. "I'm sorry. Shhh, don't talk, it's okay," putting his cold arms around her, half-carrying her into the bedroom.

•

The next morning when the alarm went she hit at it groggily, forcing herself not to slide back into the warm comfort of sleep.

Conrad. She remembered what had happened like a sudden jolt. She got out of bed smiling, looking at the ordinary things around her as though they had been transformed, were full of new meaning. Conrad was getting better; Conrad had said her name. She wished she could go to see him right now—

And why shouldn't she? Why should she wait? It was too important to put off until after school. She had to make sure the doctor came; she had to do everything she could.

She phoned the Dispatch Centre, said she was sick and would they send someone else to Oakdale. It would have been her third day at the school, and an easy one, but Conrad was more important.

When thoughts of Richard pushed into her mind, she forced them away. Later, she told herself, pulling up to Matheson Pavilion; I'll worry about Richard later.

Nurse Nice looked up in surprise. She was wearing three small roses pinned onto her cap; it made her look especially cheerful today. "You're here early," she said.

"There was a change in Conrad. Didn't they tell you?"

"A change. No. What sort of change?"

"He said my name yesterday. And his eyes were trying to focus on me, really trying to see me."

"That does sound like a change." Nurse Nice put down her clipboard. "I saw him this morning, though, and he seemed the same."

Vicky was already heading down the hallway. "He's *not* the same," she said over her shoulder. "I'm sure of it."

But when she went into the room Conrad was sitting in his chair as usual, his eyes vague and distant. She knelt down in front of him.

"Conrad. It's me. It's Vicky." She searched his eyes, willing them to see her. But there was nothing of what she had seen yesterday. She blinked back her disappointment.

Nurse Nice was at the door. "Dr. Lansky will be making his rounds in about an hour. Do you want me to have him stop by?"

"Yes, please. Of course."

She spent the hour doing everything she could to provoke some response from Conrad. She read to him, talked to him, touched him, rubbing his hands and shoulders, trying to turn his head to face her, to make his eyes see her.

Then, just before the doctor came, he made a sound, lifted his hand.

"Vicky," he said.

"Yes! It's Vicky!" She knelt by him, took his hand, pressed it to her cheek.

It was how Dr. Lansky, a jowly middle-aged man whose head sat directly on his shoulders without the nuisance of a neck, found them. He stopped at the door, as though he had intruded on something embarrassing.

"Come in," Vicky cried, stumbling to her feet. She took his arm, began pulling him across the room. He laughed uncomfortably, tried to tug free.

"So you think he's better, do you?"

"He just said my name! And he did yesterday, too. He's never repeated one word like that, so deliberately."

Dr. Lansky leaned over, looked carefully at Conrad's face. "Conrad," he said loudly. "Do you hear me?"

Conrad's lips pursed, relaxed, pursed again.

Dr. Lansky picked up Conrad's wrist, felt for the pulse, looked at his watch.

"Vicky," Conrad said, jerking his wrist away. Dr. Lansky stepped back, startled.

"See! See!" Vicky cried.

"Well," Dr. Lansky said. "That's quite interesting."

"He says my name, and you can tell from his face he's trying, he has a real expression."

Dr. Lansky nodded, frowning. "There might be something there, all right." He bent down to Conrad again. "Conrad? Can you hear me? Can you say something else? Do you know who we are?"

Conrad's eyes skipped around the room, lighting on the bed, the door, Vicky's elbow, Dr. Lansky's ankle.

"I tell you what," the doctor said after a minute. "I'll have the neurologist give him some tests tomorrow. He'll be able to tell you more definitely if there's been any real change."

Tomorrow: it seemed like forever. "But what do you think?" she said. "Doesn't it seem to you as though there's some improvement?"

Dr. Lansky hesitated, watching Conrad. "He does seem to be a bit more involved," he said guardedly. "And his repeating your name is a good sign. But after all this time, well, you have to understand it would be unusual for him to suddenly recover. There was major brain damage, you know that."

"But it's not impossible, is it, a recovery?"

"Well, nothing is impossible. There have been rare cases where locked-in states like your husband's abruptly, well, unlock. As though there had been a kind of electrical disconnect that suddenly re-fused itself. There was a man in Wisconsin who suddenly 'woke up' after eight years and began talking after being given Valium for some dental work."

"Valium! I did it with poetry."

The doctor laughed. "A non-prescription drug," he said. He tugged at his right ear, which seemed elongated from years of such pulling.

"A few days ago," Vicky said, suddenly remembering, "I saw he was dreaming. I hadn't seen him do that before. Do you think it's significant?"

"Dreaming? Well, yes, I suppose it is. Especially if it's something new." He held up his hand, as though he needed to stop Vicky from walking into him. "But, really, the brain isn't my specialty. We'll get some tests done, and a neurologist in here, and maybe they'll be able to tell us more." He moved to the door.

"In the meantime," Vicky pressed, not wanting him to go, "what should I be doing?"

"Whatever you have been doing, I guess."

Whatever you have been doing. Richard, last night. She had gone to him even after what he had said; she had gone to him like a sleepwalker, opened the door and let him take her.

She stayed at the hospital all afternoon, going out only for lunch and, later, when she could feel herself starting to doze in her chair, a walk around the block. She phoned the mother of the Vietnamese student she was supposed to tutor after school and canceled, saying she was ill.

Conrad said her name several times in the afternoon, with what seemed to be growing imperativeness, and his restlessness increased until she became alarmed and called an orderly, who wanted to give him a tranquilizer.

"Maybe we shouldn't," Vicky said, remembering the Valium and the man in Wisconsin but afraid of sedating this new energy. The orderly shrugged, went away.

She fed Conrad supper, with which he seemed particularly impatient, knocking the fork to the floor.

"Vicky," he said, beginning to rock a little back and forth, something he had never done before. "Vicky," he said, his back hitting his chair. "Vicky. Vicky."

But after supper he became listless again, let his head drop forward, and fell asleep. Vicky knew she had to go home. She couldn't afford not to answer her phone messages, to do without work two days in a row. She put her hand on Conrad's cheek, tenderly, not wanting to wake him, and left.

When she got out of her car in her driveway she looked around, nervously, half expecting Richard to be there again, in the dark, asking her questions she had no answers for. But the lights were out in his house, so, relieved, she went inside, answered her phone messages and agreed to sub the next day at Robert Hurst Junior, not her favourite school, but it was too late to be choosy.

She made herself a careless meal of leftovers, warmed-up hamburger uninvigorated by the ketchup, and as she ate she thought of Conrad sitting across the table from her, telling her about his day. The cat meowed crankily and pressed himself against her leg.

"Conrad," she told him. "You remember Conrad."

She had just finished washing her hair, was wrapping a towel around it and wondering whether she should bother to put in rollers, when the doorbell went.

She had to answer; she couldn't pretend they didn't have things to say to each other.

"Hello," he said, unsmiling, standing on her doorstep with his right arm crossed over his chest as though it should be in a sling. The beam of the porch light slid down his shoulders.

"Hello." She made herself hesitate before she said, "Come in." She tightened the twist on the towel on her head. It was the one he had given her, the most absorbent she had.

He sat down in his usual armchair, still holding his right arm like a guardrail across his chest, a strangely defensive posture she hadn't seen him use before. She perched uneasily on the arm of the sofa.

"How was Conrad today?"

Well, he wasn't going to waste any time. Vicky clenched her hands into the folds in her robe. "I don't think I was mistaken yesterday. He said my name quite a few times, and he seemed very agitated. As though he was struggling to remember, or communicate. The doctor saw him today and said he thought there might be some change, too. A specialist is going to see him tomorrow." She was relieved to say it all, hiding nothing.

And hiding everything. Using facts to avoid telling him anything. She went over to him. "I'm sorry," she said. "I know how you must feel."

"You've no idea how I feel."

"I didn't plan this. I didn't plan to have you in my life, either."

"But now I am," Richard said. "You can't just make me disappear."

He got up, so abruptly she stepped back, nudging the phone table and rattling the receiver. He stood close to but not touching her and let his arm at last drop to his side.

"I want you to choose. Him or me."

"Richard, for god's sake. I don't want to choose between you."

"So you want us both. Some sort of bigamy."

"Don't be absurd." She pushed at his chest with one hand, and he stepped back, let her sidle away.

"It's not absurd to want some commitment from you."

"He's my husband; he needs me, now more than ever." It sounded like a line from a movie, nothing she could ever have imagined herself saying.

"And what about us?"

"Well ... Why can't we go on as we have? Conrad is better, but he's a long way from well." It wasn't the right answer, but it was all she could think of to say.

"I see. So, as he gets better, where's the magic point? When do you decide, well, now he's really my husband again? When you sleep together?"

"Please don't."

A motorcycle went by outside, sounding so loud Vicky wanted to put her hands over her ears, to press and press, shut out everything, the silence and the noise.

"When it comes down to it, then, you choose him."

She couldn't answer.

"I see," he said harshly.

He took a step towards her, pushed at her, as though she were in his way. She fell backward, against the stereo cabinet, jarring it against the wall. The arm she put out to steady herself hit one of the speakers, knocking it over, sending the cassettes piled on top flying across the room. Some of the boxes opened, spilling tapes onto the carpet.

She sat sprawled on the floor, her back against the cabinet. The arm that had hit the speaker felt numb. The towel around her hair had jarred loose and began unfolding onto her right shoulder.

Richard stood very still, the hand that had pushed her pressed against his thigh, the fingers splayed. After what seemed like a long time, he knelt down, picked up one of the tapes, put it back into its box, set it on the coffee table.

"I'm sorry," he said. "That's the last thing I wanted to do. Act like some thug."

"You better leave," Vicky said, pulling her robe over her legs and tucking them under her. The towel dropped to the floor, and her hair fell wetly onto her neck.

Richard got up, not looking at her, and walked to the door, opened it, went out.

"Don't come over tonight," Vicky called after him. "I won't answer the door."

But, still, that night she lay awake for a long time, expecting to hear him at the door, promising herself she wouldn't, couldn't, answer, but waiting, in a kind of eager fear.

She realized, finally, he wasn't going to come.

So now it's over, she thought; it's finished. He's forced me to choose and I did not choose him. Somehow they would have to live next door to each other and become strangers again.

.

She was so tired at school the next day she drank twice as much coffee as usual, even took a cup with her to each of her classes. Her arm hurt from where it had hit the stereo cabinet, and she could see a purpling bruise starting to spread under the skin. Images of Richard would leap at her unexpectedly, like ambushes, like drug flashbacks, and she would have to turn her eyes abruptly away from the blackboard or textbook or student whose face had suddenly become his. Conrad, she would tell herself—in five hours, four, three, she would be able to see Conrad.

At lunch break she sat in the staff room and drank more coffee, imagined her brain overheating, perking with caffeine. Two more hours, and she would be at the Matheson Pavilion, would find out what the doctors said. Even if the tests showed nothing, she knew something had changed. She had reason again to hope. She could see him, rocking back and forth in his chair, saying her name.

She smiled vacuously at the other sub across from her.

"... so I told the teacher she just didn't understand Sarah, that she's a very sensitive little girl...."

When it came to their own children, Vicky thought, teachers could be surprisingly myopic. She crossed her legs, uncrossed them again, trying to pay attention.

"Vicky Bauer?"

Startled, Vicky turned around. It was one of the secretaries. "Yes?"

"There's a phone call for you."

It's my father, she thought, following the secretary to the office, god damn him, what is it this time, his remote fell on the floor and he wants me to pick it up, the toilet paper ran out and he wants me to put on a new roll.

She jerked the receiver to her ear. "Yes?" she snapped.

"Mrs. Bauer?"

It wasn't her father. More politely, she said, "That's right."

"This is Dr. Lansky. I'm afraid we have some bad news." He paused, cleared his throat. "Your husband died this morning."

"What?"

"I'm so sorry. Your husband died this morning."

Vicky put her hand on the counter, leaned forward. "Oh, god," she whispered.

"I'm so sorry."

"What? Oh, god. How could it— He was getting better...." She felt dizzy, faint, unable to draw in enough air.

"I'm sorry. I know this is a shock."

"But how ... What happened? What could have happened? Was he, I mean, was he killed?"

"Killed? Oh, no, no. He ... died. He just died, Mrs. Bauer. Peacefully. In his sleep, we think. Probably from an aneurysm."

"I see."

"We could do an autopsy, if you like. We'd need your consent."

"I ... I don't know." The room seemed to be darkening, as though someone were slowly dimming the lights. "What difference would it make now? He's dead."

"I'm so sorry, Mrs. Bauer. I know how hard this must be."

Vicky shook her head. No, she thought, you don't, but she couldn't speak. A hot pain gripped her throat.

JESUS CHRIST

*E*RNEST AND HELEN came over and, sitting uneasily on her sofa, assured Vicky they would look after everything.

"The Memorial Society will handle the cremation," Ernest said. He was wearing a navy blue jacket and new jeans with brittle creases. "And then a small service on the weekend, we thought." He leaned forward, slid one foot ahead of the other as though he might suddenly have to leap to his feet.

"There probably won't be a lot of people, will there?" Helen asked.

She was a tiny, energetic woman with shrill red hair that seemed particularly at odds today with her black suit and shoes and handbag, the strap of which she kept pleating nervously in her lap. She had always seemed to Vicky like the kind of woman who had found in adolescence a personality that had suited her ever since, and like most adolescents she could be simultaneously endearing and annoying.

"No," Vicky said. "We didn't really know many people here."

"Well, then," Ernest said. "We'll call you when we've reserved a ... a venue."

"A venue," Vicky said.

"Well, you know." Ernest cleared his throat. His thick-lensed glasses were misting over at the tops. "A place. A funeral parlour."

"Yes, of course. Thank you."

Her calmness was unnerving them, she knew.

"Is there any particular music you'd like to have them use?" Helen asked.

Vicky thought for a moment. "There's an old Blood, Sweat, and Tears song called, 'And When I Die.' Conrad said once it would be a good one for a funeral. That line about swearing there ain't no heaven but praying there ain't no hell."

She had definitely shocked them now. What had made her say such a thing, anyway, when of course it had been she, not Conrad, who had made the comment about the song?

"Whatever they usually play will be fine," she said.

Helen smiled, relieved. "It's usually something classical."

"That'll be fine."

Helen got up, touched Vicky's arm. "Do you want us to come pick you up?"

"Sure," Ernest said quickly, getting up, too. "We can do that."

"That's all right," Vicky said. "My friend Amanda can probably give me a ride."

"You'll be okay," Ernest said abruptly. "You'll see."

"*Sehen ist nicht glauben.*" Seeing isn't believing. It was what Conrad had said to her once in Germany. It surprised her as much as it did Ernest to hear herself say the words now.

•

The funeral chapel was small, as such places went, although so high-ceilinged it seemed as though more storeys than one had originally been intended. The walls were a beigy pink, the room dimly lit with recessed lights. Except for the benches, which connoted pews, there was nothing to suggest a church; even the music, although not Blood, Sweat, and Tears, was easy-listening, no organ in earshot. The secularity should have made Vicky feel more comfortable, but it didn't.

She sat politely listening to the minister's ten minutes of feigned sincerity, telling herself what did it matter if he did say "Brauer" instead of "Bauer." After, she stood murmuring polite replies to condolences. "You're so brave," someone said, and she smiled and answered, "Thank you. So good of you to come."

Even when, outside in the parking lot, her father, as they waited for his van, declared, "Well, it's for the best," she didn't get annoyed, although even Leo winced and, perhaps deliberately for once, changed the subject.

Amanda took her home, came in with her. "Are you sure you don't want to talk about it?" she asked anxiously. "I mean, you didn't even take a day off work, and you kept on tutoring...."

"I'm all right, Amanda."

"Have you cried? You should cry."

"Don't worry about me, Amanda. I've accepted it. He was gone from me already for a long time."

"Well, yes. But then those last two days, when you thought he was getting better ..."

"I suppose I hadn't really believed it yet. Now they say his increased energy was probably just a sign of something going wrong."

Amanda rubbed absently at a hangnail on her thumb. "You know that myth about Pandora, where Hope is the last thing left in the box? And we interpret this today as the one note of cheer in a host of horrors? But the Greeks believed Hope was the cruelest evil of all."

Vicky thought about it for a moment. "I suppose they were right," she said.

"Well, just so you're aware that maybe your mourning isn't over. Remember what Virginia Woolf said, something about how we experience the death of someone we love not at their funeral but when we come across a pair of their old shoes."

Vicky smiled. "I should be all right then. Ernest came over yesterday and helped me collect all Conrad's clothes and shoes and gave them to the Sally Ann."

"Did he? He's been rather helpful, hasn't he?"

"He has, actually. I'm surprised. But he feels guilty, that's all."

Amanda glanced away, and Vicky wondered if she might be thinking that Vicky had been referring to herself, too, to her own guilt.

"I'm all right, Amanda. Really."

Amanda's look was dubious. "Well, I hope so. Stiff upper lips are bad for your health. 'Courage' has the word 'rage' in it, too, you know."

"I don't have the energy to do much raging. I just feel kind of ... drained. 'Tired' has the word 'I' in it."

•

It was the fourth evening, Tuesday, when something crumbled in her. She was taking a cup from the cupboard when it slipped from her fingers and broke into three pieces on the floor, and as she bent to pick them up she suddenly began crying. She sank to the floor, sobbing, and curled herself up tightly, clenching her hand around one of the shards, not feeling that it cut her.

The phone rang several times, and someone may have come to the door, but she was aware of nothing except her grief. Eventually, her right side numbed with cold from the linoleum, she got up, opened the cupboard door above the refrigerator and reached for the bottle of gin.

She wasn't supposed to, ever. My name is Vicky and I'm an alcoholic. She unscrewed the top, drank from the bottle. The hard taste almost made her gag, but she took another swallow, another, and felt the familiar warmth under her skin, in her stomach, the warmth that would soon rise to her brain, making it soft and dull and easy. Another swallow, another.

"Unconscious," she said, leaning her forehead against the refrigerator door. "Please. Unconscious."

She had done this too often in her life, wished herself into alcoholic sleep. Until she had promised Conrad she would quit, and she had. But Conrad was gone now.

Finally, her eyes squinting to focus, she screwed the top onto the bottle and pushed it back into the cupboard, and then she stumbled around the house and pulled all the curtains tightly closed and went to bed. She pressed her eyes shut, trying to squeeze out the remaining light from the room, from the day, from the westerly sun still yeasty with life.

She was aware of a period of darkness, night, and some internal timer woke her at six-thirty and made her call the Dispatch Centre to cancel her teaching. She fell immediately back to sleep and woke up in the afternoon. She would probably have lain there longer except that she was enormously thirsty, and the cat kept clawing at her bedroom door. Her head ached and her body felt stiff and sore, as though she had fallen down a flight of stairs. A cut in her palm had bled into the sheets.

She spent the rest of the day wandering around the house in her pajamas, not bothering to brush her teeth or comb her hair, bursting into unexpected fits of crying or anger so fierce she had to grit her teeth to stop herself from throwing things against the wall. It took all her strength of will not to open the cupboard above the refrigerator. She could feel her mouth go dry, her hands start to shake, at just the thought of it. But she didn't give in. She had promised Conrad.

She spent the next two days wandering about the house in a fever of anger and grief, but by Friday she was better, and she accepted a half-day contract at Oakdale. The principal looked at her kindly, murmured something about "her loss." She thanked him politely, pressing her fingernails into the Band-Aid on her palm to stop herself from feeling anything but that easy, physical pain.

.

When she got home that night there was a message on her machine from Ernest, wanting to come over and discuss Conrad's life insurance policies.

"His life insurance policies?" she asked, when he arrived an hour later. "I didn't know he had any. Surely he'd have told me."

Ernest perched on the couch, so close to the edge that the sofa cushion lifted up in the back. He was wearing a grey suit whose pants were too tight, a white shirt, and a blue paisley tie to which he reached up now and loosened the knot.

"Actually, he took them out only a few weeks before the accident. It was, well, lucky, I suppose."

"The lawyer didn't say anything to me about life insurance policies."

"Well, he probably didn't know." Ernest clicked open the slim briefcase he had brought and took out three clipped pages. "Conrad left the policies with me, and I didn't want the lawyer taking a chunk of them. Or to bother you about it. Until now, of course." He handed her the papers.

It took Vicky only a few moments to scan the pages, to see the amount. "Two hundred thousand dollars? He left me a life insurance policy of two hundred thousand dollars?"

"Yes, he did."

Vicky kept staring at the papers. The settlement from the auto insurance, the lawyer had assured her, would be "very comfortable." And now there was this.

"Why didn't Conrad tell me about it?"

"I'm sure he meant to."

But he would have known Vicky would snort and say it was paternalistic and a waste of money and that she could manage perfectly well without him. Her throat tightened.

She wouldn't cry, not in front of Ernest.

It wasn't until he was going out the door that she thought to say, "You mentioned policies. Insurance policies. Was there more than one?"

Ernest looked down at his shoes, rubbed at the snap on his briefcase. "Yes. There was another one." He cleared his throat. "I was the beneficiary. Or rather, the company was. The company wasn't actually doing all that well, as you know...."

"No. I didn't know." She could feel a cold dislike of him hardening in her chest.

"So we each took out a policy naming the company as beneficiary. We each did."

"I see. But Conrad was just your employee."

"I was going to make him a partner. I was going to have the papers drawn up. You know I was. Conrad wasn't just an employee." Ernest looked up at her then, met her eyes. He was trying unsuccessfully to smile. "He was family. I miss him." His voice was becoming hoarse. "I miss him a lot."

"So do I," Vicky said. But she felt her hostility ease.
There wasn't anything wrong with what Ernest had done,
was there? "Well. Thank you for these." She gestured at the
papers she had set beside her on the hall table.

When Ernest had gone she picked the papers up again.
She could feel the tears pressing against her eyes. Two hundred thousand dollars. So much money. Not enough to buy
back one life.

.

Since the night he had pushed her down and she had told
him to leave, almost two weeks ago now, although it
seemed like much longer, she had not heard from or seen
Richard. Everything between them seemed to have happened years ago, when she was a teenager, the details hazy.
When she thought of him, it was mostly with a sting of
regret, but there was something else, too, a sting of shame,
because, when she let herself remember the awful phone
call at the school, she knew that what had leapt, mon-
strously, into her mind was that Richard could have had
something to do with Conrad's death. She could hardly
believe, now, that she could have thought such a thing, at
such a time; but there it had been, a sudden and cruel
judgement on both of them.

Sometimes she thought of Lisa, too, feeling remiss, as
though she had abandoned her. She hadn't seen Lisa
around, although she had noticed Jason several times in his
back yard, playing with his hockey set, shooting broody
looks periodically at her house. But he didn't come over,
didn't try to talk to her, didn't try any more of his strange
tricks. Perhaps, since she was no longer seeing Richard, the
boy no longer needed to try to frighten her away.

She wondered if Richard might know about Conrad's death, if he was avoiding her because of that and not because of what had happened between them. But of course he couldn't know, she told herself; he was staying away because whatever was between them had ended.

She hadn't counted on Birdy. The day after Conrad's death she had pushed through Vicky's mail slot an enormous sympathy card and a half-pound box of chocolates with a note attached saying, "Good for everything that hurts." So Vicky should have expected the news not to stay a secret in the neighbourhood.

Still, when she picked up her mail that Friday afternoon and opened the letter, her breath caught when she saw Richard's signature. His writing was firm, pressed strongly into the paper, although sometimes the words were so close together she had trouble distinguishing them from each other.

Dear Vicky,
I'm so sorry to hear of Conrad's death. If you
need anything, anything at all, please let me know.
I feel terrible about our argument. Please forgive me.
Your friend,
Richard

Your friend. It sounded so deliberate, so ... prim. She read the note several times, telling herself not to be suspicious. And, yes, she couldn't deny it—a part of her was glad to hear from him. But it was (and it surprised her to realize this) the part that *did* want him to be a friend, only a friend. She glanced at her arm, where the bruise was still faintly visible, a dull yellow, and looked quickly away.

She made no response to the note. Later, she told herself, as she had so often before—she would decide what to do about Richard later.

The next day, Saturday, she had just opened the door to pick up the litter of fliers on her front steps when she saw Lisa coming down the walk towards her, carrying what looked like a casserole bowl. She was wearing a long brown parka that went almost to her ankles and that Vicky thought belonged to Richard.

Vicky straightened, smiled, walked down the steps to meet her. "Hello," she said. "It's nice to see you."

The girl handed her the bowl, blinked up at her. "Hi," she said. "This is from us. Me and my dad. He said you're sad right now because somebody you liked died and this is to cheer you up."

"Well, isn't that thoughtful. Thank you very much." She took the bowl. "What is it?"

"Zawnya. My dad made it."

"Lasagna? I love lasagna. Do you want to come in for a while?"

Lisa looked down at her feet, kicked the toe of her right shoe lightly against the side of her left one, and shook her head. "My dad says I shouldn't. He says you want to be alone now."

"That's true, I suppose, more or less. But maybe you can come back later. When I feel better."

"Okay." She took a few steps back.

"Well, thank your dad for me."

The casserole bowl felt warm in her hands, as though it had recently come from the oven. She could imagine Richard watching her, and she struggled to keep her eyes from flicking up to the window that faced her house.

Thank your dad for me. She knew what that meant. Later, she had kept telling herself, but it wasn't later at all, and she had as good as invited him over.

•

He waited until Sunday, and then he phoned.

"It's such a nice day," he said. "I'm going for a walk down to the beach, and I wondered if you'd like to come."

It sounded harmless, neutral. Still, if she said yes she would be agreeing to more than just a walk. She was quiet for so long that finally he cleared his throat, said, "I'll understand if you don't want to, Vicky."

"All right. Just for half an hour. I've got other things to do."

He came to the door, wearing his paint-stained T-shirt and jeans, smelling faintly of turpentine, and waited on the stoop as she got her jacket.

What did she feel, seeing him again, after all that had happened? As she put on her coat she glanced at him furtively, his profile broken into a thousand tiny pixels, through the screen door she'd just put up for the summer. There was not, she was relieved to note, that leaping of the pulses she had always felt before at the sight of him. She felt, still, oddly numb, incapable of arousal, faintly incredulous at the very idea. That should help to make her, she thought, wary now, cautious. She mustn't forget what had happened the last time she'd seen Richard. Conrad was gone now; he had been a limit that Richard knew she could no longer impose on him. And even if she didn't feel anything sexual for Richard now, she was still vulnerable. She would have to be as wary of herself as of him. Conrad was no longer her excuse, her safeguard, her husband.

"I'm ready," she said.

They walked past Birdy's and down to the end of Balsam Street, to the stairs that led to the beach. They didn't speak except to remark, once, on a flowering quince spread against a carport and charmed by the sun into hundreds of red blossoms. It was so warm that she took off her jacket.

At the top of the stairs they sat, without either of them suggesting it, on the bench facing the ocean.

Semiahmoo Bay glistened in the sun. On the beach at Blaine, just past the Indian reserve and the border crossing, they could see slim crescents of sand as the tide went out. Beyond that rose the cloudy scapulae of the San Juan Islands. It wasn't quite clear enough to see the mountains of the Olympic peninsula across the Juan de Fuca Strait. To the west, the long brown tongue of the White Rock pier lapped at the bay. They could just see the top of the huge, eponymous white rock on the beach. Erratic, it was called in geology: a solitary boulder transported by a glacier from some distance away.

"My sister lives straight south from here," Richard said. "Port Townsend. There's almost nothing but water between us. If they made strong enough binoculars I could probably see her house. If I wanted to."

They were quiet again, looking out across the water.

Richard cleared his throat. "I want to tell you," he said, "how sorry I am about Conrad. You probably won't believe that, given the way I behaved, but I am. Losing someone you love is ..." He picked a dandelion growing near the leg of the bench. "Christine didn't die, of course, but it felt like she had. I fell apart after we separated. With Jason, with everything, I'm improvising. Putting storm windows on a collapsing house. Running five minutes ahead of every crisis."

"That's better than five minutes behind."

He laughed, twisting the dandelion between his fingers. "I didn't mean to go on about myself. You're the one who's really lost someone, who deserves sympathy."

"I don't really want sympathy." She looked across the bay spread out blue and white and grey in front of her. Two sailboats were frisking south from the pier into the open water. "I'm not sure what I want. Time to heal, I suppose, simplistic as that sounds."

"I wish it *were* simplistic," Richard said. He handed her the dandelion.

"Thank you," she said, taking it. "A *pissenlit*." He looked at her oddly. "It means 'piss-in-bed.' Amanda says it has something to do with the leaves being a diuretic."

"*Pissenlit*," he said, in a better accent than hers. "Those poetic French." He did not sound amused, and Vicky remembered, then, his surname, Menard, and that his father had been French-Canadian.

A woman carrying a large sketchpad came wheezing up the steps, gave them a panting grin. "Out of shape or *what*," she gasped, stumbling past them.

"We'd make a good picture," Vicky said. "Two Wounded People On Bench, Holding Dandelion."

They walked back using another route, past the lawn bowling club where two old men were tossing a Frisbee back and forth, laughing like young, wobbly children whose reach exceeded their grasp. When they got to her house, Vicky remembered the casserole dish, so she had to ask Richard in.

"I won't stay," he said. "I know you've got things to do." He stood on the stoop holding the screen door open until she returned with the bowl.

"It was delicious."

"Good. Lisa helped me make it." He took the bowl. "When are you going back to work?"

"I already went on Monday and Tuesday. It was foolish, I guess. I felt as though I were sleepwalking, but I had to go. I need the money."

She wasn't aware until she'd said it that it was a lie now. She couldn't exactly retire, but she would no longer have to panic over missing a few days of work. She could miss a few *years.* But she didn't say anything to Richard, some old superstition of her father's surfacing in her that you should always pretend to be poorer than you are.

"I wish I could have helped somehow."

"There was nothing you could have done."

"Still," he said. "Still."

Perhaps he made some slight move towards her, or perhaps she was only afraid that he would, but she pulled back. Richard let go of the screen door and it slowly swung shut between them.

"Look," she said. "About us. We can't just, you know, pick up where we left off. We can't just start sleeping together again as though nothing's happened."

"Of course," he said. "I understand that."

"I mean, a lot has changed. Everything has changed."

And she knew she should go on to say that she wasn't talking just about Conrad's death but also about how Richard had behaved, how if he ever laid a hand on her again ... But it seemed unnecessary, somehow, too much as though she would be envisioning, inviting even, a future where there could be such passion between them again.

"I don't expect you to do anything you don't want to, Vicky. I mean that." He reached out, let the back of his hand brush lightly across the screen, let it drop.

She would remember that gesture (yes: she thought of it now, watching the policeman walk down the corridor toward her, slowly, his shoes making no noise as the heels struck the floor), the reaching out and not touching, how exactly right it was.

•

Fraser Secondary. Imagine that. Another teacher who didn't know her history here.

As she walked down the hallway to Jesus Christ's office to pick up the daybook, she was surprised to find that she was not afraid. Uncomfortable, yes, and who wouldn't be at having to see Jesus Christ, but not afraid. Was it having money that made her less fearful of him, of what he could do to her? Or had Conrad's death simply made her more fatalistic? She'd have to think about that.

When she entered his office, he looked up, said, "Mrs. Bauer." He had obviously been expecting her. Around his throat, she noticed, just above the level of his rigid white collar, was a row of lumpy red blemishes from ingrown whiskers. Either that, or someone had recently tried to hang him.

"I'm subbing today for Carol Otley." She returned his absence of a smile. "You have her daybook?"

He gestured at it and the stack of texts on the corner of his desk. "Everything you need is there," he said. "I've checked it."

And Carol Otley would have been so grateful for *that*, Vicky thought. She picked up the books. "Thank you."

"You may be wondering," he said suddenly, "why you have another assignment here."

Of course she was wondering. But she made herself not say, yes, please, tell me.

"Well," he said, a frown wadding up his face at her silence, "I'm sure it won't surprise you to hear it was none of my doing."

She made herself stand still, just look at him. Inside her shoes she allowed her toes to curl, clench, against the soles.

"I might as well tell you, then, before you hear it from them." He put a slight, unpleasant emphasis on the word *them* and glanced at the wall, where, Vicky deduced, he was probably not referring to the Rocky Mountains picture-framed there but to the occupants of the staff room behind the wall. "I'm being replaced as vice-principal. It appears my performance appraisals were not ... acceptable to the superintendent."

"I see."

"I thought you'd like to know. That you're not the only one who's been held up to evaluation and ... found wanting."

Vicky laughed. "'Found wanting.' Is that how we've been found?"

Jesus Christ stirred his fingers among the assortment of pencils on his desk. "I'm glad you find it amusing."

"I'm not particularly amused." But she was, oh yes she was. "The truth is, I don't think you're good at being a vice-principal." Oh, the nerve of her.

"And maybe you're no good at being a sub."

Touché. "Maybe I'm not. Maybe what I'm good at is being a regular classroom teacher."

They eyed each other tensely. It was Jesus Christ whose gaze dropped first, settling on the flap of Vicky's purse. "I suppose God has His reasons for denying us what we want."

"Of course," she said cruelly. "But He does it for our own good, doesn't He?"

He tightened his lips. "We are often tested, Mrs. Bauer."

"I can't argue with that."

She turned to go, but something made her pause at the door and ask, "By the way, did they ever find out who trashed your car?"

"No," he said. He cleared his throat. "Perhaps it was simply another test."

She smiled. "Perhaps."

"I will tell you, Mrs. Bauer, that it occurred to me that it might have been you."

She stared at him. "*Me?*"

"I considered anyone who might have had, well, both the nature and the motive."

Vicky began to laugh. "The nature and the motive." She couldn't stop laughing.

"Well." Jesus Christ frowned, his eyes flicking around the room in small pendulum arcs until they lit on the phone. His hand reached out for it, as though it had been ringing. "I have a call to make, Mrs. Bauer. If you'll excuse me."

"Of course," she said, swallowing another burst of laughter. Let him have his last moments of importance, of power.

As she walked down the hall to her first class she might have begun laughing again if she hadn't pressed a fist to her mouth and coughed instead.

The nature and the motive: good grief. He must have been disappointed at her reaction. How was he to know she would be so difficult to humiliate today? To know she might even see such a character assessment, considering its source, as a compliment? Jesus Christ demoted: maybe there really was a god. Of course, the man would simply be put back into full-time classroom teaching, which from her perspective was hardly a punishment, but the point was, she supposed, that it was a punishment for *him*, that it was, as he said, denying him what he wanted.

When she got home that afternoon, the first thing she noticed was her house key lying conspicuously on her kitchen counter. She had left it with Richard so he could let in the plumber to fix the leak in her downstairs sink. She smiled. Richard was doing nothing wrong, she thought. Nothing at all.

There was a message on her machine from Amanda, saying, "Guess what I heard about Jesus Christ?" so Vicky phoned her back.

"I know," she said. "He's history. He told me himself."

"He told you *himself*?"

"Yup. Then he told me he thought I might have been the one who trashed his car. And it just made me laugh. I burst into this uncontrollable laughter."

"You *laughed*? Vicky, you take me quite aback. Not my favourite position. I can't believe you *laughed*. Maybe you have coprolalia. You know, the involuntary utterance of vulgarities. It's a later stage of Sub's Syndrome."

"It felt quite liberating."

"Still, you better be careful."

"Careful? What's happening to you, Amanda? You're sounding awfully proper suddenly."

Amanda sighed. "I know, I know. I'm sucking up so hard at that school I'm inhaling the furniture. But when they do hire someone you can bet the only battle scars they'll be looking for are lobotomy scars."

"Well, you don't need to ingratiate yourself with Jesus Christ anymore. What did he finally do, anyway, that got him dumped? I thought these positions were like king for life."

"Not sure. I know he got transferred from Elmhurst because the principal couldn't stand him. There were rumours of him making a girl get down on her knees in his office and pray."

Vicky laughed. "It's not funny. Why can't I stop laughing?"

"I told you. Sub's Syndrome. How are things with you and Richard?"

Amanda and her whiplash segues. She could be as bad as Leo.

"Fine," Vicky said. "He's being really good. Not pressuring me about anything. Tonight he and Lisa are taking me out for supper."

"Lucky you," Amanda said. She was probably being sarcastic, but Vicky could tell her heart wasn't in it.

At the restaurant later, just the local IHOP but she was glad it wasn't somewhere more expensive, she told Richard about Jesus Christ.

"Not often you have the satisfaction of seeing the people with power over you get their comeuppance," Richard said, paging through the menu.

"What's 'comeuppance' mean?" Lisa asked. She was wearing the frilly blue dress she'd worn the first time Vicky had met her.

"A penalty," Richard said. "Someone who hasn't been nice getting what they deserve. Someone mean being punished."

"Like Jason," Lisa said.

Richard's hand went still on the page he was turning. He lowered his menu, looked at Lisa. "That's not exactly the same," he said. His voice had a sternness in it, a warning.

"Why not?" Lisa asked. She stared back at Richard. There was something of Jason in that gaze, Vicky thought. It was a look that rebutted a challenge, that pushed back.

To her surprise, Richard's gaze dropped first, down to his menu.

"Besides," Lisa said, "it should be called 'comedownance.'"

"Clever girl," Richard murmured, his eyes not leaving the page.

The waitress, a tall, olive-skinned young woman with fingernails so long they began to curve down, asked if they were ready to order.

"I suppose so," said Vicky, when Richard didn't answer. "I'll have the fettucine."

"And what will your daughter have?"

Lisa giggled, looked at Vicky, then at her father. Vicky

began to laugh, too, as giggly as the child.

"I'll have the same as my mom," Lisa said.

Richard said little as they drove back to Vicky's for coffee and dessert, a chocolate cake she had bought the day before. He sat down on the sofa, turned on the TV, began flipping through the channels with the volume off.

"Can I have another piece of cake?" Lisa asked. She was barely half-finished her first piece.

"No," Richard said, not taking his eyes from the set.

"*Please?*"

"Ask Vicky."

"Can I?" Lisa turned to her.

"We better not. Too much cake is bad for you."

"Okay." She gave Vicky an odd little smile, just pulling her bottom lip up. Vicky had the feeling she hadn't really wanted another piece of cake.

She returned the girl's ambiguous smile, set her plate on the counter, and sat down beside Richard, watched the channels flick past.

"Wait," she said. "Go back. Was that Bernadette Peters?"

Richard flipped back two channels. "Looks like it."

"I think it's *Slaves of New York*. I had a reference to it in my thesis. It's about, well, New York, and this rather useless woman."

"Sounds fascinating."

"And she lives with a painter."

"Ah. Well, then." Richard turned the volume up.

The film suddenly began running two scenes simultaneously, superimposing images of a couple making love on images of the man's apartment being vandalized.

Richard peered at the screen. "Is this happening on purpose? It looks like a mistake."

"It does, rather," Vicky had to agree.

"Is the man fantasizing about slashing his paintings while he's making love?"

"No, no. It's two separate events, happening at the same time. It's supposed to be clever, a variation on the split screen. Creating a double exposure using a double negative. So to speak."

"What's that mean, that double thing?" Lisa asked, licking the icing from her plate.

"A double negative? Oh, here it's just the way they made the movie, but it usually has to do with speaking correctly. How if you say no two ways in a sentence it's like saying yes." Hadn't Amanda said the opposite to her once? *No plus no does not equal yes.* "So if you say, 'I don't want none,' it's like saying you do want some."

"What about if you say, 'I don't *not* want none'?"

"That would mean, well, the same as wanting none. You're getting awfully complicated here."

Lisa grinned. "I know." She lay down on the floor and began playing with the cat.

Vicky watched the screen. The film was irritating her, looking amateurish now instead of original, and she couldn't imagine why she had once thought differently. Had she changed that much?

"The book was better," she said weakly.

•

Richard was at her house the next day when she got the call from the hospital.

"What's wrong?" Richard asked, as she put the phone down.

How could she have forgotten? A wave of guilt and self-recrimination swept over her.

"It was the hospital," Vicky said, not looking at him.

"They want me to come and collect Conrad's things. It's been over two weeks. They shouldn't have had to remind me."

"You had enough to think about."

"Too much," she said. "The wrong things."

He didn't answer. She picked up her purse from the coffee table, turned it in her fingers as though inspecting it for damage. "I should go right now," she said.

"Do you want me to go with you?"

She shook her head. "You better not."

"Are you sure?"

"Yes. I should go alone."

"I don't mind. There might be boxes to carry."

"No. Please. I'll have to pack things. The nurse said she wasn't sure even where they all were."

"Oh, I'm sure they're not that disorganized. That nurse—the one you call Nurse Nice?—she'll find it all. She seemed like a sensible enough person."

"I want to go on my own, Richard."

Richard stepped back, raised his hands slightly. "All right. All right."

At Matheson Pavilion Vicky stood outside the door for a long time, and then someone came and held it open for her, so she had to say thank you and go in.

Nurse Nice smiled at Vicky warmly. "Thanks for coming," she said. "We thought you must have forgotten about his things."

Vicky knew she hadn't meant it as a reprimand, but still she winced and mumbled something to her feet, ashamed to meet the woman's eyes.

"We have it all ready for you," Nurse Nice said. She set two cardboard boxes on the table. Then she picked up the large flowering cactus sitting beside her in the grey ceramic pot with red flecks and set it on top of the smaller box.

"Oh, I don't really want that," Vicky said. Why would the nurse have thought she would?

"Well, it's yours. It was in his room."

"I don't think so."

"Really. It was definitely in his room."

"Are you sure? I never saw it there."

"I thought maybe you'd sent it to him. It was delivered just before we found ... I mean, just before he died." Nurse Nice lowered her voice a little on "died," as though she were betraying a secret.

"*I* didn't send it."

"Well, someone sent it. Or brought it. There's still a card with Conrad's name on it, see? I was here when the man came and took it down to Conrad's room."

"All right," Vicky said helplessly, wanting only to get away. "I'll take it then."

Nurse Nice helped her carry things out to the car, and when they had packed everything into the back seat, Vicky realized she would probably never see the woman again. It suddenly seemed a difficult loss, even though she knew she had tried hard all along not to see her as anything more than peripheral to her life. But she had become important to Vicky, her cheerfulness a comfort she depended on.

"I don't even know your last name," Vicky said. She didn't say that she remembered her first name only because it was on her name tag. Gail.

"Mendelson."

"Thank you, Gail Mendelson."

"Anytime," Gail Mendelson said, smiling, turning away. She was used to such farewells, Vicky thought, watching her go. Perhaps the nurses had code names for their patients and visitors, too, a way of distancing themselves. She wondered what they would have named her.

When she got home Vicky put the boxes in the basement, telling herself she would open them later, when she was better able to face them. Later: it had become her favourite word. She took the flowering cactus upstairs, set it on the sill of her dining-room window. It was beautiful, dozens of red blossoms sleeving the blue-green arms. Still, there had obviously been some mistake; nobody would have sent this to Conrad. Well, it was Vicky's now. She gave it some water and picked off a shrivelling flower.

WORK

"*IT'S GORGEOUS*," Amanda said of the cactus the next day when she came over to cut Vicky's hair, a job she did better than professionals. "What are you going to call it? Spike? But then of course you don't believe in naming the so-called lower species." Amanda looked down at the cat sleeping on his back with his legs stuck in the air like an upturned stool.

"I call you Amanda, don't I?"

Amanda clicked her scissors in Vicky's ear. "That's what van Gogh said to *his* barber."

She began cutting. Vicky watched the little chunks falling to the floor, the grey more obvious lying there than she had allowed herself to see in the cloudy bathroom mirror. She should colour it, she thought vaguely. Later.

"So do you see much of that kid? Jason?" Amanda asked.

"Hardly ever. When I do, the best responses I get from him are mumbles and scowls. He's spending more time with his mother, but he doesn't seem any happier. Poor kid. I wish I could do something for him, but I admit I'm not eager to get involved."

"But you're eager to get involved with the girl."

Vicky shifted in her seat. "It's not fair, is it?"

"Keep still. Not from Jason's point of view, I expect."

Vicky sighed. "I should tell Richard to bring him over sometime. Make a real effort."

"If you and Richard are going to keep seeing each other,

I suppose you can't pretend he doesn't have this kid. Tilt your head forward."

Vicky felt the cold blade of the scissors snipping across the nape of her neck. "As long as Conrad was still alive it was easier. I didn't really have to think ahead about Richard. Everything was so ... daily, you know?"

"Mmm," Amanda said. The scissors stopped clicking. She put her left hand on Vicky's shoulder.

"You're not finished already, are you?" Vicky lifted her chin.

"I have something to tell you," Amanda said, failing completely to sound casual.

Vicky turned, looked up. "What?"

"I'm afraid to tell you."

"What, for god's sake?"

"They offered me the new job at Fraser Secondary."

"Really? That's wonderful. Why would you be afraid to tell me?"

Amanda brushed at the hair on the towel around Vicky's neck. "Well, I thought you'd feel crummy because I got an offer and you haven't. Yet."

"I'd feel crummy no matter what. Now at least I can be glad for you."

But deep inside she felt the ugly prick of resentment, envy. Something had changed between them, suddenly.

"It *does* bother you." Amanda should have been a psychic.

"A bit, I suppose. It'll affect our friendship."

Amanda took her hand from Vicky's shoulder. "What do you mean, it'll affect our friendship?" She came around and stood in front of Vicky. Vicky fiddled with the edge of the towel, wouldn't look up.

"Well, you know. What made us friends in the first place was our being subs. It gave us a common enemy to bitch about."

"And that's the only reason we're friends?"

"No," Vicky fumbled, "but ... in a way we're not really equals any more—"

"Oh, for shit's sake. 'Not really equals any more.'"

"I mean, you'll be making new friends, I'll just be a reminder of the bad old days and make you feel guilty."

"Look, Vicky—when you started hanging around with Mr. Hunk did I say, 'Oh, we're not equals any more' and 'You've got new friends now,' et cetera?"

"Yes, as a matter of fact."

Amanda waved the scissors dismissively. "Oh, all right. But that's *men*. I'm talking about a *job*." From the lugubrious emphasis she had given each word it was hard to tell which she thought more important.

"I've seen it happen before, Amanda. A friend of Conrad's got a promotion and soon they barely nodded hello. One of the secretaries at my school in Edmonton took teacher training and then asked not to work at her old school because she'd feel too uncomfortable around the secretaries. A change in status, that's all that had happened." Vicky picked a thread loose and then tried to push it back into the towel. "Remember how when you were into your second week at Fraser Secondary you didn't even want to tell me that?"

The fridge clicked off, leaving a hard residue of silence. Amanda moved back behind Vicky and rummaged in her hair, parting off a section, pinning another back. The scissors made a coarse, raspy sound.

"Maybe I've just sold out," Amanda said abruptly. "Being part of the underclass gives one a certain honesty. The best way to silence someone is to give her what she wants."

"Like Bismarck."

"Who?"

"Bismarck. He's in Socials 9. It was his tactic."

"Smart man," said Amanda. "Kill 'em or co-opt 'em."

"You're at least dangerous enough to kill or co-opt."

"You're more dangerous than you were."

Vicky laughed, bitterly. "I haven't even had any interviews. They're never going to erase my record. If I were permanent I could be a psychotic pedophile and they'd have to give me my job back. But I'm a sub. They don't have to give me a damn thing."

Perhaps for the first time the words did not sound to Vicky like the required complaining. They sounded like simple truth.

She stared at the spice rack on the far wall and made herself say it: "I'm never going to be hired full-time. I better face up to it."

"There *are* jobs," Amanda insisted, letting the scissors rest on Vicky's shoulder. "And there's always the tutoring. I've got over twenty people registered with me and I can give you all my files, the whole business. With the contacts you've already made, it could be practically full-time work."

"I suppose," Vicky said halfheartedly. "And the insurance money will keep me going for a while." She hadn't dared tell Amanda how much there might actually be. A change in status: was that why she'd been reluctant to tell her? But that was *money*. They were talking about a *job*.

"Sure," Amanda said. "Now let me finish this haircut before I raise my rates."

•

For the next few days all Vicky could think of was that moment of awareness: *I'm never going to be hired full-time.* There it was, hanging like a big sign on the spice rack in the kitchen. The morning she drove to Glen Shepherd Secondary she could see it in shop windows, in the rear-view mirror, on bumper stickers on the cars in front of her.

By the time she got into her first classroom she was in a reckless, antagonistic mood. It was Geography 12, her favourite course, but she found herself impatient with it, with her old deference to the daybook and students, to the texts with their careful evasions.

"To say that one of the most important benefits of alpine glaciation is to make the Rockies a major tourist industry is pretty absurd, isn't it?" she said, tapping the offending text.

The students stared at her.

"Look, forget about plotting mean temperatures. Instead, write to your MP telling him what you think he should be doing about the greenhouse effect."

They did. She could hardly believe it was so easy.

Her Socials 10 had even more obvious material for sub-version.

"'The provincial and federal governments strictly control the emissions and disposal of waste from pulp mills,'" she read, saying "strictly control" with a sneer. "Do you think our air quality would be as appalling as it is if the mills were 'strictly controlled'?"

A boy near the front put up his hand.

"Yes?" she snapped.

"We already *fin*ished that chapter."

"*Have* you?" She slammed the text shut so hard he jumped. "Have you finished with your *life*? Do you know what dioxins and sulphur dioxide and nitrogen oxide do to you? Do you know how much particulate you're inhaling into your lungs right now? Do you care? Or have you *fin*ished that chapter?"

He shrank down in his seat.

"Okay. Those of you who don't particularly want to die of cancer or drought or CO_2 concentration, look at question 4, page 324." The question read, *Discuss ways the forest industry has improved its logging practices.* "Write 'not' between 'has' and 'improved.' Read the chapter again and you'll find the answer between the lines. Write it down, hand it in. If you get it right, you get to live. Then start reading the next chapter."

They stared; they frowned; they smiled; but they all, every single one of them, began to write something down.

When one of the boys crumpled up and threw away several pieces of paper into the waste basket, she made him dig the pages out and put them in the recycling box by the door.

"Let me tell you a story," she said, striding across the front of the room. "When I was your age I had a summer job in a bank. One day the manager sent three of us tellers to the basement to look up some old records. We found boxes of them, from the beginning of the century, and each piece of paper was written on over and over, both sides, in pencil and then in pen, between lines and on top of lines, straight and slanted, in all the margins, every corner squeezed full. Boy, did we laugh." She pointed her chalk at the student. "Do you think that's a funny story?"

The boy, who had an Adam's apple as large as a Golden Delicious, mumbled, "I guess not."

"Good. Because people a century from now won't be laughing at how we use paper today."

The boy swallowed, his Adam's apple leaping, and said, "You can't blame us for the way your generation screwed things up."

"Absolutely! My generation screwed up big time! And now we're handing you the problems we created. And you better not screw up as badly. Just blaming *us* won't help because, hey, we'll be dead, we won't care." She grinned.

In the Socials 9 class, one she'd taught before and with which she'd had discipline problems, she made herself be tough, a bully. She sent four students to the principal when they misbehaved, not caring if they went there or not. When the vice-principal found two of them wandering in the halls and, annoyed, brought them back to the class-room, as though she must have mislaid them, she threw them out again a few minutes later.

"Bitch," one of them snarled on his way out.

"Same to you," she said, before the door slammed.

Nothing they could do could touch her. Not since she'd had her own classes in Edmonton had she felt such confidence. Amanda was right: she was more dangerous than she used to be. She looked out over the roomful of bent heads, smiled, and sat down at the desk. She hadn't, she realized, had the slightest urge to snoop through it.

It was after that class, the last one of the day, that the principal called her into his office. She hesitated at the door, preparing for the worst.

But all he said was that the regular teacher would be away for the rest of the week and would she be able to continue?

"Sure," she said. "I'll be glad to."

"That's a relief," he sighed. "It's so hard to get good subs these days."

Amazing, she thought. She had broken every good-sub rule she could think of, had behaved like an anarchist, and here was the principal relieved that she could come back. She could hardly wait to tell Amanda. But maybe now all Amanda would tell her was, as a student essay once had about Trudeau, that she was getting too big for her bridges and was sure to fall off.

.

By the time she got home she was no longer in danger of falling off any bridges. Yes, it had felt good, very good in fact, to be so aggressive. But she knew she wouldn't be able to get away with it too often. Teachers expected their day-books to be followed; administrators expected a sub not to involve them with her unruly students; the ministry expected its curriculum to be respected. What the students expected was, of course, irrelevant.

As she walked through the kitchen, stooping to pick up a stray strand of her hair, she thought of Amanda again, her news. A full-time job.

"I don't think so, either," she told the cat, who turned and licked his little puckered pink bumhole. It seemed an appropriate answer.

She sat down, pulled a piece of paper towards her and made a list of her options.

1. Be a sub forever.
2. Get out of teaching entirely.
3. That PhD in Film?
4. Tutor full-time.
5. Apply to teach in the North/Alberta/the US

She doodled a picture of a cat in the margin and then crossed off number one. Her pencil hesitated over number five. The idea was oddly exciting: to move away, to start again: an adventure. She didn't cross it out.

She felt better, having made the list, as though the choices hadn't been real until she made them visible on a page. When the insurance money came through it would buy her more than enough time to make a transition.

She tossed the list on top of a pile of books and papers she kept meaning to organize, and when the furnace fan kicked in that evening it blew the paper down and skittered it across the floor into the hallway, and when Richard came over later to return the ice pack he'd borrowed for a sore shoulder he picked the list up.

"What's this number five?" he exclaimed. "'Apply to teach in the North/Alberta/the US.'"

Vicky reached over and tried to snatch it from his fingers, but he pulled it out of her reach. "I was just trying to convince myself that I had some choices."

"You could have told me you were thinking about this, Vicky." His voice sounded hurt, accusatory.

"I just wanted to feel I didn't have to be a sub for the rest of my life."

"Here," Richard said, "I'll show you the best choice." He picked up the red felt marker on the coffee table and, anchoring Vicky's list under his splayed fingers, crossed out the four items Vicky had left. Then he wrote: "6. Let Richard decide."

She laughed. "How very godlike of you." He was only joking, she told herself.

When he was leaving, Vicky remembered what she had promised herself about Jason.

"About Jason." She tried to put some conviction into her voice. "I was wondering if I should, you know, try a little harder with him."

Richard looked at her in surprise. "What do you mean?"

"I mean, it's not fair to him that I obviously prefer Lisa. Maybe I should, we should, I don't know, do something with him sometime. Supper, a movie, bungee jumping. Something."

"That's really good of you, Vicky. I know Jason's a hard kid to like."

"Would he *want* to come if I'm along?"

"I'm sure he would." Richard rubbed his hand up and

down his cheek. Vicky could hear the soft rasp of bristles. "How about next week sometime?"

"Sure. Okay."

"Thanks." Richard reached over and patted her arm.

And Vicky felt, at his touch, the familiar tingle, a current, buzz through her, and she knew, more dismayed than excited, that what had stopped in her when Conrad died had restarted, and that it would not be long before she would be sleeping with Richard again.

He nodded at the piece of paper they'd left on the coffee table. "Just don't leave town without telling us," he said.

"I won't." She smiled.

But when, a week later, she found the list under an old TV guide, she shuddered and jerked her hand away from it as though the red ink were smears of blood.

Because of what happened Saturday.

JASON

RICHARD HAD PHONED her Saturday morning and asked if she would mind babysitting Lisa. A co-worker had had to leave early, it would just be for a few hours, it was an imposition, he knew that, but the high-school student who usually took her was away, and please.

"Of course," she said.

So she spent the morning with Lisa.

Richard had brought over some videos for her, so they watched one together—*Batman*, a film Vicky hadn't seen, and she found it interesting watching such a movie with a child, found herself disturbed more than usual at the violence and sexism and joylessness of it. But Lisa watched it breathlessly, laughing a little wildly at parts Vicky couldn't imagine anyone finding funny. She was relieved when it was over.

Except for the first time Lisa had come over, returning her towel, Vicky had never been alone with the girl for more than a few moments, and even the half dozen or so times Lisa had been here with Richard he had taken her home after about an hour. So, Vicky realized, perhaps it shouldn't surprise her now to still feel somewhat uncertain around the child. If she felt uncertain around *Lisa*, she thought gloomily, what would she feel like next week when she'd promised to spend time with Jason?

They went for a walk down to the corner store to buy some milk and light bulbs, and Lisa insisted on carrying them home, swinging the bag so that Vicky was afraid it would go flying into the street, but she restrained herself from criticizing.

"I like your dress," Vicky told her instead. It was dark blue, a cotton blend, lined, with a shirred bodice and an attached belt that tied in the back. The colour matched, for a change, that of her big, rectangular barrettes. "Is it new?"

"Yeah. My dad got it for me. I think maybe he can get things at Sears for less than other people because he works there."

"That must be nice," Vicky said. "I'd love to get clothes at a discount."

"I think you have to be a relative," Lisa said. "But I can ask him for you."

"Oh, no," Vicky said hastily. "Please don't."

Lisa, more talkative than usual, prattled on then about school, about a project on the West Coast Indians, how she was making a basket out of cedar bark. The day was warm and sunny, spiced with birdsong and the smells of fresh-cut grass. In every yard they passed something was blooming, azaleas, rhododendrons, broom, lilacs, wisteria, dozens of smaller flowers Vicky was ashamed not to know the names of when Lisa asked. Other walkers they met seemed to be in bloom, too, smiling and saying hello instead of hunched and zippered up against the rain and one another.

At home they made hot chocolate and Vicky showed Lisa how to play a card game called Sixty-six she remembered from her own childhood. She was astonished at how quickly the girl learned, but Lisa became bored with the game after they had played it twice, so Vicky put in another video, a cartoon show taped from TV, and went into the kitchen to make lunch. Listening to the explosions, screams and women's hysterical voices, Vicky began to think *Batman* was probably benign by comparison.

She cut the sandwiches in half and put them on plates,

then decided to go to the bathroom before they ate. If it hadn't been for the sound of the cartoon show filling up the living room behind her with a burst of percussive noise, making her envisage the child sitting there and watching, it would probably have occurred to Vicky that the closed bathroom door meant Lisa was inside. But, her mind on what entertainments she might offer after lunch, Vicky opened the door and stepped into the room.

Lisa was standing in front of the toilet bowl. Her panties were puddled around her ankles, and she was holding her dress aside with one hand. With the other hand she was directing the flow of urine from what was unmistakably a penis.

Vicky gasped. The child turned towards her, the pee spraying in a small parabola against the sink, the cabinet, the floor. The child screamed, a shrill, high-pitched scream of fear and panic. The pee dribbled to a stop.

Vicky couldn't move. She stared at the child before her, the small limp penis.

The child reached down and pulled up his underpants, frantically, stumbling, almost falling. He smoothed the dress down, pressed himself against the bathroom wall.

"It's okay," Vicky said. "Don't be afraid. It's okay." She was speaking as much to calm herself as to calm the child. Her heart was beating so fast she pressed a hand to her chest.

"You're Jason, aren't you?" she said, trying to keep her voice from shaking.

"I'm Lisa," the boy whimpered. "Lisa, Lisa, Lisa." He began banging his head against the wall, moaning the name. "Lisa. I'm Lisa."

"You're a boy. Lisa's a girl. Lisa's your sister."

"I'm *Lisa*!" he screamed at her. "Don't you see? I'm *Lisa.*"

And then she did see.

"There is no Lisa, is there?" she whispered. "You don't have a twin sister. You're ... Lisa, too."

He stopped banging his head. "I'm Lisa," he said. He began to cry, steady, mournful sobs.

She made herself go to him, crouch down. Her knees cracked as she knelt, and he winced at the sound. She put her arms uncertainly around him. She expected him to hit out at her, to push her away, but he didn't; he stayed limp in her arms, crying until she could feel the wetness soaking through her blouse onto her shoulder. She put her hand on his head, pushed her fingers gently into the thick, curly hair, tightened her fingers a little and pulled. The wig slid off to the side, to the floor, the two heavy barrettes still attached. It was the barrettes she'd always noticed more than the hair: they were a misdirection, a magician's trick.

Her mind was dizzy, thoughts snapping across synapses in search of something, anything, in her experience to help her understand. But there was nothing, only the slow horror of it.

"Was it some game you were playing?" Clutching at straws. "Did you want to see how long you could fool me?"

He didn't respond, except to keep crying. The noise from the cartoon in the living room seemed to get suddenly louder, a voice shrieking, "Don't jump!"

So then she had to say it. "Did your father make you do this?" But of course she knew the answer already.

Jason went rigid. She held him a little away from her, tried to look into his face. She kept seeing Lisa, Lisa who didn't exist. He turned away, his eyes squeezed shut.

"Please don't be afraid. You can tell me. I'm going to help you. It's all right." Platitudes, lies. It wasn't all right. And how could she promise to help, when she was as frightened and confused as the child?

But the boy only kept his head turned to the wall, his eyes squeezed shut. He twisted his hands into each other in front of him, the small knuckles turning white.

"Does your mother know about Lisa?"

He turned to face her, his eyes leaping open, so quickly Vicky started.

"No," he cried, as though the question had released him, let the words spill out. "Mom doesn't know. It was a secret, between Dad and me. I wanted to be Lisa. And Dad said if you found out you'd hate me. Everybody would hate me. I had to be Lisa or you'd all hate me." He began to cry again, long keening exhalations of breath.

"Oh, god," Vicky said. She put her arms around him again, drew him to her. He didn't resist, didn't respond, stood in her embrace emptied of volition.

I had to be Lisa or you'd all hate me. How often had she told Richard how much she liked Lisa, how different she was from Jason? They'd only given her what she wanted.

No, she mustn't blame herself, mustn't make it easier for Richard. She breathed in, deeply, slowly, then out. She had to be calm, clear-headed.

"Did he ... hurt you? Your father? Did he hurt you?" She couldn't bring herself to be more explicit. She closed her eyes against the sudden images of Richard, of making love with him.

"He hit me sometimes. When I was bad."

"You're *not* bad. Nobody should ever hit you." Yet when Richard had grabbed and shaken and pushed the child so hard he fell she hadn't interfered, had offered no real help. Richard's contrition had been enough for her; she hadn't wanted to know anything more. She was guilty, too, the crime of the bystander.

She swallowed, made herself continue. "Did he touch you ... down there?"

She gestured in the direction of his genitals. What were the right words? How could she make him understand without upsetting him even more? Perhaps she shouldn't ask; perhaps she should leave it to a professional, who would know how to do it with a minimum of damage. But she had to know.

"Not like they tell us about in school, not like my mom warned me about. Not like in sex."

Vicky sank back a little, felt a tremor of relief. But then why had Richard established this grotesque charade? Why would he do something like this to his own son? Surely it wasn't just to please her.

"Your father—when did you first start being Lisa? Can you remember?"

Jason rubbed his hand under his snotty nose, wiped it on the dress. Vicky reeled off a foot of toilet paper and handed it to him, but he didn't take it.

"Can you remember?" she prompted. "How long ago did it first start?"

"I don't know."

"Was it before you moved here?"

"Sometimes. When Mom was out. But not very often. Not like after we came here." He ran his hand under his nose again.

"I see." It wasn't something, then, Richard had started after he met her. His reasons went beyond that.

"Don't tell my dad you found out, okay? He'll be real mad if you tell him." Jason began to whimper again, pulling back from her against the bathroom wall.

So now she had to decide. What *should* she do? She didn't doubt the boy's assessment—of course Richard would be angry. She had seen Richard angry.

She tried to think of him objectively, as someone disturbed, damaged by his own brutal father, not the man she knew. There had been warnings all along, of course there had been, and she had ignored them, wanting him on her own terms, not asking questions she wouldn't like the answers to. Even now, the evidence indisputable in front of her, she felt her mind cringe from it, try to find another route around the facts, to stop at the memories of him smiling at her, touching her, putting his hand fondly on Lisa's shoulder—

There *was* no Lisa. He had imagined her into existence.

For one frantic moment she thought, *All right, we won't tell him; you can just keep on being Lisa.* She had to stop herself from whimpering, too, just for thinking that, for having no better answer.

She would have to report it. To whom? The police, she supposed. At best, they would take Jason away, and he would blame himself, as children did when their parents failed them.

"It's not fair," Jason shouted, understanding what her silence must mean. "You can't tell my dad! It's not fair!" He pushed past her, knocking her back against the tub.

"Jason!" she cried, scrambling to her feet. What if he ran outside, oh, god, would she be able to catch him, hold on to him?

But he only ran into the living room, threw himself face down on the sofa. Vicky came over to him and put her hand carefully on his shoulder. He winced, pressed himself further into the back of the sofa.

"We have to do something, Jason. What your dad did to you is wrong. We have to make him stop."

"It's not fair," he said, his voice muffled.

"I know," Vicky said helplessly. "It isn't fair."

"I want my mom," Jason said.

Of course. Why not take him to his mother's? She was the one who should decide what to do, what would be best for the boy. It seemed unlikely that Jason would have lied about her ignorance of what was going on. Even if she wasn't the most responsible parent she had to be better than Richard. And it was where Jason wanted to go.

"All right," Vicky said. "Let's go to your mom's."

Jason sat up. "You mean it?"

"Yes, I mean it. If you want to."

"Yeah, I do." He stood up. "Right now? Can we go right now?"

"She might not be home."

"She's always home in the afternoon. She works at home. On her computer."

"All right, then." It was two o'clock. Vicky wasn't sure when Richard would be back. Her eyes flicked to the door, could already see him there.

Jason went to the hall closet and pulled his windbreaker from the hanger. He was eager now, almost cheerful.

"I don't know where your mom lives, though," Vicky said. "Will you be able to show me?"

"Her address is in the phone book."

"Her last name is Menard?" Vicky pulled out the book, opened it.

Jason nodded, fidgeting with the zipper on his coat.

And there it was, circled in red pencil. *Christine Menard.* A chill went up Vicky's back. "How did that red circle get there?" she asked, her voice unsteady.

Jason seemed pleased at her surprise. "I did that," he said. "I came into your house once and did it."

"I see." Vicky looked at the clue he had hidden here, waiting for her to find it.

She copied down the address, somewhere in Burnaby, on Halifax Street. She found it on a map, not far off the Lougheed Highway. It was a long way but shouldn't be hard to find.

They were going down the back steps before she realized that when Richard got home he would find them gone. He would be worried, annoyed, maybe suspicious. She had to keep him from being any of those as long as possible.

She ran back inside, started to write him a note. "Dear Richard—" She crumpled it up and threw it away. She couldn't call him "Dear," even as a formality. What should she say? What excuse should she offer? She looked nervously out her front window, afraid she might see him suddenly coming down her walk. Finally, writing so fast she scarcely lifted the pencil between words, she wrote, the first thing that came into her mind:

> *Richard—*
> *Sorry I had to go out. I've taken Jason*
> *with me to my father's. See you later—*
> *Vicky*

Her writing looked faint, barely embedded in the paper, like a loose thread only basted onto the page, one he could pull free with a tug of skepticism. But she didn't want to take time to do it over, so she ran over to Richard's house and slid the note through his mail slot, jerking her fingers back quickly, as though something inside might bite her. Then she ran around to the back of her house, where Jason sat on the steps petting the cat, who had crawled out from under the hedge. The cat's hair rose up in leaps of static under Jason's hand.

"Okay," Vicky said. "Let's go."

"Can I take the cat?"

"No."

"I want to take him."

"No, you can't. He doesn't like going in the car."

"I'd hold him. He'd like it if I hold him."

"He wouldn't. Cats don't like going in cars."

"Some of them do."

"Well, that one doesn't."

"Maybe he would. I want him to come."

The cat had his ears back now and was twitching his tail, as though he knew what they were negotiating. Jason had stopped petting him and was simply holding on to him to prevent his escape.

"*No*. Please, Jason, let's go."

"I bet he'd like to go for a ride."

"No, he wouldn't."

"I want to take him."

Vicky clenched her teeth, felt the urge to grab him by the arm and drag him to the car. He was Jason, all right, not Lisa.

But looking at him sitting on the step, wearing the blue dress, she saw Lisa again, Lisa who might have had her hair cut too short but who was still the little girl she knew.

"No! We're not taking the cat, and that's final. If you want to go to your mother's we have to leave right now." She started walking towards the car.

She could hear Jason get up, follow her. She gave an apparently casual glance behind her to make sure he wasn't carrying the cat.

On the drive to Burnaby the boy behaved as though nothing were particularly unusual, as though it were perfectly normal for him to be sitting here beside her like this, dressed as a girl. He kept pulling out and retracting the seat belt, playing with the radio buttons, pointing out cars like his mother's.

"You really had me fooled, Jason," Vicky said finally, cautiously. "I really believed you were Lisa."

"I know," he said. He sounded proud, gleeful even. "I

thought for sure you'd figure it out the time we forgot about Lisa's shoes, but you didn't even *notice!*"

We. Something he and Richard did together, a father and son thing, like going camping or playing catch or building a model airplane.

"No," Vicky said. "I didn't notice." She glanced down at Jason's runners. They were new, clean, with carefully tied pink laces.

"It was that time we went out for supper. I can't believe you didn't notice!"

"Not very observant of me, was it?" It would spoil it for him to say that even if she had noticed it wouldn't have seemed significant; at best she'd have thought that Lisa was just wearing Jason's shoes.

"That's okay. But I thought for *sure* you'd guess the time I said the name of my school, and of course it's the school Jason goes to, not Lisa." He giggled, covering his mouth with one hand. "Lisa's supposed to go to the one in Burnaby."

Jason. Lisa. He said both names as though they were other people. Would anyone be able to help him, make him into one person again?

Suddenly she felt she might be making a mistake, taking him to his mother. Even if most of what Richard had said about her was untrue, she might still be part of the problem. Shouldn't Christine Menard have sensed something was wrong? But then Vicky reminded herself that most of the times she thought Jason was with his mother he was really still with Richard; his mother obviously saw him only rarely. But wasn't that by choice? Perhaps she really didn't care. There must have been reasons she hadn't been awarded custody.

Vicky's foot was easing off the accelerator. She was on the freeway already. But it wasn't too late. She could take the next exit, turn around, go back. And then what? Perhaps she could leave the boy at Birdy's while she tried somehow to discuss this with Richard, to make him explain. She tried to imagine the conversation, her asking the questions, calmly, reasonably—

But Richard wasn't reasonable. The man she had slept with, the man she was falling in love with, was not a reasonable man. No explanation he could offer would justify going back to him now.

She pressed down again on the accelerator. A red sports car that had pulled into the passing lane behind her roared past, then cut in again so sharply she had to brake. This anonymous highway aggression, people shooting their cars at each other like guns.

She took the Willingdon exit, checking the map to see where she should turn next.

"This isn't right," Jason kept saying. "This is the wrong exit. Don't you know how to drive?"

"I know where I'm going."

"No, you don't."

"I can get to Halifax Street from here. Be patient."

"I told you. It's the wrong exit." He began banging his heels against the seat. Vicky gritted her teeth. She should have phoned Christine Menard first. If she wasn't home then what would they do? She didn't know how much longer she and Jason could stand each other.

She took a wrong turn and wound up in a shopping centre, but when she managed to get out of it she found herself on Halifax Street. "See," she said to Jason, in childish triumph. "Here we are. Now we only have to find the house."

"It's not the right way to get there," Jason said. But he stopped banging his heels and looked eagerly out the window, gnawing at his thumbnail.

Vicky drove slowly, peering at the house numbers. "This should be the right block. Eighty-three, eighty-five—"

"There it is," Jason exclaimed. "The green one." He pointed. "That's her car in the driveway."

It was the rusty red Toyota she had seen a couple of times in front of Richard's place. Vicky pulled into a parking spot across the street, looked at the old house with green aluminum siding, at the front yard which might not have seen a lawnmower the whole previous summer.

Jason was already out of the car, running across the street. By the time she realized what he was doing, that he would be showing up at his mother's door unannounced, wearing a blue dress and brought here by a woman she had never seen before, he had started up the front walk.

"Jason, wait," she shouted, jumping out of the car and running after him. A car had to swerve to avoid hitting her.

As she reached the front walk, Jason was already at the door, pounding on it, as though he were fleeing from her, desperate to be let it.

She had just reached him when the door opened. A chubby blond woman about Vicky's age and wearing jogging pants and a red sweatshirt that stretched tightly across her large bra-less breasts stood there. Her gaze flicked across Jason with no sign of recognition and settled flatly on Vicky.

"Hi, Mom," Jason said. He must have known the impression he would make. He grinned up at Vicky, conspiratorially. It was hard to believe he was the same boy who only an hour ago had pleaded hysterically with Vicky not to tell his secret.

The woman's eyes leaped down to the boy. Her mouth fell open as she stared at him. Vicky was relieved to see her unmistakable expression of shock.

"Jason!" Her voice was gravelly and harsh, as though

she might have just woken up. "What the hell is going on? Why are you dressed like that?" Her eyes shot back up to Vicky, turning angry now, accusatory. "What's going on?"

Vicky made herself smile politely, keep her voice calm. "I guess that's what I'd like to know, too."

"Who are you?" The woman took her hand from the doorknob and took a long, trembly drag from the cigarette she was holding. Her eyes went back to Jason, staring at him as though still trying to identify him.

"I'm Jason's neighbour. Vicky Bauer. I wanted to bring Jason here to talk to you about ... this." She gestured vaguely at the boy, the dress. "I was hoping you'd know what to do."

Jason slid past his mother into the house, and Vicky could hear the high-pitched barking of a dog, Jason saying, "Leroy! Here, Leroy! Good boy!"

"I guess you'd better come in," Christine Menard said.

CHRISTINE

"GO PLAY," his mother said to Jason.

Vicky could remember that order so well herself from childhood. It was the job of children to play, to work at playing in order to stay ignorant of adult life. A little too late for that for Jason, she thought. But he gave them each a squinty, evaluative look, and then he picked up his dog, a terrier pup with stiff hair that looked to be in permanent contact with a Van de Graaff generator, and took him into the living room. They heard the TV go on.

And then, sitting at Christine Menard's kitchen table, Vicky told her everything, from the day Richard and Jason had moved in next door, not sparing herself, trying to be honest. When she finished, she sank back in her chair, which tilted so far she had to grab the table for fear of falling over backwards. The table quivered, nearly spilling the disorderly pile of computer printouts off the end. Her throat felt as though she had run it over a cheese grater.

Christine Menard sat looking across the room at the door of her refrigerator, which was cluttered with magnets anchoring store coupons and recipes and several child's drawings, which Vicky assumed had been done by Jason and which looked no stranger than any child's.

She waited so long before she spoke that Vicky wanted to shake her.

"Jesus," Christine said at last. She took a long pull from her cigarette, exhaled slowly. She set the cigarette in the ashtray and turned it round and round, a pencil in a sharpener. "So he told you I was a lesbian, did he?" She laughed harshly.

Vicky stared at her. She had told the woman a horrifying tale of how her child had been abused, and now she was laughing and saying, "So he told you I was a lesbian."

"Yes," Vicky said.

"Well, I'm not, you know. Not that it's anybody's business. It was just his way of rationalizing how I could want a divorce."

"But about Jason," Vicky said, leaning forward in her unstable chair, "what should we do about that?"

"Yeah," Christine said.

Vicky waited for her to say something more, and when she didn't she prodded, "I mean, he's really been abused. He needs help, protection."

Christine sighed, took another long pull on her cigarette, held the smoke a moment before releasing it. Vicky had to stop herself from waving the cloud irritably away.

"Look," Christine said, "I made sure Jason knew about sexual abuse. Inappropriate touching, all that stuff. I made him promise to tell me if it happened. You told me yourself he said it didn't. And Jason's not an ordinary kid. He's tough. And smart. He's learned how to defend himself. He's better at it than I was."

"But he's just a child!" Vicky exclaimed. "Richard made him dress up and behave like a girl. That's a terribly damaging thing to do."

"I wasn't saying it's *healthy*." Christine looked at her through narrowed eyes. They were a hazy blue, as though the smoke had permanently fogged them. "I'm saying Jason would have found a way of handling it. He'd have made a game of it. He's always liked acting, playing dress-up."

"This wasn't just a game. Richard was making him be Lisa almost all the time he wasn't in school."

"Maybe Richard was *letting* him be Lisa. Maybe it was like, let's play a game, Jason. See if we can fool the nice lady."

"Well, of course Jason *participated*. But Richard set it up, he was the one in control. Look, you should have seen Jason when I found out. He was hysterical, terrified of my telling Richard, crying—"

"All right, all right." Christine stubbed out her cigarette as though it were something alive she was grinding to death. "I hear what you're saying. I'm not trying to minimize what Richard's done. I'm just saying that Jason—"

In another room, a phone rang. Christine, without apology, got up and went down the hall. Vicky heard her pick up the phone somewhere, say hello. Vicky must have sat there for ten minutes, fidgeting, annoyed, listening to the TV in the living room and the occasional murmur of Christine's voice on the phone.

Finally Christine came back, flicking a lighter at a new cigarette. She sat down. "So what was I saying?"

"You weren't trying to minimize what Richard's done."

Christine gave her a twitch of a smile. "I was *going* to say that Jason knows how to push your buttons. If he thinks you expect tears and hysteria, he'll give them to you. He's his father's child, after all. Richard could cry on cue when he wanted something from you."

He could cry on cue. More than once, it had been his tears that had made her forgive him. *When he wanted something from you.*

She made herself concentrate. She had to think about Jason, not herself.

"Anyway, you can't let Jason go back to him. You can get a restraining order or something. I'll tell the police what I know."

Christine walked over to the stove, poured herself a coffee from a carafe sitting between the front burners. "Want one?" she said, holding the pot up.

"Yes, please." She had never needed a cup of coffee more. "Just black."

Christine lifted a blue mug, which may or may not have been clean, out of the sink, poured it full of coffee and handed it to Vicky. She took her time with her own cup, stirring sugar into it, meditatively, while she rubbed her left ankle slowly with her other foot. She was wearing a pair of matted slippers with holes in the sides.

When she sat back down she said, "Look. I admit I wasn't a very good mother. And Jason's a difficult kid. I was exhausted all the time, I thought my life had just gone down the toilet. So when we divorced I thought, well, it's damned well time Richard did his share. He wasn't a bad parent, he was better with the kid than I was. And I didn't want to keep Jason, I admit it." She glanced towards the living room, lowered her voice. "I don't want to keep him now."

"Please," Vicky said. "You have to."

Christine looked into her cup. After a moment she sighed deeply and said, "Yeah, yeah. I suppose I have to try."

"And you'll let the appropriate people know? The social workers, the police, a lawyer?"

Christine sighed again. "I suppose so. Jesus. This is going to be such a mess. The courts don't look kindly on a mother who didn't want to keep her kid. And I didn't fight Richard about the lesbian allegations. I was kind of flattered by them, actually." She gave a little laugh.

"But about Jason. This time there'll be my testimony, too. It won't be just Richard's word against yours."

"One man's word against that of two bitter women? The courts will believe him."

"There's Jason's word, too."

Christine hesitated. "You can't always count on Jason."

"But you can't let him go back to Richard. Jason needs help. He needs counselling."

"All right, all right. I said I'll try. Okay?"

Vicky leaned back again, the tension in her easing, and the chair, whose back had lost its tension long ago, threatened to dump her over backwards. She grabbed the edge of the table, reached for her coffee with her other hand, took a sip. It was so strong she could feel her tongue melting, but she made herself swallow.

"I still don't understand how Richard thought he could get away with this," she said. "He must have known I'd have to find out sooner or later about Jason."

"Maybe a part of him wanted to be found out. Isn't that what a shrink would say?"

Vicky thought of Jason, the clues he had left for her, but perhaps Richard, too, had been offering her clues: move in with me, Vicky, so you'll have to find out; let me forget to make Jason put on the right shoes; let me tell you a hundred times, let me show you, how hard I find it to cope with him; let me leave him with you today, just after he showed us in the restaurant how he was starting to want to stop being Lisa, just after you said you'd be willing to spend some time with Jason.

"Or maybe," Christine continued, "he thought that by then you'd be so crazy-in-love with him that you'd accept whatever explanation he offered."

Whether Christine meant that as a comment on Vicky's stupidity or on Richard's Vicky wasn't going to ask. She said instead, "But why would he want to do this to his son? How could he? Did he want a girl instead of a boy?"

"Not that I was aware of."

"So why then? Do you think his father might have

done the same thing to him, dressed him as a girl?"

Christine sucked at her cigarette. A little frill of ashes littered her sweatshirt. "His father." A slight smile tugged at her lips. "I suppose Richard gave you his sob story about how his father sexually abused him."

"You mean ... he didn't? But Richard was so ..."

"Convincing? He always is."

Vicky felt dizzy. "But he ... But it's hard to imagine, that he would make up something like that—"

"Okay, if you don't believe me, ask his sister. Yvonne. She lives in Port Townsend. I was starting to have my suspicions about damn near everything he told me so I asked her about it. She told me she was as sure as she could be that nothing like that ever happened. And this woman is no fool. She's a lawyer, for Christ's sake, she knows about this stuff. She knows Richard. When I told him what she said, he just shrugged, said 'What would she know?' but I could see on his face I'd caught him."

"But maybe the sister didn't know, couldn't know. When it's in your own family, well ..."

"Let me just ask you this. Did Richard pull out the child-abuse stuff at pretty convenient times, like when you'd just caught him in a lie and he needed to wriggle out of it, when he suddenly needed an excuse, needed you to feel sorry for him?"

Vicky tried to remember, tried not to remember: after he hit Jason, after she found out about Sears ...

"He did, didn't he?" Christine said, unable to keep the triumph from her voice.

White spots began flickering in front of Vicky's eyes. She blinked hard, forced them away. "Richard has to see a psychiatrist," she said. "Maybe the police can make him go."

"Nobody can make Richard do anything. Look. Don't

start feeling sorry for the man again. There's something about him that's so, so screwed up nobody can fix it. He's good at getting your sympathy, at trying to please you, but only so he can own you. He has to own you. I can see you thinking, oh poor Richard, poor handsome Richard, maybe his father really was a monster and he deserves understanding and love. Well, I've been there. And I can tell you, forget it. You can't help him. Don't try. Or you'll be sorry."

"Well ... thank you for the advice—"

"You can't just go back to him."

"I won't, of course I won't. If I'd intended that I wouldn't have come here."

"Wouldn't you?" Christine said. "You've got rid of Jason, and he was the problem, right? So now you can go back to Richard, cure the poor man, and live happily ever after."

Vicky stood up. "That's not true. Why do you think I have sinister motives just because I'm trying to do the right thing for your son?"

"Okay, okay." Christine shoved a hand abruptly through her hair, leaving it standing in little spikes.

"I suppose I should go," Vicky said stiffly. She took a piece of paper out of her purse, wrote her name and address and phone number on it, and set it in the middle of the table. "You can reach me there when you need to."

Christine nodded.

"Can I say goodbye to Jason?" Vicky asked.

"Suit yourself."

Jason was lying on his stomach on the living room floor, watching TV. Vicky wondered if he had heard any of their conversation. She couldn't imagine him lying here watching a soap opera when he could have been eavesdropping on a more interesting drama in the kitchen.

He had taken off the dress and was wearing jeans and a

short-sleeved red sweater, but still Vicky could see Lisa lying there, the child she had grown to care about. She must still be there, somewhere. Vicky didn't know whether she should wish for her to disappear forever or not. What would the psychiatrists make of him, the two faces of Jason? Would they find it impossible to believe he could have deceived Vicky as long as he had? She found it almost impossible to believe herself. And she wouldn't have found out, even now, but for an accident. She thought of the strange things he had done when they'd first moved in, trying to get her attention, and how she had ignored them, not wanting to understand, thinking only of herself, herself and Richard, making it two adults instead of one in collusion against him.

She took a deep breath, stepped into the room, which was large and sunny, with several big leafy ivies hanging in the corners. The dog was lying on a threadbare towel underneath one of the plants, chewing on a mangled tennis ball.

"Jason. I'm going now. I just want to say goodbye."

He turned his head a little, not enough to really see her. He said something, but his voice was so low she couldn't hear. She knelt down beside him.

"She doesn't want me. She'll let my dad take me back."

"Oh, Jason." She put her hand on his shoulder. She could feel him tense at her touch, pull his shoulder down, away from her hand. "That's not true. Now that your mother knows what he did she won't let you go back."

Jason said nothing. His eyes were fixed on the TV. In the corner the dog began to whine, dropping and picking up the ball, imploring a game.

"She promised me," Vicky said, trying to convince him, convince herself.

"You don't know," he said, his voice so hard and bitter

and full of adult understanding that she drew back, took her hand from him.

"There *are* people who care about you, Jason," she said weakly. "Really there are." People like herself, she thought, ashamed, people who say things like that as they say good-bye.

He didn't answer. He was holding a remote control, and Vicky saw his finger move over to the volume button, push. The sound from the TV increased slightly.

"If you ever want to talk to me, your mother has my number." She hesitated. "And you can look it up in the phone book, too. It's under Bauer. C. Bauer." C for Conrad, she started to say, but couldn't, the name, the loss of him, how she would never be listed under C. Bauer again, hitting her, a punch in the stomach, taking her breath away. She swallowed. "Everything will be all right, Jason. You'll see."

"Sure," he said.

She got to her feet, stood there helplessly. She had to go. She had to trust the boy's mother to look after him now. Look after him: it wasn't the same as loving him. *She doesn't want me.* Vicky opened her mouth to say something, some last reassurance that he wouldn't believe, but finally she only turned and walked back into the kitchen.

Christine was stacking the dirty dishes into the dish-washer built in beside the sink. She straightened when Vicky came into the room. "Okay?"

Vicky nodded, not sure what she was agreeing to. She picked up her purse, assembled an appropriate-for-depar-ture smile and stepped to the door.

"Just for curiosity's sake," Christine said behind her, "did Richard show you a bunch of amateur-looking paint-ings, lines at right angles mostly, and say they were his?"

Vicky turned. "Yes, he did. You mean they—"

"Aren't his. They're mine. Interesting, huh? I didn't want them. He had a dealer come to the house once and I couldn't believe my ears when I heard Richard tell him they were his own. When I confronted him with it you know what he said?"

"No." There was no memory of Richard she could keep. One by one they had turned into cheats, betrayals.

"He said he was afraid to show him only his own. Because he thought they were too strange. He wanted some that looked normal." Christine laughed, said again, "Looked normal."

"There were some of hands. Were they his?"

"Oh, yeah, those were his."

"They didn't seem ... not normal."

"Yeah, well, normality is in the eye of the beholder. He did another whole series called *The Other Family* that was basically like family portraits, following several generations, each picture with faces deleted or added, meticulously realistic, except that in each there was one face that was distorted, like a gargoyle's. If you followed the half dozen or so works for each family you could see how that face passed on from parent to child. Afterwards, I wondered if maybe he needed to invent a history for himself to explain his art. Instead of the other way around."

"He didn't show me any of those."

"That's because they all sold." Christine slid a plate between two spikes in her dishwasher. Her voice suddenly softened, became almost gentle. "Richard was incredibly talented. In the art class in Spokane where we met he was by far the best of us. The instructor arranged a showing of his work, and everything sold. He adored Richard. So did I."

Vicky put her hand on the doorknob, turned, released it. "Well," she said, "I should go."

She made herself open the door. In the living room the dog gave two sharp barks. She wondered what Jason was doing, what he was thinking, if he was listening. He must have known the paintings Richard showed her were his mother's. It was why he had come in and made the sneering comment and kicked at them and why Richard had gotten so angry, had needed to silence him.

"Look, it would have been a *game* to Jason," Christine said, seeing the direction of Vicky's gaze. "I know you think he's had this huge traumatic experience, but he's tougher than you think."

"He's just a kid. He shouldn't have to be tough. He did this because he wanted to be loved. He feels alone and helpless and he just really needs you to, well, to love him."

She could tell she had overstepped her bounds. Christine said nothing, began wiping the counter with the dishcloth. Her lips were pressed thin and tight.

"Well," Vicky said. "Call me if you need me." She stepped outside.

"Yeah, yeah," Christine said.

Back in the car Vicky sat for a long time looking at the house she had just left. Christine Menard had been a disappointment, no doubt about that. Could Vicky trust her to keep Jason, get him the counseling he needed? Christine had never met Lisa; perhaps she couldn't know how convincing the boy had been, that he had been able to become a whole different person, that he really had been damaged.

Vicky leaned her head back and closed her eyes. Why hadn't she gotten suspicious sooner herself? She had been a blinkered horse, trotting mindlessly along—no, worse, because she knew there were frightening things to the side she would have to see if only she dared to look; but she wouldn't turn her head, had shut her eyes against the glimpses in her peripheral vision.

A headache hammered at her temples.

She had done what she could for Jason. It was up to his mother now. Meanwhile, she had to go home, tell Richard what she had done. The thought made her shudder. She hadn't let herself think that far ahead. How could she face him? Who knew what he might do? But maybe there was still some way of reaching him. You can't help him, Christine had said; don't try. But how hard had Christine tried?

No. She had to get herself out of Richard's life. Period. Again and again she had let him come back, had stumbled to the door like a sleepwalker to let him in, no matter how firmly she had told herself, no, it was over, there she would be, full of excuses for them both. Well, she was awake now. She had stopped making excuses.

She started the car, headed home. The beginnings of rush hour were quarreling at the streets, and finally, after she made a wrong turn, she gave up and pulled in at a restaurant.

She ordered a sandwich, although she didn't feel hungry, and made herself eat. She watched two men at the next table, the way they gestured with their hands, laughed loudly at each other's jokes. She could tell by the way they slid sly glances at her that the jokes must be about women. They would never have to be afraid of going home, she thought, of facing someone stronger than they. She remembered a boy from high school engaged to her friend Dianne, who beat him once at arm-wrestling and he broke off the engagement, saying he couldn't marry someone physically stronger than he, that he would always feel he couldn't trust her.

She made herself take another bite of sandwich.

How had she gotten involved with such a man as Richard; how had she gotten so desperate?

She looked dully at the napkin dispenser on her table, her teeth chewing mechanically. The sandwich tasted rancid.

When she raised her eyes she saw one of the men at the next table looking at her. He glanced away, shifting a little in his seat, pretending to be watching something out the window behind her. She forced herself to keep looking at him. He was a small, slight man, nobody to be afraid of, she told herself. He had a pug nose and a reddish moustache, which he stroked now with the thumb and forefinger of his right hand, the way Conrad used to do the year he grew a beard.

Conrad. She thought of her last day with him, the way he had repeated her name, given her that terrible hope. And the next day he was gone, the timing for Richard so perfect it was as though he had planned it, as though he had made it happen.

As though—

She began to cough, a piece of sandwich gagging her.

That nurse. She seemed like a sensible enough person.

Dear god. How could he say that, unless he had gone to the hospital himself?

She began to tremble, as though the temperature of the room had suddenly fallen below zero. Her hands felt icy. She wrapped them around the coffee cup, pressing hard.

It was absurd. How could she imagine something so grotesque?

But it had been almost her first thought, hadn't it, on hearing of Conrad's death: that Richard could have killed him. Conrad had seemed to be getting better; then she had had the argument with Richard about him; the next day Conrad was dead. If the doctor on the phone hadn't reacted with such surprise to her use of the word "killed," perhaps she wouldn't have been so quick to dismiss it, to tell herself it was impossible, to let her shame at the very idea stop her from remembering the things she was remembering now.

The cactus. *The man took it down to Conrad's room.* Could he—his hands around Conrad's throat, squeezing—or the pillow over the face—

She twisted her head to the side, not wanting to look, to see. When the doctor had asked if she wanted an autopsy she had said no, and when Ernest had asked if cremation would be okay she had said yes. As though some deep, black part of her knew what might have happened.

No. It was madness. She forced herself to take another bite of her sandwich.

The waitress, a thin, nervous woman in an oversized blue uniform, came by with the coffee pot and asked if she wanted a refill, and she heard herself say, "I'd like a drink."

"Oh, we don't have a liquor licence," the waitress said.

"Just as well." What was wrong with her? A drink was the last thing she needed. She had to stay clear-headed, to think.

She *knew* Richard. Yes, he had done all that bizarre stuff with Jason, but that was a far cry from cold-blooded murder. Wouldn't the two things involve wholly different kinds of personality, of personality disorders? Murder: she would know if he was capable of that. Surely she would. She had scoffed at murderers' wives who insisted they'd had no idea. How could they not at least have suspected?

Of course, she had known Richard barely six months. Christine was the one who had been his wife. Christine would suspect him. *He has to own you.* How far would he go to own her? *He tries to please you so that he can own you.*

Psychopaths were like that. They could fool anybody, the police, psychiatrists. They were good at sensing what people wanted from them, at giving it to them, at getting what they wanted in return.

Good at sensing what people want. Good at. What I wanted from him. What I. What I thought he wanted. *It's what you want, isn't it?* Good at.

It had started as soon as they met, him giving her things she wanted: the barking machine abruptly silenced, the eavestrough repaired. Sex. Lisa. What else? Maybe it had even been Richard who trashed Jesus Christ's car, giving her something else he thought she wanted, hoping she would guess it was him.

He could have done it. Richard could have killed Conrad. She made herself think the words, form them slowly in her mind, one after another, as though they were being printed out on a screen behind her eyes. Richard could have killed Conrad.

It went beyond *could have.* It went all the way to probability. Richard probably killed Conrad.

"Are you all right?" The waitress was leaning over her.

Vicky nodded, didn't look at her.

"You were making this funny little sound. Are you sure you're okay? You want me to call somebody?"

Vicky shook her head. "I'm okay," she made herself say, and she smiled numbly at the waitress until she went away.

She would be able to prove nothing. The police would shrug at her accusations. They would put them together with her claims about Jason, and they would shake their heads, laugh incredulously, think she was the mad one. And, no, Christine Menard would have to admit, she hadn't actually seen Richard ever dress her son like a girl; Vicky had simply brought him to the door that way, and maybe Vicky was the one ... Even if Jason corroborated her story about what Richard had done to him, they would never believe her about Conrad. "Where's your proof?" they would ask, patiently. "Bringing a plant to your husband isn't proof of killing him."

And how could she go home now? How could she bear it, having him live next door, believing him capable of murder? The police would probably not even arrest him on the charges Christine would bring; at best they would give her custody of the boy. Vicky would be too afraid of Richard to accuse him to his face. She would have to pretend she didn't suspect. She would have to let him get away with it.

She was shivering. She pulled her coat over her shoulders, shoved her hands down between her thighs. She wanted a drink, desperately, a craving she remembered too well, the kind that made her weak-kneed and disoriented, that made her think she couldn't stand it without one. Get a grip. For god's sake. She made herself take deep breaths, expel them slowly, through her mouth, and after a while the feeling passed.

Well, she couldn't sit in a restaurant in Burnaby for the rest of her life. Richard could be home by now, and he would have found her note that said she had taken Jason to her father's and he would be starting to wonder why she wasn't back yet—

The note. She said she had taken Jason. But Richard hadn't left Jason with her. He had left Lisa.

He would think she had written the note that way deliberately, telling him she knew.

Her heart thudded wildly; she could feel its reverberations in her skull. So what would he do? She said they'd gone to her father's. He knew where her father lived. He would rush over there, furious; she had even shown him where her father kept his key; he would storm in—

And her father would shoot him.

She made herself pick up her cup of coffee, take a sip, swallow, feel the hot liquid run down into her stomach. Her father would shoot him.

Breathy bursts of laughter pulsed up from her throat.

She stifled them quickly, pressed her hand over her mouth, but even so the men at the next table looked at her, startled.

What was wrong with her? She was imagining her father killing the man she had been sleeping with; she was sitting here laughing about it, a madwoman. But if he had killed Conrad, Richard deserved to be dead, too. It would solve everything, wouldn't it? And her father, well, the police would lay charges, but he would get off. He was a frightened old man shooting an intruder.

It took her longer than it should have (she would think later, sitting in the police station watching the officer walk towards her in his mysteriously silent shoes, trying to prepare what she would tell him) to stop sitting there in the restaurant thinking about it. What made her move, finally, was no concern for Richard, no concern for the morality of what she was imagining, no concern even for herself and her own murderous desires.

What made her decide was her father. She couldn't do this to him. She had told herself she didn't care, it served him right. But, in spite of everything, she did, she must, still care about him. Maybe she had no choice. He had been imprinted on her. Some families would call it love.

This wasn't the time to try to sort out her feelings about her father. She had to decide what to do about Richard. If she rushed over to her father's there was a chance she could get there before Richard did. And then what?

If she could get hold of her father's gun she could shoot him herself. It excited and horrified her, the thought of it, the gun in her hands, having that power.

She stood up, abruptly, almost bumped into the waitress. "Is there a phone here I could use?"

"By the door." She gestured with the coffee pot.

Vicky picked up her coat and purse, walked to the phone, listened to the quarter clattering down the throat of the machine. Her father answered on the first ring.

"Dad? Look, has Richard phoned or come over there by any chance?" She tried to make her voice casual.

"Who? Of course not. I'm alone here. As usual."

"Okay, okay. I just ... I'll come over, all right?"

"Yeah, whatever."

"I'll see you in half an hour or so, then."

After she hung up she stood staring at the round pocked face of the phone dial for several moments. When she finally opened the restaurant door to leave, her arm seemed to have caught on something; she tried to pull it free, but it wouldn't come. When she turned to look, she could see the waitress had hold of it, was looking at her pleadingly.

"You forgot to pay," the woman kept saying, until Vicky heard.

FATHERS

*V*ICKY MANAGED TO GET BACK onto the freeway without making any wrong turns, but then she was stuck in the slow, jerky spasms of rush hour. Why hadn't she warned her father about Richard, told him to take his spare key in and keep the chain on? Stupid, stupid. She might get there and it would be all over. Whatever *it* might be.

At last she was over the bridge, the traffic like racehorses leaping for the open extra lane and straining up the hill. She got stuck behind a tractor-trailer crawling along in the middle lane and lost so much speed she couldn't accelerate into another lane. She knew she was tailgating, her front bumper only a foot or two from the tractor-trailer, but she could feel only an irrational fury at being delayed, watching cars zoom past on either side.

"Damn it!" she heard herself yell. "Hurry up!"

At last she was able to squeeze into the exit to Guildford. She was filled with such urgency, but what would she actually do, say, to Richard if he came to her father's? She'd have to play it by ear, she thought. Play it by ear: meaning opposite things, both to extemporize and to recite from memory. Vicky wasn't particularly good at either. She concentrated on her driving: gear down, brake, turn here, change lanes, gear up, stop, go.

An ambulance with its siren and lights on came up behind her and she had to pull over. Hurry *up*, she thought, tapping her fingers on the wheel, watching it in the rear-view mirror.

When she reached her father's apartment building, where the dogwood tree by the sidewalk was just starting to unwrap its cream-coloured blossoms, she looked around for Richard's car but didn't see it. A dog barked nastily at her from across the street, and she thought for a moment of the barking machine and wondered how Richard had made it stop.

An elderly woman held the outside door for her so she didn't have to buzz up, not that she ever did, anyway; it was a big building and there was always someone there to hold the door, even to leave it propped open, because the intercoms often didn't work. It had never worried her before. She made sure the door clicked shut behind her.

She walked down the hallway nervously, throwing glances behind her several times, expecting Richard suddenly to emerge from around a corner, a doorway. What if he were already inside the apartment, waiting for her?

But of course he wasn't. Her father answered her knock by shouting, "It's open! Come in!" and when she did she found him sitting in his wheelchair watching TV, with his gun on the end table beside him.

"Why don't you lock the damn *door?*" she said, slamming it shut behind her. She turned the lock and put the chain on.

"I thought you were the Meals-on-Wheels person," he said. "If I'd known it was you I might not have said to come in." He was wearing what looked like a pajama top underneath overalls with a bleachy stain on the bib. On his lap was the crocheted red and white afghan she had bought him once at a crafts show.

"Thanks a lot," she said, dropping herself onto the sofa.

"What did you want, anyway?" He turned the volume down slightly on the TV.

"I just missed your cheerful, smiling face."

"Huh." He turned the volume up, louder than it had been when she came in, and moved his chair again to face the set. A news report was on, something about the Middle East, war.

Vicky began to watch, too, numbly, the television a black hole sucking in everything around it.

Her father snapped the set off. Vicky started. He turned his wheelchair to face her.

"So," he said. "What are you doing here?"

"I, uh ..." She glanced at the gun on the end table.

"Well, *what*? You never come over without a reason."

"I was just worried about you, okay?" she snapped.

He snorted. "That'll be the day."

She remembered the feeling she had suddenly had for her father in the restaurant, how she had thought it might be love. Well, it didn't mean you loved a person just because you didn't want him to shoot someone.

Not just someone. Richard. She glanced at the door.

What should she tell her father? He was involved in this now, whether he wanted to be or not. She ran her thumb back and forth along the sofa cushion, feeling the slow burn of friction. "I have to tell you something, Dad. About Richard."

"Yeah? Richard? The new boyfriend?"

She winced at the word. But that was what he was, after all. They hadn't even broken up. The changes had taken place only in Vicky's head. Richard might still be considering her his girlfriend. *Boyfriend. Girlfriend. Broken up.* It was a vocabulary of childhood.

"Yes," she said. "Now please listen to me. This is important."

And so she told him. About Richard, about Jason, about Conrad's death. Her father kept his eyes on the corner of the sofa as she was talking, and Vicky had the feeling he wasn't hearing her at all.

"So I think he's going to come over here," she concluded. "I'm sorry. I didn't intend for it to work out this way."

Her father was quiet for a long time, frowning at the sofa. Finally he looked at her. "So what do you want me to do?" he asked. "Shoot him?"

Vicky laughed, wildly. "No. Of course not."

"So what then? What are we supposed to do when he comes?"

"Give me the gun, all right?"

"Why? So *you* can shoot him?" He gave a harsh cough of laughter. "That'll be the day." He picked up the gun and slid it onto his lap underneath the afghan.

"I want him to know I'm serious. I want him to think I could do it. I'm almost certain he killed Conrad. I can't stand to think of him getting away with it."

The afghan was slipping from her father's lap, and he pulled it back up with his left hand. His right stayed firmly clamped around the gun.

"Okay, so this guy is kind of warped, all that stuff with his kid. But you don't know he killed Conrad. You don't know for sure he even went to the hospital. And even if he did, maybe he just wanted to do something nice, to bring Conrad this plant so you'd see it and think it was nice of him. To say he was sorry about your fight. It's not his fault Conrad died so soon after that."

What he said made sense. His were the arguments the police would make, and even her father had made them sound persuasive.

"I just think he did it, Dad. The timing, it's just too great a coincidence." She was trying to convince herself now as much as him. "Of course you're skeptical. You only saw Richard once, when he was being charming. Richard is very good at being charming."

"So it makes him a murderer, being charming?"

She frowned impatiently. "Of course not. What I'm saying is that Richard is, well, he's not a normal person. If his son displeases him, well, he'll turn him into a girl who *will* please. If a lie is easier than the truth, he'll use the lie. If I choose someone over him, he'll eliminate that person."

Her father shook his head, made a "tsk" sound. "I dunno," he said. "A lot of imagination in there."

"I'm not *imagining* all this, Dad."

"Get me some coffee, will you?" her father said. "There's some Leo made in the pot on the stove. Although it's probably stone cold by now. Better make some more."

"This is important! Forget about the coffee."

"A cup of coffee—is that too much to ask? That you get me one cup of coffee? It takes a couple of goddamned minutes."

"We might not *have* a couple of minutes!" Vicky leaped to her feet, pointed at the door. "Richard could be here at any time. This isn't some stupid joke!"

"So I can think better with a cup of coffee. Quit acting like a hysterical woman, for god's sake."

Vicky stalked into the kitchen, plugged the kettle in, slammed the filter into the holder so hard it split. She filled it with coffee anyway; what were a few grounds in the coffee going to matter?

Outside the kitchen window two crows settled on the power lines. She could hear their loud, squawky conversation, a sound that had always grated on her. Conrad saying you can't blame them for being successful survivors, for wanting to live where people did, Vicky saying "a murder of crows" wasn't a collective noun as much as an imperative verb. She looked quickly back at the kettle, the tendrils of steam in the air, tried not to hear what the crows said.

It occurred to her to phone Amanda, entreat her to

come over, but she decided not to. There was nothing Amanda could do to help.

When the coffee was ready she poured them both a cup, brought her father's out and set it on the end table. He grunted, picked it up, took a noisy sip. Then he put his forefinger to his tongue, pulled his finger away and looked at it. "Got grounds in here," he said.

Vicky didn't reply. She took a sip of her own coffee. It had grounds in it.

"I still don't know what we're supposed to do when this Richard gets here," her father said.

Vicky sighed. "I don't know, either. I just think he's going to come."

"You going to let him in?"

"I don't want him to come in. He's dangerous. And he's going to be furious about my taking Jason to his ex-wife's."

"You going to tell him you think he killed Conrad?"

She didn't know what to answer.

"Well?"

"I can't. I have no proof. And I'm too afraid." She began pacing around the room, running her hand over the furniture.

"I'll shoot him for you if he gets out of hand," her father said. It was impossible to tell whether he was being serious. "You want me to phone Leo to come over? He's got more guns like this."

Good grief. "No. Don't call Leo. And I wish you'd give me that thing. Please."

Her father shook his head. "Nope. Forget it. It's my gun." He patted it gently in his lap, as though it were a pet.

Vicky sat back down. "Oh, god," she said. "This is such a mess. Maybe I should just leave. If he comes you can yell at him through the door that I've gone home."

"Wait a little longer. Until that TV show comes on. I

want to watch that. The one with the wheel. You know."

"No, I don't," Vicky said. She slumped back, looked at the cup clenched in her hands. Her mouth felt gritty.

"So this Richard. He dresses his little boy up to look like a girl."

"That's what I told you." If he laughs, Vicky thought, I'll strangle him.

"Why would he do that?"

"I've no idea. Some way of keeping the boy under his control, I suppose. Some game he was playing with me. I don't know."

"Huh." Her father scratched at his nose with his thumbnail. "I wasn't a very good father, but at least I'd never do something like that."

I wasn't a very good father. Imagine him saying that.

"You weren't all that bad," she said, "until you left."

"You were better off without me."

"Oh, of course we were. Gee, Mom said every day how much better off we were without you. The day she died she was still saying it."

"Well, I *thought* you were better off without me. I guess I was wrong." He put his hand on his chair wheel, rocked himself stiffly back and forth. "I'm too old to know anything anymore. I'm going to go have a piss. Let me know if the boyfriend comes."

He turned his chair and began to wheel himself down the hall to the bathroom. Vicky watched him go, the back of his head with its bristly fringe of white hair that needed to be washed and cut, the thick rinds of his ears that seemed, like his nose, to get larger every time she saw him. *I guess I was wrong.* That was quite an admission, for him.

The bathroom door closed, thunk, hard, a slam, keep out. Vicky sighed. Probably they would never cease annoying each other. In some unhealthy way she might even have needed him to be the way he was, to give herself the satisfaction of anger at someone who deserved it, at someone who expected nothing better of her.

She thought of the photograph tucked between pages 22 and 23 of her high school yearbook. The photograph of her real father. How often she had thought of it with nasty anticipation, of the day she might be able to wave it in his face, exclaiming, "*This* is my father! Not you!"

Maybe she'd known all along she would never do it. There might have been a time when such an act would have freed them both, but now it would only be a useless cruelty. Perhaps she had even kept the picture there just as some kind of protection against her confused feelings for him. She remembered him introducing her once to someone when she was little, saying, "She's not much, but she's all I've got." She'd probably known he was joking, but still she'd seethed with indignation. Maybe it was what she could say of him now: he's not much, but he's all I've got. He was more than a photograph of a teenage boy she had never met.

Perhaps, she thought, he had known all along he wasn't her biological father. Perhaps she had known he knew, and couldn't bear to face it. The ironies almost made her laugh out loud.

Her eyes settled then on the photograph on the record cabinet. Her mother, younger than Vicky was now, standing with her arm around her daughter's waist. Caring about her father felt suddenly like a betrayal. Perhaps she had never believed she could love both of them.

The toilet flushed, jerking her mind back from its wanderings, housework she had given it to tidy itself up, ready itself for something more important. For Richard.

Maybe he wasn't going to come after all. Maybe he was just waiting for her at home. She considered phoning his house, hanging up if he answered. But he would know it was her. Where *was* he, damn it?

She could phone Birdy. All Birdy would have to do was look out her upstairs living-room window and she could see if Richard's car was home.

Vicky grabbed the phone book, found the number, dialed.

"Birdy! It's Vicky. I'm glad you're there. Could you do me a favour? Could you look out your window and see if Richard's car is in his driveway?"

"Sure," Birdy said. "Just a minute." It took her less than that to come back and say, "Nope."

"Oh, okay. Thanks."

It wouldn't be that easy to dislodge Birdy. "Is anything wrong? Should I go over and knock at his door?"

"No, really—I just ... I'll talk to you later."

She had only made the woman more curious. "Are you okay? You sound kind of strange. Is Richard okay?"

"Probably not," Vicky said, wishing immediately she'd said something more neutral. "Just ... don't go over there, okay? Don't talk to him."

"Don't *talk* to him? Gee whiz, Vicky. Anyway, I haven't talked to him since he told me Conrad died. But why—"

"What? *He* told *you* Conrad died?"

"Yeah. Why? Shouldn't he have?"

"No, it's just—I'd assumed he'd heard it from you." Vicky was gripping the receiver so tightly it began to tremble.

"How would *I* have found out?"

"When did he tell you?"

"Let's see. The day before I left you those chocolates, I guess. Vicky, what's going on?"

"I can't talk now. I'll explain later."

She hung up, her hand still shaking. How could

Richard have known about Conrad, have known about his death the very day it happened?

But the police would still say the evidence was all circumstantial. And unless they believed her, unless they could charge him, how could she accuse him? He lived next door. If he knew what she had found out she would never feel safe. She could sell the house, move, but he knew too much about her; he would always know how to find her.

She walked around, picking up things and setting them back down. The water running suddenly through the refrigerator sounded cold, a stream under ice. She heard the bathroom door open, her father come out and drop into the wheelchair he'd left in the hall.

She should have gone to see if he'd left his gun in the chair while he was in the bathroom. But she doubted he would have given her such an opportunity. Maybe she should go ask Leo if she could borrow one of his. He would probably be only too happy to give her one.

Her father came back into the living room. "Who were you phoning?"

"Just my neighbour. To see if Richard's car was there."

"And?"

"It wasn't. But she told me something else. She said Richard was the one who told *her* Conrad was dead. I thought it was the other way around. How could Richard have known, unless he'd killed him?"

"Someone else could have told him."

"Like who? Who else knew both of us? It was the very same *day*, for god's sake. I hadn't even told Amanda, or you, or even Ernest!"

Her father rubbed his thumb across his chin, thinking about it. At last he said, as though begrudging it to her, "I guess that's odd, all right."

There was a knock at the door. They froze.

"Is that him?" her father whispered, his breathing loud and raspy.

"I don't know," Vicky whispered back. "Probably."

She walked over to the door, slowly, on tiptoe, stood pressing her ear against it, listening.

Another knock, longer, louder. Vicky jumped at the suddenness of it.

"Who is it?" Her voice was pitched so high it sounded as though she had been breathing helium.

"It's Richard. Vicky, is that you?"

"Yes."

Unexpectedly, she could feel herself calming. He was here. It was what she had been waiting for. She couldn't afford to be panicky, to make mistakes.

She opened the door, let it move inwards slowly until it hit the end of the chain.

"Open the door," Richard said.

He was rubbing his hands together as though they were cold. He folded them over each other and raised them to his mouth, blew into them, obscuring half his face. Vicky looked at his eyes. She could read nothing in them, nothing to tell her what he was thinking, what she should expect.

"Jason isn't here. I took him to his mother's."

His hands dropped slowly from his face, opening as they fell. She had surprised him, she thought: good. It gave her an advantage.

"Why did you do that, for heaven's sake?" As though he didn't know.

"I know all about Lisa, Richard." She could see him so poorly through the narrow crack. He shifted his position, and now she could hardly see him at all, just a piece of torso, a leg, an arm. He was wearing a navy-blue suit and tie and a grey silk shirt; he mustn't have changed after work.

He shifted his position again, lunged into her vision so

abruptly she cringed back.

"Vicky, I know how it must look. But it was just a game. It was Jason's idea. He likes playing games."

"How long were you going to let it go on?"

"I know it's upset you. I was going to tell you—"

"This isn't about *me*. Don't you care about Jason at all? If you leave him with Christine—"

"Christine. Christine doesn't want him. If she told you she did she's lying."

"Anyway, that's not the point. The point is that you did something very damaging to Jason. He needs help. So do you."

"Let me in. We can talk about it."

He pushed against the door. It rebounded a little from the chain, and he pushed again, hard. "Take the chain off. I hate when you do this, this little coy thing, make me talk at you through a crack in the door." She could see his face, a knot of muscle hardening in his cheek.

"I don't want you to come in. I don't want to see or talk to you ever again."

"Stop this, Vicky. Let me just explain—"

"I don't want to hear any more of your lies. I don't want to ever see you again. Don't come over to my house. Or I'll call the police. I mean it. Now go away."

She started to push the door closed, but he still had his hand on it, forcing it open. She could see anger undisguised on his face now, a vein pulsing in his neck.

"Damn it," he said. "I just want to talk—"

She was pushing hard at the door, with both hands, but unable to latch it. Behind her she heard her father say something, and she turned, removing her pressure on the door.

And suddenly she was reeling backward, as the door flew open. The plate that had been anchoring the chain to the jamb had torn loose, its screws popping free as easily as if they had been implanted in sawdust. Richard stumbled into the room, caught himself on the door, a look of surprise on his face.

"Jesus," he said. "I'm sorry."

He closed the door behind him, gently, keeping his hand on the knob. The dangling chain, with the torn-off plate still attached, went clink, clink, clink, in the tense silence as it swung against the door.

"You get the hell out of here!"

Richard hadn't seen Vicky's father until he spoke, and the voice from across the room, so loud and fierce it frightened Vicky, too, made him take a step back so that he was pressed up against the door.

Vicky's father was standing behind the wheelchair, clutching the back with his left hand and holding the gun in his right, pointing it at Richard. There was a slight tremor in his hand.

Vicky looked at Richard, still pressed, motionless, against the door. His eyes were fixed on the gun. Slowly, he raised his arms out to the sides, as though to embrace someone. His lips pulled back a little, a poor pretense of a smile.

"Hey," he said. His voice was unsteady. "Take it easy."

"Get out."

"I just want to talk to your daughter." He twisted his head slightly in Vicky's direction, not taking his eyes off the gun. He lowered his arms slightly.

"She doesn't want to talk to you."

"I'm sorry about the door. I'll pay for the damage."

"Right now! Get out or I'll shoot you!"

"Come on. You wouldn't shoot me."

"You just broke into my house. I got a pretty damned good excuse to shoot you." Her father waved the gun a little from side to side.

Richard took a step forward, his smile rigid. He raised his right hand slightly, palm open. "I don't think you'll shoot me," he said. He took another step forward.

Her father did something to the top of the gun, cocked it, Vicky supposed, remembering the motion, the sound, from TV shows. Why couldn't she move, speak? She was standing halfway between them and to the side, over by the sofa, watching them as though they were strangers, actors in a movie.

Richard took another step. She had to do something. She licked her lips, but her mouth was so dry it brought no moisture with it.

"He means it, Richard. He'll shoot you."

He stopped, looked at her. The smile had begun to look grotesque, something of which his mouth could not rid itself. "Don't you think that would be a good idea?"

"Maybe it would."

Her answer was not one he had expected, she could tell. He turned to her father, said bitterly, "So go ahead, then. Do it. Why not? I'm just this loser, this fucked-up loser."

"You shut up," her father said.

"Shut up," Richard mimicked. "Shut up. That's what my father liked to tell me. Did Vicky tell you what he was doing while he was saying it? That my earliest memories of dear old dad are of him shoving my face into my pillow until I nearly passed out while he tried to ram his dick up my ass? That my mother pretended not to believe it? That he—"

"Don't listen to him, Dad. It's all lies."

Richard turned to her. "Oh, I see. You know that, do you? More of Christine's little theories." He put his hand to the knot in his tie, wrenched it loose, then jerked the tie free and shoved it into his jacket pocket.

"What I know is that there's no excuse for what you did to Jason."

"What I did—" Richard eyes went squinty for a moment, and he blinked hard "—saved him. My father never touched my sister, only me. So long as Jason was Lisa he was safe from me."

So long as Jason was Lisa. He spoke of Lisa the same way Jason did, as though she really existed. But might he believe what he had just told her, that he had saved Jason? No. No. It was all just more of his clever lies.

"Did you kill my son-in-law?"

Vicky gasped, turned to stare at her father. Stop, she wanted to cry, you can't tell him!

"What?"

"Dad, please ..." She mustn't panic. She couldn't make her father unsay the words.

"Did you?" her father repeated.

Richard began to laugh, a harsh, bitter sound. "You think I killed Conrad, Vicky? My god, is that what you think?"

She made herself look at him, right in the eye. Maybe she should be glad her father had accused him. She would never have had the courage. Who knows how long she would have gone on living next door to him, filled with helpless hatred?

"I think you could have," she said.

"Oh, I see, I see. I somehow could make him have the aneurysm, or the heart attack, or whatever the hell it was."

"I think you could have gone down there with that plant, and then you, you could have killed him. Suffocated him, strangled him, something. It would have been easy."

"What, what? Are you crazy? I killed him with a plant? What plant?"

"You know what I mean."

"No, I don't know what you mean. How can you imagine anything like that? That I'd kill your husband? What could possibly make you think that?"

"It was you who told Birdy Conrad was dead. How could you have known?"

"Oh, for god's sake." He lifted his hand, gestured at the air. "I kept trying to call you the day after I, well, you know, after I pushed you, I wanted to apologize, and there was no answer, not even your machine, so I thought you must be at the nursing home, so I called there, to see if that's where you were, to see if the change in Conrad was like you'd said, if he really had improved. And the nurse told me. If I'd had something to hide, would I have been so stupid as to tell your next-door neighbour what I knew?"

"Why not? You have such a good, innocent explanation. Maybe you did even call the hospital afterwards."

"That is so—I can't believe how ridiculous that is. It would be funny if it weren't so goddamned ridiculous."

She could feel herself wavering. His explanation *did* make sense—

But what she'd learned from Birdy wasn't her only evidence. She had almost forgotten what had alerted her in the first place.

She kept her voice firm, even; she mustn't let him see her falter. "Someone saw you there. Nurse Nice. Gail Mendelson."

And she could see from his face that he knew what she meant. Something in her had still kept hoping she was wrong, but she wasn't, oh god, she wasn't. She looked away, couldn't stand to see the truth in his eyes.

"She'll be able to identify you," Vicky said, her voice surprising her with its steadiness.

"All right," Richard said. "I did go to see Conrad once. The day after you said you wouldn't take me. I was ...

annoyed, I guess. I couldn't see the harm in going. I just wanted to see him, just once. If I were going to come back later and kill him would I have stopped to talk to the nurse, given her any reason to remember me?"

"I won't listen to any more of your lies. Of course you wouldn't call them lies, just omissions."

Richard's pale complexion had darkened. "You want to believe I killed Conrad? All right, go ahead. My life is so fucked-up, why not? Why not have killed someone? Yes, I'm so fucking desperate to have you I killed your husband. There, is that what you want to hear? Does that make you feel better? I killed Conrad. You're so clever you must have a tape recorder running somewhere." He looked wildly around the room, shouted into the bedroom, "Did you get that? I killed Conrad!"

The room was still. The air smelled sour, stale.

"That was a good performance," Vicky said coldly.

Never in her life had she felt such pure hatred. And he would get away with what he'd done. She would phone the police; she would tell them everything, but she knew there wouldn't be enough proof. There would never be enough proof. Maybe she *should* have had a tape recorder running. He had confessed, after all.

And then her eyes were suddenly drawn to a slight movement behind Richard, at the door. It was opening, slowly.

Richard must have sensed her shift of attention because he turned, following the direction of her gaze. Vicky could see from the corner of her eye her father draw back the gun, set it on the table beside him. They were all three of them rigid, watching the door.

"Jason!" Vicky exclaimed.

He was wearing the same jeans and short-sleeved red sweater as when she had last seen him, lying on the floor watching TV at his mother's, where, Vicky thought, her mind refusing to understand, he was still supposed to be, safe.

"What are you doing here?" she asked.

He didn't answer her, just looked from one to the other of them, his face wary, his eyes blinking, hard.

"I told you to wait in the lobby," Richard snapped.

Jason took his hand from the doorknob. "I have to go to the bathroom."

"Jesus, can't you wait?"

Jason shook his head, looked down at his feet.

"All right, go." Richard waved his hand down the hall. "Hurry up."

Jason came into the room, making small sideways steps and staying as far away from all of them as he could, his right hand behind him feeling his way along the pieces of furniture. When he reached the hallway he backed down it until he was almost at the bathroom, and then he turned and ran inside and slammed shut the door.

"What's he doing here?" Vicky asked. She felt tired, defeated. Everything she had done had only made things worse for the boy.

"We're on our way home from Christine's," Richard said.

"How did you know he was there?"

"Christine called me."

"Christine ... called you."

"Christine doesn't *want* him. Can't you get that through your head? I know you think I've done this terrible thing to him, but he's better off with me than with her. Christine doesn't love him. At least I do, at least I love him."

"You can't—"

The door to the bathroom was opening. Jason came out, closed the door behind him. He looked around at all of them, not speaking.

"Go down to the car."

The boy didn't move, stood by the bathroom door, holding his arms awkwardly in front of his chest.

"Did you hear me? Go to the car!"

Jason began to walk forward, slowly, small steps, until he was beside the table. A flick of his eyes gave him away.

"No!" Vicky cried.

She rushed forward, but, to sidestep Richard, who stood unmoving, she bumped against the side of the sofa, and it shook her balance enough that by the time she reached the table Jason had already picked up the gun.

If only she had pushed Richard out of the way, she would think later (and was thinking now, as she watched the officer, looking at the heels of his shoes hit the carpet and realizing, of course, that was why they made no sound) she might have reached the gun before Jason did.

"Put it down, boy," said her father. "That's no toy."

Jason backed away until he was pressed against the wall. He lifted the gun. It looked enormous in his small hands.

"I know," he said to Vicky's father.

"Give it to me," Richard said. "This isn't a game." He walked toward Jason, his hand out. "Give it to me."

"No." Jason pointed the gun at Richard.

Richard kept walking toward his son, his hand out, palm cupped upwards.

"Stay away from me," Jason said. The gun was shaking in his hands.

Richard stopped. He was trying to smile. His fingers were only inches from the gun when Jason shot him.

AFTERWARDS

*I*T WAS THREE WEEKS after Richard's death. Vicky had gone to her father's to return the toaster she'd had repaired for him and to pick up her toaster oven she had lent him in the meantime. As she opened his door she thought about how she wouldn't have to worry about him sitting there with a gun in his lap. The police, of course, had taken it. It was unlikely they had believed his dithery story about having gotten it from someone in a bar, but they didn't press charges. They had a more complicated story to work on.

"So what happened to that kid, finally?" her father asked, grunting down into his wheelchair.

"He's in a group home somewhere. I don't know what will happen to him. Richard's sister has apparently been in touch and may eventually become his guardian."

"That mother." He shook his head. "Some mother, not wanting her kid."

"Just like some fathers."

"Huh."

But Christine Menard's refusal to take Jason had upset Vicky, too, more than she dared to let on. She had been angry enough to phone Christine, who had snapped, "Look, who are you to tell *me* what to do? It wasn't *my* father who gave him a loaded gun to play with."

And what could she say to that? If it hadn't been for her father's gun, Richard would still be alive.

Maybe it was only for Jason's sake that she wished he

were. She looked at the place by the kitchen entrance where he had fallen, where the police had only two weeks ago allowed her to throw away the bloodstained carpet she had been unable to shampoo clean. Her father had been surprised at her coldly industrious approach, and she couldn't explain to him her apparent detachment, her wish only to erase Richard from her life, from her memory, the way he must have wished to erase Conrad.

"Well," she said now to her father, "I have to get going." She took his toaster to the kitchen, plugged it in. "Where's my toaster oven?" she called, not seeing it on the counter.

"Oh, I forgot." Her father wheeled over to the doorway. "I lent it to Leo."

"For heaven's sake. Couldn't he buy his own?"

"He wanted to try one out first, that's all. Don't be such a grouch." He coughed, scraping up phlegm in his throat. "We can go get it. He's out but I got a key."

Vicky sighed. "Okay, give it to me. But I have to hurry. I have someone coming over for tutoring."

"That your new job, eh?" He began rummaging in a kitchen drawer.

"Yeah. I phoned Sub Dispatch and told them to take my name off the list. That felt pretty nice."

"You like this, this tutoring?" He held up a key with a gummy twist tie saying "Leo" threaded through the hole.

"Sure, I guess so. I like it a lot better than subbing."

She reached for the key, but he snatched it back. "I'll do it," he said.

Vicky swallowed her impatience and followed him down the hall to Leo's door, where her father fumbled the key into the lock. The apartment was a mirror of her father's, only messier, smelling of stale clothes and cigarettes, and the furniture was newer and more expensive, with plush finishes and high, moulded backs on the two identical blue sofas. Vicky smiled. Leo bought two of everything. A large cabinet with one glass door open stood against the open-ended wall separating the living room and kitchen, and a set of barbells, big ones, sat beside the cabinet.

"You can go look in the kitchen," her father said. Vicky was already heading toward it.

She stopped. On top of the cabinet sat a cactus plant, with unusual bluish leaves. The flowers had dried and fallen into the pot, a grey ceramic one with red flecks in it.

Leo bought two of everything.

"Dad," she said carefully, "tell me everything you know about Leo."

She could hear her father's wheelchair creak behind her as he got up. She couldn't take her eyes from the plant.

Her father came around beside her, dropped onto one of the sofas.

"The reason I stopped writing," he said, "the reason I stopped sending money—"

"I don't care any more. Tell me about Leo."

"I was in jail."

She turned to stare at him. "*Jail?*"

"You have to understand," he said, licking at his lips. "I got in with some bad company, that was all. I was just the driver. They were the ones who went in and actually did the stickup."

"Stickup? *Stickup?*"

"I didn't do anything. I just waited in the car. It was them others who—"

"Leo? Leo was one of them?"

"No, no. I met Leo in jail. He was, well, nice to me. He protected me. He was tough, people respected him."

"What was he in for?"

"He, uh, killed someone. His ex's new husband. He

said it was self-defence but they didn't believe him."

Vicky had started to shake. She put her hand against the wall to steady herself. There seemed to be both too much light and too little air in the room.

"What's wrong?" Her father struggled to his feet, stood holding on to the arm of the sofa.

She opened her mouth, made some small sound, but there were no words.

"Vicky, has Leo done something to you?" Her father sounded frightened now.

She made herself turn to face him. "Yes, maybe. Why would you think he has?"

Her father's leg was wobbling. He sat down again. "Well, he, uh, he has this thing for you. You know."

"This thing for me."

"I didn't think anything about it. I thought it was harmless. He just ... wanted to do things for you."

"What sort of things?"

"Nothing, nothing really. Well, there was that time with that vice-principal ..."

"What time?"

"Well, it was *you* who kept complaining about him. Once when Leo was there. Maybe I mentioned the name of the school to him afterwards, that's all, that's all I did."

"And?"

"And, uh, well, Leo did something to the man's car, I think."

"Why didn't you tell me, for god's sake? Why didn't you tell me?"

"Well, I knew you'd be mad. I knew—"

"You knew *nothing*! Oh, god. I feel sick." She swallowed several times.

He just wanted to do things for you. How many times had her father said that she was better off without Conrad?

How many times had Leo heard?

She had been so certain that Richard had killed Conrad. Richard had died knowing she believed him a murderer, knowing she thought him capable of that. And how long had Jason been standing outside the door, listening? As far as she knew, he had told the police nothing about her accusations, but if he had heard them, might they have influenced him, given him the extra determination he needed to pull the trigger?

Her father was whining something about how it wasn't his fault, whatever had happened it wasn't his fault.

She made herself concentrate. "Leo keeps guns, you said. Where?"

"What do you want with—"

"*Where?*"

"I don't know. Maybe one in a kitchen drawer ..."

The kitchen smelled of built-up grease and of garlic. On the counter sat her toaster oven, and the sight of it filled her with sudden revulsion—she would never want it back, now that he had touched it. Her shoes stepped on something gummy on the floor; she didn't look down, began rummaging through the drawers.

The gun was in the third one she looked in, lying on top of a mess of pliers, wrenches, wires, and something red and cylindrical that for all she knew could have been a stick of dynamite. She took the gun out, laid it in her palm. It was, of course, identical to the one he'd given her father.

And what now? Could she shoot him? Did she hate him enough? Was she sure enough, this time, that he was the one? She had no more proof of his guilt than she'd had of Richard's.

The front door. She froze.

"Arthur! What're you doing here?"

"Oh, ah, well, we came to get Vicky's toaster thing."

Her father's voice was so strained she scarcely recognized it.

"Vicky's here?"

She could hear his footsteps, coming towards the kitchen.

She put the gun on the counter, grabbed the toaster oven and pulled it in front of the gun. She was reaching out to unplug it when Leo came around the corner.

"Hiya," he said. The smile she had always thought of as shy now seemed repulsive, sinister.

"Hi, Leo." Her heart was beating so loudly she was sure he must hear it.

His eyes dropped to the drawer. The open drawer. When he looked up he met her eyes. He was still smiling, but she could tell he knew. His body had gone very still, an animal's, tensing for a spring.

Vicky picked up the gun, in both hands, pointed it at him, backed away.

"Hey," Leo said. "Hey." He stared at the gun.

"Tell me the truth, Leo," she said.

Perhaps it had been exactly the right thing to say. Leo seemed to relax a little, and he reached his hand up to run it over his head, smoothing back his pale, thin hair.

"Come on, Vicky. He was no good to you that way."

That was all she had had to do, ask him to tell her the truth. She almost began to laugh, hysterically.

"Ah, Leo, no, no." Her father had shuffled up behind her, from the back entrance into the kitchen, and stood at her elbow. His voice cracked. "You didn't."

"You said. You said she was better off without him."

"I didn't mean—ah, Jesus, Leo—"

"Tell her to put the gun away. I got my own, anyway." Leo slid his hand into his jacket pocket.

"Don't," Vicky said.

But Leo, with such casualness it was as though he had

forgotten what she was holding, as though he was only reaching for something to show her, took out another gun, weighed it in his hand, approvingly, smiling slyly at it.

"Cock yours," her father hissed at her. "Vicky, cock it. Pull back the hammer thing."

Vicky looked at the gun, saw what he must be referring to. She lifted her thumb, pushed down on the little catch, heard a click. Cocked: if she pulled the trigger, right now, she could kill him.

"Call the police, Dad."

"Hey, hey," Leo said. "No police. I ain't going back to no jail. Not for doing you a favour."

The smile was gone now from his face. Vicky could see the anger forming in it, pulling his brows down, curling his upper lip. His hand tightened on his gun, but he didn't raise it.

"Dad—call the police!"

"No police!" Leo shouted.

"Now, Leo, calm down, calm down."

Vicky could sense her father backing away, could hear his raspy breath.

"Goddammit, Arthur. Arthur! You listen to me. I said no police!"

Leo raised the gun, pointed it several degrees to Vicky's right, where she knew her father must be.

Vicky pulled the trigger.

•

She asked to go home first, to change her clothes, she said, because there was blood on them. Improbably, the officer driving her agreed. Maybe it didn't really matter to them, she thought; maybe if they hadn't actually arrested her (yet?) she could do as she liked.

But the man came in with her. He could have waited in the car. It must mean they didn't trust her all that much. She went into the bedroom, closed the door, and called Amanda.

"Of course I'll come down," Amanda said. "Jesus. Of course. God, Vicky."

Vicky sat on the bed, her hand still on the receiver. She should get up, she thought, and change her clothes the way they expected her to, but she kept sitting there, her hand on the phone, as though it knew she had to make another call. And then she was picking up the receiver and asking the operator for Information for Port Townsend, Washington.

There was one Y. Menard. Vicky wrote down the number. If she got a machine, she told herself, she'd hang up. She dialed, closed her eyes. Straight south from her there was almost nothing but water between her and where the other phone was ringing, and if they made strong enough binoculars, she and Richard might have seen the house the day they sat on the bench and looked across at the Olympic Peninsula.

"Hello?"

She opened her eyes. She hadn't thought at all of what she would say.

"Oh, hello. Is this Yvonne Menard?"

"Speaking." A businesslike voice, brusque.

Vicky took a deep breath. "My name is Vicky Bauer. I was a friend of your brother's."

There was a pause. "You're the neighbour."

"Yes. I'm sorry to intrude, but, well, something's happened that makes me think I was wrong about Richard, I mean, I thought he did something worse than he did, and—I need to understand him, I guess, try to understand why ..." She didn't know how to continue; why had she called, when she didn't even know what she wanted to ask?

"... why Richard would dress his son like a girl?"

"Yes. I guess so."

The silence on the line was so long Vicky thought the woman might have hung up. At last Yvonne Menard said, her voice slow, careful, "Okay. I've had to think about it a lot, too. As I told Christine, I don't think my father sexually abused Richard. Although ... it's not something we can ever know for sure, is it? Not positively for sure." She paused. "But I can tell you that my father was awfully ... relentless with Richard. He expected so much of him. So Richard would, well, exaggerate. And Dad would be furious, he couldn't stand people lying to him, and he would punish Richard by taking away his books, his toys, his clothes."

"His clothes?"

"A couple of times he had to wear mine to school. No big deal, jeans are jeans, sweatshirts are sweatshirts. But still. Anyway, it's some connection, isn't it? For what he did to Jason."

Vicky swallowed. "It's ... maybe I had hoped there was no connection. No explanation. No excuses."

"So that he really deserves to be dead?"

Vicky winced.

"Well," Yvonne Menard said, a sudden impatience to her voice, "is that enough? Is that what you wanted to know?"

There was a knock at the bedroom door. "Mrs. Bauer?" said the voice behind it. "Are you ready? We have to go."

Vicky cupped her hand around the receiver. *Is that enough? Is that what you wanted to know?* "Thank you," she said, her voice low, into the phone. "Yes, I guess so. Maybe ... maybe I just wanted your forgiveness."

"Forgiveness." Yvonne Menard was silent for a moment. When she spoke again there was a gentleness to her tone that belied the words themselves. "I'm a lawyer,

Mrs. Bauer. I don't do forgiveness."

.

"Vicky Bauer?" asked the officer standing before her. "You can come with me now."

Amanda squeezed her arm. "Good luck," she said.

Vicky got up, followed the tall, young policeman down the hall. The room was just as she had imagined it, white, square, austere. As she entered, a man sitting at a desk with his back to her turned, raised himself slightly from his seat, in what might have been some awkward chivalry, and gestured to the chair in front of the desk. She sat down. The man and the desk were between her and the door now: a deliberate arrangement, she remembered from some police show.

"Corporal March," he said. He was dark-haired and olive-skinned, with a terse moustache. "And you're—" he glanced at a file on his desk "—Vicky Bauer."

"Yes." She glimpsed her face in a mirror on the wall, and she wondered if it was one-way, if anyone sat behind it, watching her.

"Mind if we tape this?"

"No."

"All right. Just tell us what happened."

What happened. She had been thinking so much of Richard that it amazed her to realize that of course they wouldn't care about him, that what she was guilty of with Richard was irrelevant to them. It was Richard she deserved to be punished for, but all they cared about was Leo.

"How is he?" she asked.

"He was hit in the thigh," the policeman said, using the neutral, passive voice. "He'll live."

"He killed my husband."

The corporal's finger hesitated over the red "record" button on the tape machine in front of him. "He did admit to that." His voice had softened a little. He gave her a slight smile. "He's not exactly Einstein. Ready?"

He pushed the red button. She could hear no sound from the machine. It was professional, doing its job, listening. She told it what happened.